DETACHED

DETACHED

A NOVEL

WENDY WEISS

gatekeeper press

Columbus, Ohio

Published by Gatekeeper Press
3971 Hoover Rd. Suite 77
Columbus, OH 43123-2839
www.GatekeeperPress.com

Library of Congress Control Number: 2017960686

ISBN: 9781619848122
eISBN: 9781619848139

Printed in the United States of America

For My Father,
M. Richard Weiss

Special thanks to Ken Hutchinson,
Lisa & Dan Peck
And
Missy the Dog

PART 1
Now

CHAPTER ONE

At 6:00 AM, the sun had not yet appeared over Southwest Florida. Lindsey Blake was walking her usual route along the chain-link fence, earbuds in place, listening to her audiobook. Crows jumped from the fence to the trees making her shoo them away when they flew too close.

The sky above her was gray, and she heard a rumble of thunder from the north where darker clouds hung low. The air was thick, humid, and palpable, and her T-shirt and shorts clung to her in uncomfortable places. But she was used to it now, having lived in the climate for nearly four years, since leaving her life and son behind in Boston.

Hearing another rumble, she glanced at the northern sky and pulled out her cell phone to check the local weather radar. It was nearing the end of the spring season, which meant rain and storms would come nearly every day. It was a strange place to live at times, but it was mostly sunny, and the humidity felt like a warm embrace. She couldn't imagine moving back to her old life with the snow and sleet, and the ice-cold toilet seats. But she missed her son.

Lindsey was at a full fast-walk pace when the narrator's voice in her ears suddenly stopped. She scrambled to pull the phone out of her pocket hoping that she hadn't accidentally called someone.

Her hands were sweaty, and she lost her grip on the phone, juggling it back and forth until it cleared her finger tips-gravity pulling the earbuds from her ears. She lurched forward in an attempt to catch the assembly before it hit the pavement, but was shoved as she did so, going down hard, like a great weight on her upper body was forcing her, pushing her down. Her legs and hips scraped the rough pavement opening her skin. Someone grabbed her arms, and she tried to look back, but now she was being pulled up and simultaneously pushed forward. She tried to scream but couldn't get the sound out.

A car pulled along the sidewalk, and the trunk opened. A fleshy hand covered her mouth, and blood rushed to her face, her eyes bulging, pleading. A muffled "NO!" came up from her throat. She writhed and kicked but couldn't get control of her body. Then cruel hands lifted her off her feet and slammed her against the carpeted floor of the trunk. Then darkness. Her body lurched to the rear, and her head hit something sharp as the car raced forward. She lay there stunned, eyes darting back and forth. Terrified.

CHAPTER TWO

D R. JASON SMITH sat behind his desk at Unified Health Insurance Company and looked at his watch for the umpteenth time. His plan was officially in play. Lindsey Blake was locked in the trunk of a car and on the way to Casey Key. Her kidnapping was crucial to his plan; there was no turning back. He would have to find a way to live with what he'd done. But first, he needed to hear that they'd arrived at the cottage and Lindsey was unharmed.

Sweat beaded on his face, and he wiped his forehead with his shirt sleeve. He picked up the framed picture of his family that stood cornered on his desk. He tried to focus on the image, but stress blurred his vision. He squinted and breathed heavily through his mouth.

The picture had been taken at the beach about three years ago when his daughter, Hanna, was ten. She had been in full remission for over a year. The leukemia was gone . . . again. She did cartwheels in the sand that day, and stood on his shoulders, before diving into the warm, gulf water. Her smile was toothy and wide. She was beautiful. And his wife Donna was laughing and happy.

He set the frame face down on the desk and, in his mind, replaced the image with what she looked like today. She was thirteen now, and her hair was thin and falling out. Her skin was pale, and her eyes appeared sunken and dull. Donna's beauty had faded in synch with Hanna's decline, and she nagged him constantly about being at the office, away from home, and away from her and Hanna. He audibly groaned.

He closed his eyes and leaned over facing the floor, touching his fingertips to the carpet. Sometimes when a panic attack was looming, he could scare it off in this position, slowly counting to ten, but it wasn't working. Then the room began to spin, and he reached for the trash can, aiming his face, just in case. But nothing happened. Instead, he could start to feel himself detaching, lifting, and looking down on himself, but his fog was interrupted by a vibration in his pocket. His mind and body quickly reunited and he jumped up, steadying himself against the desk as he pulled out the burner phone.

"Are you there?" Jason asked.

"Yeah, we're here. Everything is cool. She's out." Ben replied.

"What do you mean, she's out?

"She's a feisty bitch. I had to knock her out."

"With the sedative?"

"Um, well no . . . I gave her a little tap on the forehead, and she went down. I swear it was just a light tap. She'll have a little bruise, but she'll be fine."

Jason's face flushed and his temples pulsated. He lowered his voice and pressed his mouth closer to the phone.

"I told you not to hurt her."

"I didn't have a choice." Ben's voice escalated. "She was crazed . . . all over the place."

"If anything happens to her the deal is off. Do you understand me?"

"Yeah, calm down. She'll be fine."

Jason shut the phone and stuffed it in his pocket. A moment later his regular cell rang. Donna. *Can't deal with her right now.*

He pushed the button on the top of the phone and sent her to voicemail.

An image of Lindsey Blake's battered face flashed in his mind, and he reached for the trash can again. His empty stomach heaved. No relief. He breathed fast and heavy. Drops of sweat rolled off his face onto the carpet. He straightened himself, peeking over the cubicle wall to make sure no one was around to witness his apparent sickness.

He hoped Lindsey wasn't scarred or worse. Why did Ben have to hurt her? His orders were clear! They were not supposed to harm her! Ben should have used the sedative if she fought back. It was so simple! He could have poked the needle in anywhere, and she would have relaxed.

Jason sucked in a deep breath fully expanding his chest, forcing the band of tension to loosen its grip, and then he sat in his chair and faced his computer monitor. His hands shook as he typed in his user ID and password. It took him three attempts before his fingers were steady enough to type the correct combination. He clicked on his calendar, and the eight-thirty meeting reminder popped up. Lisa Simmons' medical review meeting. He had to call in. It had to be a regular workday.

He picked up his cell and opened a text message to his daughter. "Love you, Baby. See you after lunch." Then he reached for the desk phone and dialed into Lisa's conference call.

The meeting today was a review of a new medical device, a type of shunt that helped to drain fluid from the brain. There was an uptick in the number of pre-service requests. Jason had asked for a report that included a list of the doctors, and the related patient information. He wanted to read the information and then deny their requests. The shunt was expensive, and there were cheaper alternatives that performed the same function.

He listened to Lisa's voice on the phone and wondered what her reaction would be when she learned about Lindsey. Shock and fear he assumed. He glanced at his watch again. It was just a matter of hours. The thick band around his chest tightened a few notches, and his eyes searched for the trash can once more.

CHAPTER THREE

THE OLD 2012 Mercury used to be a shimmery beige that glimmered in any light, but the south-east sun was cruel, and after so many years, the once shiny car had faded to a dull, flat tone with spots of rust visible along the undercarriage. The car was a hand-me-down from Cliff's grandmother and still had a good engine despite its 160,000 miles. Ben drove the car cautiously. Fully aware of the live cargo in the trunk, he tried his best not to jerk it around the turns.

Cliff shifted his weight in the passenger seat causing the springs to make a loud, creaking sound. He reached down, pulled a dirty rag from under the seat, and wiped the sweat from his forehead, leaving a streak of dirt.

"You hungry?" he asked.

Ben glanced at his partner and scrunched up his face.

"Fuck, Cliff, you stink! And wipe that shit off your face. How can you think about food now? We just kidnapped a fucking woman!"

"Do we got any beer left in the back?"

"Jesus, you're like a little kid! No, we'll get some beer later." Ben glanced at Cliff. His grip tightened on the steering wheel and his biceps flexed.

Cliff was a large, white, bearded man in his early thirties with a huge beer belly that had a life of its own.

His gut wiggled and bounced when he walked, giving the appearance that his belly arrived at the scene before the rest of him. His cotton T-shirt was worn thin and had likely been white at an earlier time, but years of wear had colored it gray with deep, yellow sweat stains. He lost one of his upper front teeth in a bar fight a few years ago, and as a result, had a lisp or a whistle that made him sound mentally challenged.

The two men had met at a local bar in Tampa, near where Ben worked part-time at a liquor store. They sat next to each other drinking beer several nights in a row before Ben started the conversation. It didn't take long for Ben to grasp Cliff's low intellectual bandwidth and his lack of a moral compass. He was unemployed, pliable and needed some fast money. Ben knew that he needed a powerful physical presence in addition to his own and figured Cliff could do the job.

Ben pulled the car onto the highway and glanced in the rear-view mirror. No one appeared to be following them, and he was confident that the ride would be uneventful, despite the woman pounding herself against the inside of the trunk. He had taken the precaution of removing the trunk release and reinforcing the rear lights to ensure that she could not kick them out. They both just needed to stay calm, follow the plan and get this job done as quickly as possible.

Cliff shifted his weight again causing the springs to grind even louder.

"What's your problem, man? It's a short ride. Can't you sit still?"

"I got a spring up my ass." Cliff chuckled.

Ben rolled his eyes.

"Maybe it's time for a new car after this is over."

"My Grandma gave me this car. I ain't getting rid of it. I'll just go the junkyard and get a new seat."

Ben glanced at him seriously questioning his decision. The more time he spent with him, the less confidence he had in Cliff's ability to even follow directions without getting sidetracked. They had clear instructions not to hurt the woman, but Ben knew that Cliff was a mean drunk. He would have to work hard to keep him in line, and that would mean limiting his beer consumption.

He pulled the car off the exit and Cliff's head cocked, gawking out of the passenger side window.

"Can you stop there? There's a store at the gas station."

"No, dumb ass. We're not stopping anywhere with that woman in the trunk! We can't risk anyone hearing her pounding in there. What the fuck is wrong with you?"

"I just wanted to run in and grab some beer."

"Fuck the beer, Cliff. We'll get it later!" You are so fucking annoying with the beer. Maybe you need some AA."

Cliff's pudgy face was instantly red, and he clenched his fists, a seething expressing on his face.

"Watch your mouth, asshole. I ain't needing any fucking AA. I'm just thirsty."

"We got water at the cottage. You can drink that."

Cliff turned away and unclenched his fists.

They drove another mile and then turned right onto a dirt road, the thick gravel crunching under the tires. Ben slowed to a near crawl, then made another sharp turn pulling the old Mercury into the short driveway in front of the cottage.

CHAPTER FOUR

LINDSEY KNEW THEY had been driving for nearly forty minutes because her fitness tracker was glowing and she could read the time. She couldn't find the internal trunk release latch, and there was no other obvious way out. The trunk was large, and stunk of rotting carpet, old food, and grease. She was sobbing, shaking, sweating and she had to pee, but she could, at least, roll over and move her legs. The car had been driving straight and fast, so she figured they were on the highway, but where were they taking her? She reached up, scraping her elbows on the top of the trunk and felt the lump growing on the back of her head.

None of this made any sense. She kicked at the trunk and screamed, "Let me out!" *Why would someone want to do this to her? What could she possibly offer?* She took a deep breath to try and calm herself. *Think! Think!* She searched her pockets again for her cell phone but knew that it had been left behind near the chain-link fence, or perhaps the men that grabbed her had picked it up? It all happened so fast she couldn't recall the exact events. *Think!* She tried to rationalize what was happening, but her thoughts were jumbled. How could she not see this was about to happen?

She was sobbing again, which made the pressure in her

bladder even more uncomfortable. A sense of doom crept into her gut. *Was she picked at random? Had someone been following her, watching her, waiting for a day when no one was around? Would they rape her, strangle her, shoot her? How would her son learn about what happened to her? Would she end up like one of those missing women that aren't found for months or years until some hiker comes upon their decomposed remains?* Her sobbing grew more intense with every horrible thought, and she squeezed her thighs together harder. She kicked and kicked again. *Stop it and get control!* She rolled onto her back and wedged her knees against the roof of the trunk, trying to relieve the growing pressure in her lower belly.

She braced herself as the car veered off an exit ramp, rolling her onto her side as the car slowed into traffic. There were stops, or red lights, and more turns, and then one final sharp turn that threw her against the side of the trunk. She heard the wheels on gravel, and then the engine was off. They were coming for her.

CHAPTER FIVE

BEN BACKED THE car into the gravel driveway in front of the small, abandoned cottage situated in a secluded, wooded area on Casey Key, about sixty miles north of Fort Myers. The cottage had a narrow front porch that ran the length of the structure. From the top step, he could see slices of aqua colored water in the gulf when the breeze moved the branches in just the right way. Wealthy tourists and seasonal residents typically filled the key, but this particular section appeared neglected, as though the discriminating developer's eyes saw something unworthy in the land. It was lucky that they found the cottage, and even luckier that after three weeks of watching it, still no one had shown up to tend to it.

Ben had replaced the front door to the cottage, with a steel door that was obviously out of place, and the front windows had been boarded up.

The men exited the car and circled back to the trunk. The air was hot, steamy, and carried the smell of mildew. They could hear the woman whimpering and sobbing in the trunk, and they caught each other's eyes.

During the last twenty miles of the trip, the two men strategized on how they would get the woman out of the trunk without harming her or themselves. They agreed that Cliff would raise the trunk slowly while Ben braced himself to restrain her. He hoped she would cooperate. Cliff made his move and slid the key into the trunk and turned. He raised the lid slowly, and the woman started to move.

"Don't move!" shouted Ben. The woman raised her hands as if to protect her head and face from what might be coming at her. Cliff hovered over the trunk at it opened, blocking any possibility of escape.

"If you can slowly get up and climb out of the trunk without going crazy then we don't need to hurt you. Do you understand?" Ben asked firmly. The woman appeared to nod her head as if she understood, but she was still sobbing, and her body shook like a frightened dog.

"Cut the crying, bitch, and let's go!". Cliff yelled. The woman rolled forward onto her right hip and elbows and swung a long leg over the edge of the trunk. Cliff grabbed hold of the back of her shorts and pulled hard causing her to scream and pull away. He dug deeper into the trunk and gripped onto her arm pulling her forward and up. She screamed again.

"Stop, you're hurting me! Stop!"

She was up on her feet with Cliff supporting her weight while she gained her balance. Ben moved in close, blocking her next step.

"Just do what we tell you then no one has to get hurt."

But Lindsey's brain was in flight mode, and she didn't register any instructions. Her arms started flailing in an attempt to wrestle herself free from Cliff's stronghold, and she kicked her legs clumsily forward and to the side. Ben could hear her shorts ripping in Cliff's fist.

"I told you not to move!" Ben yelled again, but the woman was screaming now. Her whole body moved like a crazed doll. Cliff let go with one hand and grabbed her hair near her scalp, wrapping his fingers around her head and yanking it back. She tried to let out a scream but her neck was hyperextended, and she could only manage a yelp. She kicked forward again landing a sneaker hard on Ben's inner thigh.

Instinctively, Ben closed his fist and punched forward hitting the woman between the eyes. They heard the noise like water spilling, and they watched the yellow stream run down her legs.

"Fuck!" Cliff yelled releasing her like she was on fire, watching as she tumbled to the ground.

"Jesus fucking Christ! She wouldn't stop!" Ben yelled.

"She pissed herself." Cliff lisped and chuckled.

"Yeah, shit. Now we gotta clean her up or something. She can't stay like that".

Cliff was still laughing.

"She's gonna be out of it for a while. Let's get her up to the front porch and put her on the couch while we figure out some clothes for her. I don't want to be smelling her piss for the next two days. Give me her cell phone." Ben demanded.

The color drained from Cliff's face as he reached into his front pocket. "Um . . . I don't have it. I musta dropped it."

"What do you mean you dropped it? I asked you to do one fucking thing, and you dropped it?"

Cliff struggled to find the words to cover up his lie. It was true, Ben did tell him to grab her cell phone and shut it off when they took the bitch down, but the thrill of action made him forget.

"Like I said, I ain't got it."

"Look in the trunk, dumb ass!"

Cliff pulled a flash light from the glove compartment and searched the trunk.

"It ain't here. I'll check her pockets."

Cliff rolled the woman onto her back, her knees still turned to the side, and reached into both pockets pulling them inside out.

"Ain't here neither."

"Why would the phone be in her pocket if you had grabbed it?" Ben asked knowing he had caught him in a lie.

"Fucking A! What the fuck! FUCK!" Ben barked. "You gotta go back and get her fucking phone!"

Cliff gasped. "Fuck me, Ben. Why is it always me that has to do this kind of shit? You go fucking get it!"

Ben's neck flexed and the vein on his forehead pulsed. His eyes avoided Cliff's, and he scanned the woman lying half-sideways and urine-soaked on the ground.

"Listen, you fucking loser, get back in the car and go get the phone. Then stop somewhere and pick up some sweat pants for the woman. I will call the boss and let him know we got her here and that she's down for a while."

Cliff spun around and moved toward the driver's side door. "Wait, motherfucker! First, you can help me get her in the house!"

Cliff gaffed and shuffled his feet to the back of the car. They picked her up by her arms and legs, pushed their way through the front door and dropped her on the rotting living room sofa.

CHAPTER SIX

Jason sat behind his desk and turned on his docked laptop. *It's just a regular workday.* He read through some emails until after ten o'clock, but couldn't keep his concentration on the task. His brain was foggy and he considered going out to the car to get his bottle of Xanax, but it had started raining, and as usual, his umbrella was never where he needed it to be.

Since so many of Unified's staff worked remotely, they all had access to an online chat program to promote communication. When an employee logged into the system, their picture was attached to chat software. The color on the top of the window indicated the employee's current activity. Green meant the person was available, red was busy or in a meeting, and red with a line through it meant they were in a 'do not disturb' status. When the employee was away from their computer for more than fifteen minutes, the chat indicator turned to yellow. If the employee wasn't logged in, their picture was grayed out.

He opened his chat window and typed in Lindsey Blake's name. His heart pounded, and the tightness in his chest thickened. He glanced over his shoulder to make sure no one was behind him or entering his cubicle.

Her picture popped up, grayed out since she obviously wasn't online, but he had memorized her features. She was middle-aged, and attractive with long dark hair. He clicked the X on the window closing out her image. He rubbed his chest again, a habit that he couldn't seem to break, and then decided he needed to move around, distract himself. He weaved through the maze of cubicles to the back wall and leaned over Nancy's cubicle.

"Is Ron in the office today?"

"Yes, he's on a call in the conference room with the policy team. Do you want me to interrupt him?"

"No, it's okay. I'll catch up with him later."

He thanked her and walked back to his cubicle and stared at Hanna's image on his screen saver. The memory of her diagnosis poured over him.

"Hanna has an elevated white cell count," Dr. Jamison told them. He knew what that meant even though he hadn't practiced patient directed care in years. He knew what she was telling them. Hanna had Leukemia. Hanna has Leukemia. She still has it. Her perfect little body has cancer. It just didn't make sense.

In the days following Hanna's diagnosis, his panic attacks worsened. He had difficulty breathing, he couldn't concentrate, and he neglected his job. He sat in his corner cubicle with his head down, holding back tears.

He became angry and lashed out at Donna. He secretly blamed her for Hanna's illness, finding no other way to rationalize his daughter's defective genes. It must have come from Donna. It was the only explanation. The idea that he could have passed on a life-threatening disease to his daughter was simply not plausible. His blame was evident, resenting her for giving his daughter Cancer, resenting her for having the strength to be there day in and day out when he could not. But when Hanna went into remission for the third time, he smiled more often, laughed and participated in family activities. If only it had lasted.

He didn't tell many people about Hanna's condition. His secretary knew—she would ask him how Hanna was doing—and Ron Shay knew. He was a good friend, and during the most difficult times would always offer to help. Sometimes Ron would leave research about new cancer drugs or his desk, or the most recent statistics on recovery from different types of childhood cancers. But Ron knew that he was miles ahead of him, already having researched the same articles and making phone calls to the authors asking questions. Jason was glad he had someone to confide in at work, especially since his relationship with Donna was winding down. All she did was pick fights about his work schedule and the amount of time he spent away from home. None of it mattered anymore.

CHAPTER SEVEN

Since Unified Health had gone 'green' and paperless, Lisa Simmons' home office was neat, clean and organized. Her desk remained free from the folders and binders that she had kept years ago when she first started working for the company. She liked the uncluttered feel of the room, and how everything had its place. She filled her bookcases with family photos and knick-knacks, and had room for a TV in the corner. She liked having the news on during the workday but kept it muted. It kept her company, along with her dog, Missy. The only downside was that the office was in the back of the house and Missy was her only warning that someone was approaching the front door.

On Wednesday morning at eight am she was behind her desk with Missy was curled at her feet, tired after their morning walk.

Lisa opened her Outlook and scanned through the long list of unopened emails, and then spotted an email from Lindsey and smiled. Lindsey often made fun of her for having so many unopened emails. She opened it and read, "Thank you for opening my email." Lisa laughed out loud, and Missy raised her sleepy head to see what was so funny. She opened her chat communicator and saw Lindsey's picture grayed out. Unusual for her not to be on by this time, but she went back to her email and continued working through them, reading and responding, a necessary task that she did not enjoy.

At eight-thirty, Lisa dialed into an online meeting with her boss Tracy, and one of the medical directors, Dr. Jason Smith. Although she liked working with her boss, the medical director was a different story. He was quirky and odd with some strange mannerisms. She had met him a few times in person for staff meetings on the Unified Campus in Fort Myers. He wouldn't shake her hand, and twice he walked by her without acknowledging her, even though he knew who she was. At least, she thought he should have. During a meeting, he sat with arms crossed over his chest, like a mummy holding himself up, and he breathed loudly. Though Lindsey had never met him, they made up a new name nickname for him, calling him 'Darth'.

Lisa's meeting ended at 9:30 am, and she clicked back over to her chat window. Lindsey was still not logged in. She sent a text to her phone. "Everything okay?"

CHAPTER EIGHT

MOST DAYS DARIUS Williams was late for school because his mother or her latest boyfriend would not wake up in time to drive him. He piled on his backpack stuffed with books and homework papers and peddled as fast as he could on the mile-long trip.

He lived in a duplex style house. His bedroom, along with his mother's that she frequently shared with her boyfriend, occupied one side, and his Grandmother lived on the other side. She was a kind woman and tried hard to make sure that Darius was growing up right, but her health wasn't good. She was obese, and he noticed how she huffed and puffed when she walked even a short distance; she wasn't taking care of herself. Regardless, he spent many nights on her side of the house, laid out on the couch or the floor in front of the TV, and tried not to think about what his mother and her boyfriend were doing on the other side of the house. Sometimes his older half-brother, Darrin, showed up and tried to rough house with him. He would talk about his gang brothers and show him his latest tattoo. His most recent was a brightly colored snake wrapped around a large gun. Darius didn't like having his brother around. He knew that his brother and his gang were involved in drugs and other crimes. Darius was afraid of him and wanted nothing to do with him. Whenever he was around, Darrin would pick him up over his shoulder and say, "Don't worry, little gangsta, your time will come." Darius didn't want that time to come. He enjoyed school. He liked being away from home and playing sports in the school yard. He reveled laying in his bed, studying his football posters on the wall, and dreaming about being big and strong, running out of a stadium locker room with the crowd cheering. He wanted to play college football. He saw himself drafted into the NFL. He could imagine his grandmother's face when they made the announcement. 'Darius Williams was picked in the first-round draft' . . . and the money! The money would change his life and his grandmother's forever. Maybe even his mother would notice him, or the father he never knew would show up. But more important, he wanted to make his grandmother proud.

As he peddled along the long chain-link fence, he spotted a thin pink cord in the grass next to the sidewalk. He skidded to a stop on his bike and, still straddling the seat, leaned over and scooped up a set of earbuds, quickly discovering they were still attached to a cell phone. He scanned up and down the sidewalk to see if anyone was watching and then examined the phone. It was similar to the iPad they issued in school. He flipped the switch on the side to silence it, and then stuffed the phone and earbuds into his backpack. He would wait until he got home to see if he could tell who it belonged to, but maybe he would also make a call and check in on Hanna. He was worried since she had become sick again and left school.

He arrived at school five minutes after the bell and had to stop at the principal's office to explain. He told the secretary that he didn't have a ride and so he rode his bike instead. She shook her head and aimed her eyes at the door. "Get to class," she ordered, handing him a pink slip, and Darius ran down the hall disappearing through a classroom door.

CHAPTER NINE

ON WEDNESDAY MORNING, Ken Blake rolled over in his bed and with one eye open pushed the button on his cell phone to check the time. It was eight-thirty. He noticed a text message had come in just before six am. "I hope you have a good day off. Love you. Mommy".

Laurie had already left for work, and he was happy to have the condo to himself for the day. He could sleep in, and then spend the entire day playing his video game. When Laurie was home, he tried to refrain from playing, but there were times he couldn't resist, which led to friction between them. He thought it was prudent to spend some time apart. "Good for our marriage," he said, suggesting the idea. Laurie just shrugged and figured it was better if she was out of the house when he was deep in his gaming world. Ken set the phone back down and pulled the covers over his head.

CHAPTER TEN

CLIFF JAMMED HIS foot down on the gas pedal, spinning the tires in a grand exit from the pebbled driveway, spraying sand and rock in Ben's direction. His face was cherry red, and he was sweating anger from every pore. He continued to accelerate as he entered the paved, two-lane road that led back to the highway. He was hungry and thirsty and decided that this little road trip would include taking care of his own needs before anything else.

Just before the highway entrance, Cliff spotted an old gas station and store, with two working pumps and a red iron, antique pump on the side of the run-down building. He checked the gas level and figured topping off the tank was a good idea, though guzzling a cold beer was in the forefront of his mind. He pulled into the station alongside the pump and stepped out of the car. "Fucking heat," he mumbled using his shirt sleeve to wipe his forehead. He pulled his debit card from his wallet then hesitated, imagining Ben's angry face if they were traced because of his debit card. He dug in his front pocket pulling out some crumpled bills. He counted fourteen dollars. Not enough for gas and beer. He shoved the bills back into his pocket and pulled out his wallet again. "Fuck it." After filling the gas tank, he waddled into the store, stopping at the entrance to let the cold air from the air conditioning above blow down on him. The store was small and cramped, with narrow aisles and tall shelves. His eyes scanned along the perimeter of the small store, but he didn't see a beer cooler. A large, middle-aged woman with a round face and a pile of blonde hair clipped on top of her head was sitting behind the counter. She raised her eyes meeting Cliff's gaze and asked with a deep, southern drawl, "Can I help you, mister?"

"Yeah. Do you got any beer?"

"What kind you want?"

Her words coming at a slow pace.

"What you got?"

"Come with me," she ordered as she shifted her significant weight off the bar stool. Cliff followed behind her gawking at her backside with his mouth hanging open. His thoughts went to sex, and the crotch of his shorts bulged.

"What's your name, mister? You live nearby? I ain't seen ya'll here before". She asked her questions without turning her head.

"Just passing through. Figured a couple of beers for the ride wudn't hurt."

His expression made a question, like he wanted her permission.

He followed her through a narrow isle of dusty shelves filled with canned goods and snack foods hanging from pegs, to the back-storage room.

The door had been left ajar with the faded words 'Keep Out' stamped on its facade.

"I want some cold beer. You got anything cold?" Cliff assumed that the storage room was just for storage, but the woman didn't answer. Then he spotted the walk-in cooler off to the right behind some stacked boxes and grinned.

"How much do you want?"

"Gimme a six of Bud."

The large woman stepped into the cooler turning sideways to fit between the boxes and opened a case, pulling out a six pack of bottles. She side stepped out of the cooler and handed him the beer. Cliff surveyed the storage room and noticed a mattress on the floor in the far corner. It was disheveled as if recently slept on. He thought it was odd that she would be sleeping here but it wasn't his problem. His mouth was watering for the taste of beer, and he wanted to get on the road. He walked back to the front counter and set the bottles down waiting. It took the woman an extra minute while she wriggled herself back onto the bar stool.

"That'll be seven dollars, mister."

"For a six pack of Bud? That's too much. It's fuckin Bud, lady."

"Do you want it or not?"

"Yeah I want it but I ain't paying seven dollars for a shitty six pack of beer."

The woman reached for the beer gesturing to pull it back behind the counter, but Cliff was faster and pulled it closer to him. The woman backed off satisfied that he had given in to her price. Cliff pulled out his wallet and dropped his debit card on the counter.

"Cash only, mister."

She ordered pointing to the sign that read, 'Credit/Debit purchases over $10'.

"Jesus, lady, you're breaking my balls."

Cliff stuffed his card back into his wallet and then pulled some crumpled bills from his front pocket, shoving them toward her. "Keep the change," he said sarcastically. She rolled her eyes and watched him walk out the door.

CHAPTER ELEVEN

BEN STOOD IN the living room rubbing his sore fist and watched through the door as Cliff skid angrily away out of the driveway. He hoped that he hadn't hit the woman too hard, but just hard enough to keep her down so he could check the house one more time. Ben loomed over Lindsey's unconscious form on the old couch and noticed her hand flinch. He wanted time to make sure the house was secure, and there was no way for the woman to escape, especially since it was Cliff who had been there last. After the cell phone debacle, Ben had lost all confidence in Cliff's ability to follow instructions. He studied the woman's face again and thought of the syringes in his pocket. The idea of poking her with a needle gave him a creepy thrill, as if he had total control, like a doctor.

He had found the old cottage after a considerable amount of research on the Internet searching for foreclosed property. Although it was nearly ten years since the big real estate crash, there were still many abandoned properties scattered around the state, and some even the banks had forgotten about. He was able to see every potential property from an aerial and street view using Google Maps, and this one was far enough away from the target, but not so far away that contact with the boss would be complicated.

The size of the cottage and number of rooms was perfect for what they needed to do. He got lucky. The main room, what had once been the living room, now had a rectangular, folding table with three computer monitors, a keyboard, and a mouse. The tower sat on the floor to the right of the chair. Ben had been working on the setup over the last few days making sure that everything was in place. He was able to pirate electricity from a nearby junction box and then set up a fake account with the local Internet service provider. Once it was live, he installed a VPN. Now no one would be able to trace his IP address. If all went well, there would be no interruptions, short of a thunderstorm knocking out the power. Cliff had at least followed through on one order, and two portable air conditioners were pulled in and running.

He backed up toward the front door and decided to do a walk through to make sure that there was no way the woman could escape. The entire cottage was no more than one-thousand square feet. He turned back, noting the closed front door. Cliff had replaced the boarded up, rotting wooden door with a steel door that had a keyed deadbolt on the inside and outside. He turned left, checking the front facing windows. All three were boarded up with three-quarter inch plywood. He took several short steps into the room and turned right. The entire cottage had tiled floors, with thickened, dark grout that showed years of neglect. The kitchen was dark and had a small boarded up window over the sink. The cabinets and drawers were empty. The back door was also securely boarded up. No escape route possible.

Beyond the kitchen was a narrow hallway with three doors. The first door was the bathroom. He checked behind the rotting shower curtain and saw the small window had been boarded up with the same plywood as the living room, and then he paused to admire his image in the mirror over the sink. He knew he was attractive and was proud of his body. His face was a perfect combination of African and Asian with exotic features. The boys in high school teased him sometimes, calling him queer or fagot, but the girls hung on his every word. He had no trouble getting dates, but he never kept them around for long. He much preferred to play his video games.

He checked the door knob to make sure the lock had been removed and then walked toward the first bedroom on the left. The darkened room once again had the same plywood covering the window, but he could see the outline of the twin-sized bed against the wall. He flicked on the light switch. Just the bed. He walked into the room, backing away from the bed to see if anything was underneath. Cliff had removed the closet door. Perfect. He checked the bedroom door knob and found it replaced with an industrial style chrome knob. Just above was a keyed deadbolt. *Good,* he thought. He stepped backward leaving the room, still checking left and right. He had to be certain. He couldn't risk missing even the smallest detail. At the end of the hall was the master bedroom, though it wasn't much bigger than the other bedroom. The plywood was in place, secure. A larger sized mattress lay on the floor, but otherwise, the room was empty. No closet door. Cliff had done well. He would let him know that later when he returned with the woman's cell phone.

He went back to the living room, booted up the computer and entered a password on the main screen, which opened a window that viewed as an old DOS platform. He typed a stream of commands and then entered another password. This time a window opened on the second and third monitors with a video feed. On the first monitor, the camera was aimed at a bed with a rumpled blue comforter pushed aside exposing white sheets. He could almost make out the form of the body that had recently occupied the space. On the other side of the bed, hidden under the comforter that gently rose and fell was the woman's son, Ken Blake.

On the second monitor, he watched Lisa Simmons, behind her desk, headset on and talking. The third monitor displayed the empty single bed in the small bedroom down the hall.

The woman was starting to stir, her hands reaching instinctively to her swollen forehead. She moaned.

"Sorry, lady, but I need more time."

He reached into his back pocket, removed the small syringe filled with milky liquid, and then pulled the cap off. He leaned over the woman, and held down her left arm, feeling a slight resistance as she weakly tried to pull away. He slid the needle into her narrow, rope-like vein and pushed the plunger. Her eyes opened wide staring into space, then closed. Her arms flopped onto her belly. He grinned at his success, watching her face and body, then went back to his surveillance.

CHAPTER TWELVE

CLIFF WAS MAKING good time. He had just polished off his third beer and had driven about forty miles. He was careful to stay within the speed limit on Route seventy-five. The last thing he needed today was to get pulled over for a DUI. It wouldn't be the first time either. Not long after his mother and grandmother died, leaving him and his brother homeless, he and his brother went on a binge. They tore around town in the Mercury, whooping and hollering out the car windows until the cops pulled them over.

They were both so drunk they giggled like school boys through the entire arrest. After a night in jail, they went to court, but the public defender pleaded their case, telling the judge that they were good boys who had recently lost their mother and grandmother. The judge bought the lawyer's sob story, and both received a sentence of time served along with a week of community service. He remembered picking up trash on the side of the road, and his brother Billy got to drive the senior center van for a week.

His next arrest wasn't as fun or easy. This time he was on his own. He'd held a knife to a liquor store clerk that he knew from school, and threatened to cut his throat if he didn't give him all the money in the register. He also helped himself to a case of beer. It took less than an hour for the cops to pick him up. This time the sob story didn't work, and he spent two years in jail.

He was now only fifteen minutes away from the street where they had grabbed the woman, but then it just occurred to him, *what if he didn't find the phone? Naw*, he thought. *It will be there. People don't walk around outside that fence. They keep the kids inside the fence.* He casually flipped the tab on his fourth beer.

When he exited the highway, he sat anxiously at two very long red lights before turning onto the road next to the fence. He noticed that traffic in the area had significantly increased and the school parking lot was now full. He had to think of how to search the area without being spotted. His eyes followed a line of parked buses to the block enclosed by the chain-link fence, and he decided to circle a couple of times to try and locate the exact spot where they took the woman. "There!" he said out loud, and he yanked the wheel over.

Before getting out of the car, he glanced in the rear-view mirror and spotted two kids on bikes heading toward him. "Oh shit", he said, heart pounding, but they approached quickly and just peddled around him, talking to each other, not noticing him sitting in the car. "Close call," he mumbled.

Once the kids were well past his car, he got out and stepped toward the sidewalk. A black crow swooped in close startling him, and he waved his arms to shoo it away.

"Jesus Christ!" he yelped. "Fucking birds!"

He walked along the sidewalk with his eyes down searching for the phone but didn't see anything. He searched along the fence and was sure that he was in the right place but he kept walking, his eyes shifting left and right. By now at least fifteen minutes had passed and his flesh was roasting. Anyone that saw him could easily tell that he was looking for something.

"Shit," he said. "Where the fuck is it?" He walked past his car in the opposite direction one more time shuffling his feet in the thin grass. It was gone. Someone must have found it. Maybe one of those fucking kids. "Fuck!" What am I going to tell Ben?

Cliff dreaded Ben's reaction if he showed up without the phone. He pulled his sweaty shirt away from his skin, letting it snap back onto his belly and got back in the car. He had been gone now for nearly three hours. He wriggled his burner phone from his pocket and checked to see if Ben had called or texted. Nothing. He wiped the sweat from his forehead with his already dripping arm. He still had to stop somewhere and buy the bitch some clothes, and he needed time to think of what he would tell Ben about the missing cell phone.

He spotted a Walmart sign up ahead and pulled the car into the turning lane. Good. He could get the bitch some clothes, take a piss and get a burger at the McDonald's.

Twenty minutes later he was back in the car, with a belly full of burger and fries. He'd found some women's sweat pants and a T-shirt for under ten dollars and used the rest of his cash for the food.

Ben had given him two-hundred dollars the day before they grabbed the woman, but he had blown it all on food and beer. He might dock him some pay, but that was the least of his problems. He had to figure out what to tell Ben about the cell phone. He could buy a similar cell phone and try to pass it off as hers, but he couldn't remember what type of phone it was, and he didn't have enough money. He could tell the truth and say that he couldn't find it, or . . . he could lie and say that he found it but tossed it in a nearby pond, or off the bridge into the river. Yeah, that was it. He would tell him that he found the phone and stopped on the bridge over the river. Wasn't that why he wanted the phone in the first place? To make sure that it couldn't be traced? He would describe how he reeled it back and flung it as far as he could into the Caloosahatchee.

He wiped his forehead again with his sweaty arm, sending drops of stinky liquid all over the dashboard.

CHAPTER THIRTEEN

THE PARENT PICK-UP line ran along the full perimeter of the chain link fence. Two lines formed from opposite directions, cars on one side, buses on the other, meeting in the middle and then feeding out to the sides of the schools. Each school, one Elementary level and one Middle School held a mixture of racially diverse, upper middle-class to low-income students, a virtual student melting pot of intelligence and illiteracy, English, Spanish, Asian, of all sizes and colors.

Some parents came early, an hour before the three o'clock bell. Helicopter parents who hovered, watching and waiting, supervising. Their kids were clean and perfectly dressed, lugging expensive backpacks or musical instruments. They drove shiny SUVs and BMWs. Other parents would wait until the traffic cleared, squeezing in a few extra minutes of freedom before the onslaught of after school activities, homework and school projects. The schools had strict rules about pick-up line etiquette. No getting out of the car, no honking the horn or pulling out of the line. Parents must be seen to behave as their children should behave. Children who rode the bus were partitioned off to the right and escorted in groups to each of the numbered buses. The teachers watched them file into the seats. However, the latchkey kids were escorted to the bike rack and sidewalk and then set free, left on their own. No helicopters, no teachers, no supervision, and for some, no parents at all.

Darius Williams picked his bike from the metal jam of colored frames and pedaled on the sidewalk weaving in and out of his walking classmates like an obstacle course. When he reached the chain link fence, he quickened his pace and headed toward the spot where he found the cell phone. Darius wanted a second look. He needed to see if there was anything else mixed in the leaves or the grass where he found the phone. Why was it there? It would be easy to lose a cell phone, but this one had the earbuds still attached. And he thought it seemed new! He hadn't decided yet what he was going to do with the phone, but he needed to ride along the half-mile of fence one more time and search for clues. When he found nothing new, he took his time riding back to his house. His mother's car was gone, and he sighed with relief, though he wouldn't feel fully relieved until he knew for sure that her boyfriend was gone too.

Darius didn't understand his mother. Every guy she brought home abused her, beat her, called her names, and often, too often, Darius got caught in the middle. He heard his grandmother's voice.

"Is that you, D?"

"Yeah, Gramma, I'm home."

"Y'all hungry?" she asked.

"Yeah, Ma didn't gimme any lunch money. The teacher gave me some Ritz crackers, but I been starving all day."

"Poor baby!" His grandmother coddled him with her sweet voice. "Your ma ain't home," she reported with a disapproving tone. "I'll make ya a grilled cheese. Sit down, little D. Show me what you did at school today. You such a smart boy. You gonna be somethin' someday."

Darius unzipped his backpack without thinking, but then

remembered that he had the cell phone and earbuds stuffed between his books and papers.

"One sec, Gramma. I gotta go to the bathroom!" he yelled, grabbing the backpack and setting it on her couch. He pulled the cell phone and earbuds out and stuffed it down the front of his pants. Then he pulled some of his graded school work out to show her, went to the bathroom and then back into the kitchen.

After Darius finished his meal, he kissed and hugged his Gramma and exited her side of the duplex. He quietly opened the door on his mother's side of the house and sneaked into his bedroom closing the door behind him. A bookcase full of books that he picked up free at the school library sat next to the door. He decided not to take any chances, so he pulled the bookcase in front of the door. If his mother or her boyfriend tried to come in, they'd have to deal with the bookcase first. He took the phone out of his pants and set it down on his desk.

He pressed the round button with his index finger, and the phone lit up. It still had a nearly full battery. He noticed an unread text message and two unanswered calls. He hesitated for a moment and then opened the text messages first. "Everything OK?" A Lisa Simmons had sent the message. He wondered who she was. Her Mama maybe? He pressed the music app and scrolled. He laughed out loud. "Seriously?" Then he pushed the photo button. House pictures, and pictures of a white guy hugging a woman, pictures from another city, not in Florida. A picture of a Paul Revere Statue tagged in Boston. Pictures of rooms in a house, and selfies. She was an old white lady. Darius studied her face, trying to find something that he recognized, but he didn't. *I'm keeping it*, he thought. *Her loss. She can pay for another phone.*

He lay back on his bed holding the phone up, and one by one opened all the apps. There was medical stuff that he didn't understand, emails that he guessed were from her job, and other text messages. A string of messages between 'her' and 'Ken'. He called her 'Mom', so she must be Ken's mother. They didn't say anything important, but he did notice that each date that they exchanged text messages, the last message was always, 'I love you'. Darius tried to imagine what that would feel like, to have a mother who writes or says 'I love you' at the end of every conversation. He scrolled up through several days of texts between mother and son. There were too many 'I love you' exchanges to count. Ken would text back, 'Love you too', or 'Me too' or 'Ditto'. Darius's eyes welled up with tears.

He saw a folder of apps labeled 'fitness'. There was an app with a step counter. He scrolled through the history. "Wow," he said out loud. She walked a lot. Maybe she was walking when she dropped the phone. I'm keeping it. I need it so I can finally text Hanna. He hadn't heard anything about how she was doing these past few days, and he was worried about his sick friend. Then he spotted the book app and pressed. She was listening to, 'American Gods'. He had heard about that book and wanted to read it, but he knew that it was very long and probably too advanced. He scrolled through her library and found dozens of Steven King books. "She likes horror!" His eyes widened with excitement. They had something in common. He pushed the earbuds into his ears and opened Steven King's 'Cujo' and settled into his bed.

CHAPTER FOURTEEN

IT WAS NEARLY one o'clock, and Ben knew the woman would be awake soon. He wanted her in the bedroom where he could watch her wake up on the computer monitor.

He opened the steel door letting the hot, humid hit him hoping to see Cliff rounding the corner, but the there was no dust rising from the dirt road in the distance. He looked back at Lindsey and huffed, realizing he'd have to move her himself. The room had already filled with the stench of her urine soaked clothes. He reached under her knees and shoulders, grateful that she was a light weight. He noticed her shirt was sticking to her and her skin was warm. The smell of urine forced him to breathe through his mouth.

The bedroom door was cracked open, so he shifted her weight slightly and raised his leg to kick it in. He took two steps into the room and then with a swinging motion, flung her onto the bed. He gawked at her, laying on her back, long hair half over her face and the rest stuck behind her shoulders. Her shorts were torn, and he could see the top of her underwear. It would have been easy to take advantage of the situation, and the thought of fucking her crossed his mind, but the piss smell had already filled the room, and he couldn't breathe through his mouth any longer. He turned away, pulling the door shut behind him.

It was just a few steps to the chair in front of the monitors, but he sat quickly almost expecting to see that she'd moved, but she hadn't.

He clicked back to the video of the son and saw that he was out of bed. The bathroom door was open, and the light was on. He checked the monitor with the woman's boss, and she was still talking into her headset. He hoped that they would all cooperate and this would be over quickly. He didn't want to stay in this dump a second longer than necessary. He got up from the chair and went into the kitchen, thinking of what would come next for him, after this was over. He'd have some money and had outlined an escape plan, just in case. But he didn't have a long-term plan.

He sat back down in front of the computer and checked on the woman again. She hadn't moved, but he did catch movement on the son's feed.

Ken walked out of the bathroom in his boxers and was pulling some sweat pants from the top of a laundry pile. He appeared to be about the same age as Ben, and the condo was small but updated. Ben thought of all the crappy places he'd lived since moving out his parent's house. His father wanted him to go to college, but he'd thought it was a waste of time and money.

He watched Ken get dressed and then leave the bedroom. Ben typed a string of commands on the computer, and the view changed to the living room. Stupid, he thought. He's got smart TVs and an Xbox running in every room. He also picked up on a wireless camera, aimed out of a window onto the street in front of the building. The layout of the condo allowed Ben to see Ken's back in the kitchen. He guessed that the guy was making himself coffee. He was right. Ken walked into the living room with the coffee cup and sat on the couch. He opened his laptop, and suddenly Ben's monitor went black. Ben typed another string of commands, and the monitor lit up again. This time he had a split screen. He could see Ken sitting on the couch, and he could see the video game that he was playing on the laptop, one of his favorites, 'League of Legends'. Ben chuckled looking at his watch, then decided he would jump in and play.

Ken's screen name was 'Bagels17'. Stupid name Ben thought. He downloaded the game onto the computer and signed himself in as "BensRevenge," which he had established when he started playing the game more than five years ago. Now he had to find a way to get into the same game or be paired directly with Ken to play as his partner. He ranked the same as Bagels17—'Gold', so he knew it would at least be challenging. Ben matched Ken's move to search for a game knowing that if they searched simultaneously, there was a higher likelihood they would land in the same game. It worked.

This particular game had characters called 'Champions' that the player named, and who would represent them during the game. Ben could see Ken's champion was named 'Vinegar'. His champion was named 'Ryze'. They played each game in a 'lane'. The champions would fight, and then once the loser was defeated, he would continue to play all of the champions in the same lane until only one was victorious.

The game began, and Ben quickly discovered that Ken had some serious skills. Although Ben didn't give up easily, Ken was able to beat him in the lane within ten minutes.

Ben sat back in chair annoyed. *Stupid shit,* he thought. *I should have had him.* He continued the game with the other players in the lane, but his concentration was already on the next game. He wanted to beat him, but it might take too long.

Ben glanced at his watch again. Cliff would be back soon, and the woman would be waking up. This time he sent a friend request to Bagels17 with a message letting him know that it was a good game, and he wanted to 'duo' this time around. This meant that he was requesting that they play as partners. He held his breath and waited for a response. He accepted! *Wow, Ben thought, what a nice guy.* Under different circumstances, he would have had some respect, but he knew his loyalties were far more complex than a video game partnership. He waited until he was invited to the next game as Ken's partner and they played together for next thirty minutes, crushing their lane and continuing to win each battle until the game was over.

"Nice game; well-played." Ken typed in the chat window.

Ben responded, "Thanks, it was fun. I haven't played as often as I would like to. Been busy making money."

"Nice. How do you make your money?"

"Online."

Ken responded with, "I work at a Pharmaceutical company."

"Nice." Ben typed.

Ben watched through the Xbox camera and saw Ken close his laptop. Then he laid back on the couch and turned on the TV.

Ben got up from his chair and stepped out onto the porch. His eyes searched the distance, between the trees and caught a glimpse of the water. The breeze turned into gusts, and clouds were building to the east. Maybe the Rockies would be his next stop. *It's so fucking hot here,* he thought.

CHAPTER FIFTEEN

LISA WAS HAVING a busy day with one meeting after the next. She spotted Missy, still curled at her feet and asked her, "Do you want to go out?" Missy popped her head out and tentatively wagged her tail. "Come on; let's go!" The dog took her time getting up on all fours and padded slowly to the front door. Lisa stuffed her cell phone into her back pocket and attached Missy's leash to her pink collar. She pulled the door open, and they walked out into the hot, humid air. Lisa walked along slowly as Missy dawdled, sniffing the grass along the sidewalk. She thought about Lindsey and pulled her phone from her pocket to check her messages. There was none. It was so unlike her not to respond to a text. *What if something is wrong*, she thought. They walked for about ten minutes giving Lisa more time to think before Missy finally squatted. Did she request the time off and it didn't get posted on the calendar? She would check when she got back to her computer. In the meantime, she tested Dan. "Lindsey didn't sign on today, and I'm a little worried. She didn't respond to my text either." She could see that Dan had received the message and waited for his response.

"I'm sure it's nothing. She probably forgot to tell you that she needed the day off. If she doesn't respond by tonight just give her a call," he answered.

She supposed Dan was right, but something still didn't feel right. Whenever Lindsey took time off, which wasn't often, she always told her what her plans were. Her thoughts were going to morbid places. Should she call the police and have them go by her house? Now she was getting ridiculous. It had only been six hours since she was offline! She would check with the admin who supported Lindsey's team and see if she knew anything.

She rushed Missy through the rest of her walk and released her from the leash inside the house. Lisa was back at her desk opening the staff's calendar. There was no entry for Lindsey. She opened a chat window to Ana, the team's admin, and typed, "Is Lindsey on PTO today?" She waited for a response.

Ana typed, "No, we were wondering what's going on. You haven't heard from her?"

"No," Lisa replied.

Ana continued to type, "I will call her and see if she answers. I will let you know."

Lisa responded with the letter "K".

A few minutes passed, and Lisa's chat window lit up with a message from Ana. "No answer. I left a voicemail asking her to call us."

Again, Lisa responded with the letter "K."

There has to be a simple explanation for this, Lisa thought. She was sure she would hear from Lindsey soon, and in the meantime, she had work she needed to complete for her boss.

Developing and reviewing medical criteria was a daunting process, but Lisa enjoyed the responsibility, and she took her work very seriously. When medications, devices, and procedures were newly, FDA approved, Unified had to decide whether or not it would offer benefits to cover the new medication or services. Lisa's team wrote the policy, then developed and published the criteria for the use of the new benefit.

The Medical Director's role in the process was crucial since they had the final say on what got approved or denied. So much was at stake when considering that people's lives were depending on the work that Doctors and Nurses did behind the scenes.

Lisa went back to her email and spotted a new FDA notice on a recently approved drug called Cineth. She logged into the Unified platform that collected the pharmaceutical company's research and started reading. The new drug was fast tracked for FDA approval, passing all of the clinical trials with flying colors. She continued reading. 'Cineth, combined with other chemotherapeutic drugs, has the potential to put Philadelphia chromosome-positive chronic myeloid leukemia patients into full remission.' The new drug was approved for adult use at a per dose cost of $10,500, and so not affordable by ninety-nine percent of patients. The contracting process between the Weston Pharmaceuticals and Unified, and other insurance companies had already begun. Ultimately each insurance company would agree on an allowed amount per dose. It was up to Lisa's team to decide on the medical necessity criteria and policy for the use of the medication. She opened her policy template and began typing.

CHAPTER SIXTEEN

DARIUS LAY IN bed, earbuds still tucked in his ears, snoring when an unfamiliar buzzing noise startled him awake. He sat up remembering he was listening to 'Cujo' and studied the phone. There was a message.

"Did you take the day off today? Let me know you are OK. I didn't get a text from you." The message was from Lisa again. Darius wondered what the relationship was and what he should do, if anything. Butterflies filled his stomach. He thought about replying to the message, pretending to be the owner of the phone but then he might get into trouble if Lisa S started asking questions. Better ignore it. He laid back on his pillow, rubbing his belly, and hit the play button on the audiobook. But then he noticed that the shelf in front of the door was moving. He shot up pulling the earbuds out and shoved the phone under his covers.

"Hey, little D, Whatchu doin' in there?" It was his half-brother Darrin.

"Nothing. Leave me alone!"

Darrin pushed harder on the door.

"You must be doin' something . . . else you wouldn't be jamming up the door."

There was a final kick and the door flew open sending the

bookcase and all of its contents tumbling to the floor. "Aww, man! Why'd you do that?"

Darrin stepped over the mess and leaped onto the bed bouncing Darius airborne. Darrin reached for him, pulling him in and turning him into a choke hold.

"Let go a me!" Darius insisted.

"Not till you tell me whatchu hiding in here."

"Nothing! I was just sleeping. I didn't want Ma's boyfriend to come in here. He's always bothering me."

Darrin loosened his hold and then pushed him face down into his pillow.

"Is that dick-head picking on my little bro? I'll get my boys over here and take care of that prick. You won't never see his dumb ass again."

Darius pushed himself back from the pillow.

"No! Just stay out of it. I can take care of myself."

"Right, D. You take care of yourself. That's what you got your gang for."

Darius inspected his older brother, a dagger tattoo on his neck and numbers tattooed on his fingers. He shivered.

"I don't want nothing to do with your gang. Just leave me alone. I got homework to do."

"Okay, little D. You do your homework, but you'll be needing me soon. That's what brothers do. They look out for each other. Ma ain't gonna do anything for you. You lucky you ain't starving to death here. You lucky Gramma still alive to watch out for you." He cocked his wrist with an extended arm as he spoke.

Darrin backed out of Darius's room tripping and nearly falling over the pile of books.

"Pick this shit up, man." He ordered as he pulled the door shut behind him.

Close call, Darius thought. He got off the bed and scooped up the books, taking his time, lining them up in alphabetical order on the bookcase. He had read all of them and earned his bragging rights.

He heard another message come through the phone and went back to the bed pulling back the covers. "Mom, are you there?" It was Kenny, the woman's son. *Shit,* he thought. *Now she's got two people looking for her.* He shifted his position on the bed, and the butterflies rose again. He hadn't stolen the phone, but still, it wasn't his, and he should return it. But how would he do that without getting into trouble? He stared at the text message; then he started to peck at the small keyboard.

"Your mom lost her phone and I found it," he typed. Then his hand hovered over the send button. His thoughts turned to Hanna. He could use the phone and text her, see how she's feeling. He tapped the backspace key until his sentence was gone. He wished he could tell someone, but who? His Gramma would surely take the phone away from him and do who knows what with it. No way could he tell his mother. She'd either keep it for herself or try to sell it or swap it for drugs. Maybe he should do nothing for a while longer. By now the woman must know that she had lost her phone and maybe she was out right now getting a new one. *I'll wait and see what happens,* he thought.

The phone rang, and he saw Kenny's face on the display. *Oh no,* he thought. *He must know.*

He let it ring. A minute later another buzzing noise. He had left a voicemail. Darius opened the voicemail app and listened. "Mom, where are you? Call me back. Love you. Bye." Darius's stomach dropped. He noticed another voicemail there also. It was from an Ana. People wanted to talk to her. Tears spilled over his cheeks. Maybe he should bring it back to where he found it, let someone else worry about it. Maybe the woman has already come back to look for it. He decided that tomorrow he would return it to the spot he found it. He would listen to the rest of 'Cujo' today before he put the phone back in the grass along the fence, and he would do his homework and try not to think about it anymore.

CHAPTER SEVENTEEN

CLIFF PULLED HIS car off the highway exit and turned toward Casey Key. He was slowly passing the gas station where he bought the beers earlier that day. He nearly veered into the parking lot, then glanced at the time and figured he could wait until later for another six-pack.

He maneuvered the car down the narrow road toward the end of the key and mentally practiced the story he would tell Ben about the cell phone. Hopefully, everything in the house was under control. He yawned big, exposing his full mouth and extending his tongue, ready for a nap. He was tired from the thrill of snatching the woman, the stress of getting her out of the trunk and the trip back to find the cell phone. The air conditioning in old Mercury was barely working, and Cliff was drenched in sweat. He looked at himself in the rear-view mirror. *Shit*, he thought, *I need to get that fucking tooth fixed*, and he shut his mouth. He imagined that he appeared older than his thirty-two years, more like forty. Maybe it was time to get rid of the beard, lose some weight and get into shape. He could see the small dirt road up ahead and reached into the Walmart bag on the seat next to him, feeling inside for the Snickers bar he'd bought in the check-out line. With one hand, he tore off the wrapper and shoved the entire bar in his mouth, while turning the car sharply into the gravel driveway. He didn't see the woman on the couch and there was no sign of Ben. Again, he mentally practiced his story. Found the phone, stopped on the overpass and tossed it in the river. He will be mad, but he'll get over it.

"I'm back," he announced banging on the steel door. He didn't hear any commotion, but then again, it was a steel door. He waited a moment and then banged again. "Open the door!"

A second later he heard the deadbolt turn, and the door flew open.

"Did you get it?"

"Yeah, I found it."

"Give it to me."

"It's gone."

"What do you mean it's gone?"

"I chucked it into the river."

"What?" Ben's face flushed.

"Yeah, I figured that as long as we had the phone we could be tracked, so I stopped on the bridge and tossed it into the Caloosahatchee." Cliff grinned.

"You fucking idiot! I didn't tell you to get rid of the phone! I needed that phone here! Jesus Christ! Can't you do anything right?!

"Fuck it. It's too late now. Like I said, I chucked it." Cliff held the bag out. "Got her shit right here."

"Next time I give you instructions just fucking do what I tell you."

Ben turned away from Cliff and sat down in front of the monitors. Cliff followed, standing behind his chair. He could see the woman had turned over on the bed.

"She's waking up. I'll do the talking. You've fucked up enough for one day."

Ben kept his eyes peeled to the monitors and saw Ken back

on the couch with his laptop open, fully engaged in a video game. The woman's boss was busy typing on her computer. He could see by the focused expression on her face that she was deep in concentration.

In the room down the hall, the woman rolled back onto her other side and kicked her legs. She was facing the camera now and Ben saw around her eyes had already started turning black from his punch, and her forehead was bulging. She was in good shape, attractive . . . for a middle-aged woman, and he hoped he hadn't messed her up too much. He watched as her hands went to her face and then recoiled. For a few seconds, she stared at the wall, her eyes not moving. Ben guessed it was the tranquilizer taking its time, leaving her foggy. Then her eyes shifted to the door and she started pulling herself upright. He could see the fear starting to set in. He turned on the microphone.

"Just try to stay calm. Sit on the edge of the bed for few minutes and then everything will be explained to you. We have some clean clothes for you to change into. Just stay calm, and we won't have to hurt you again." Ben spoke evenly into the microphone. He knew she would be easier to deal with if she could keep herself calm.

The woman spotted the camera above in the corner and stared into the lens.

"Let me out of here! What happened to me? What do you want? Just let me go, and I will get you whatever you want!" Her voice was soft, still sedated, but Ben could hear pleading. "What do you want?" She was louder this time.

"Just stay calm, and we will explain everything. I am going to open your door and let you go into the bathroom to clean up and change your clothes. If you try anything we will sedate you again, so please, for your own good, just do as you're told."

He checked Cliff's expression to make sure he was calm.

"Just stay behind me. I don't think she'll try anything. She's too groggy."

When Ben set the plan for the job he decided that having the woman see their faces would not be an issue. He didn't care if she would be able to identify them later, after they let her go. He had no criminal record and he would be difficult to trace even though his escape plan wasn't well formulated yet.

As for Cliff . . . he didn't give a shit. If Cliff got caught and tried to drag him down, the cops would only spend so much time and money hunting for him before they'd give up and move on to solving the next crime. After all, he had no plans to hurt this woman, her son or her boss. In the end, it would be just another victimless crime, and he would be away sitting on the beach, or hiking in the mountains.

Ben was at the bedroom door turning the deadbolt. He cracked the door open expecting to see her on the other side, but she was still sitting on bed. He pushed open the door and faced her. "Give me the bag," he ordered Cliff. Ben took the bag, walked into the room and offered it to her.

"Here's some sweatpants. The bathroom is across the hall. You can clean up and get changed and I then I will explain what's going to happen."

The woman stood up slowly, steadying herself and waited a few seconds before stepping forward. Ben and Cliff stepped back giving her a little room.

"Just try to stay calm," Ben said with a reassuring voice.

"No one has to get hurt."

She moved slowly forward and she pulled the bag quickly from his out-stretched arm. The two men stepped back into the narrow hallway, blocking the view into the living room and Ben pointed to the open bathroom door. "There's is no lock on the door and no way out of the bathroom. Please just go and get washed and come out when you are done."

The woman tried to stretch her gaze past them toward the living room, but she gave up and looked into the bathroom.

"It's fine," Ben assured her.

She stepped into the bathroom and quickly shut the door. They could hear her play with the door knob for a moment, figuring she was checking to see if there was any way to lock it. But she gave up quickly and turned on the water. She took her time and then finally opened the door.

"Not bad," Cliff cackled at her. "She's a cougar in sweats."

"Shut up," Ben snapped.

"This way." Ben pointed toward the living room where the computer table was set up. "I am going to show you something and then explain what's going to happen. As long as everyone follows our instructions, no one gets hurt. Do you think you can do that?"

The woman stared at his face for a moment unable to find her voice and then nodded.

"Good. Sit here."

The woman sat in the chair facing the monitors, shocked at what she was seeing, and then started to cry.

CHAPTER EIGHTEEN

*O*PEN YOUR EYES! *Open your eyes!* Lindsey forced herself into consciousness. *I'm still alive!* She was struggling to wake up and rolled wearily onto one side, then the other. Something was wrong with her face. Her eyes were throbbing, and she had a massive headache. Her thighs stuck together. Finally, she forced one eye open and then the other. She was facing a wall. Her eyes closed again. They were too heavy to keep open. *Don't fall back asleep!* She rolled again to her other side and forced her eyes open again. This time she saw a door. She held her eyes open, focusing on the door. *Where am I? This doesn't look familiar. What happened to me?* She was trying to remember, forcing the memory, and then terror rose inside of her. Her heart raced, and her face throbbed. She remembered walking, then being thrown into the trunk. She reached up and touched the back of her head. *Why would anyone want to attack me this way? My face hurts so bad. Was I raped?* Her head was spinning with fear, but she was so sleepy and confused. She tried to move her eyes down to look at her body but she was too afraid that they would close again and she would slip back into darkness, and maybe this time she wouldn't ever wake up. *The door! I need to get up and get out of here.* The fogginess was slowly beginning to clear, but the pain in her face grew stronger.

She closed and then opened her eyes again. She wanted to sit up, force herself up and see her face, her head. She pushed herself up and sat on the edge of the bed, staring at the door knob. It was smooth, out of place. It didn't match the room she was in. Her eyes searched the room and saw the boarded-up window. There was no light peeking in. Just a dim bulb in a ceiling fixture. She spotted a closet with a missing door. It was empty. Then she noticed the camera up in the right corner, just under the ceiling. A red light was on. Whoever did this to her, whoever grabbed her while she minded her own business, walking right outside her neighborhood, near a school . . . was watching.

"Let me out of here!" She tried to shout, but she had no strength behind her words. She was still too groggy. More words came out of her mouth, but she didn't have full control.

"What do you want from me?"

The door knob was turning. She was trying so hard to pull her thoughts together but the pain was pulling her back down. *Are they letting me go now? I can't run like this*, she thought.

The door opened slowly and then she saw the man who attacked her. She saw another older guy, sloppy, fat . . . grinning at her, toothless. She was physically frozen but her aching brain, her bursting heart was telling her to run. The black man spoke to her quietly, calmly, trying to reassure her. She didn't know what to think. Why did he want her to change her clothes? She looked down at herself, and the smell of urine hit her. The blood rush causing her face to throb even worse. *How did this happen? I have never lost control like that.* Finally, she stood up, taking a moment to find her balance, she took the bag of clothes and followed her captors to the bathroom shutting the door behind her.

She stood for a moment, studying her face in the mirror and started to cry, but then caught herself. Crying made the pain worse. *No! I have to get a clear head if I am going to survive this. If they wanted me dead, I would be dead already. I need to figure out what they want from me. What could they possibly want from me? I am nobody. I have no money!* She took her time undressing and used the washcloth and towels that were left for her to clean herself. She filled the sink with hot water and rinsed her torn, soiled shorts and underpants, placing them on the edge of the tub, her underpants hidden underneath. Her hands were shaking. She was embarrassed and afraid, though she had no memory of how it had all happened. She slipped into the cheap sweatpants and then sat on the toilet seat to think. The crook of her arm hurt, and she held it open and examined the area. A tiny needle mark. Vomit rose quickly, and she had a strange metallic taste in her mouth. *What kind of drugs had they given her?* It took another minute to settle herself.

She leaned forward quietly pulling back the shower curtain and saw the small boarded-up window. *Fuck! No way I'm getting out through there.* She sat a little longer collecting herself and then went back to the sink to examine her swollen face in the mirror. *They hit me but I don't remember! I'm ready now and I'm going to get out of here!* She opened the door and faced her captors once again.

The black guy was striking, with piercing blue eyes and prominent features. Unusual. She stared at him wondering, had she met him before? His face was unfamiliar, and she was sure she would have remembered him. He was talking to her again, reassuring her that if she cooperated, then no one would get hurt. Her brain was still shaking off the drug, and she had to focus hard on his words. Every syllable mimicked the throbbing in her face. Then the fat guy was gawking at her. He was a pig. Hatred boiled up inside of her.

"This way," he instructed her, and she followed him into what she imagined was once a proper living room, but instead of sofas and chairs, she saw a long table with computer screens.

He guided her to the chair in the center of the table, and she sat, watching her son, watching Lisa. She wanted to reach out and touch them. Tears were streaming down her face, her whole body shaking. "Oh, my God! That's my . . . ." She stopped herself. What if they didn't know it was her son? She moved her face closer to the other monitor, at Lisa typing on her keyboard. She had never seen her home office before, but she recognized Missy, her dog, from the pictures that Lisa had texted to her over the past few years.

The black man spoke.

"We know that this is your son, Ken, and we know your boss, Lisa." They do not know about you . . . that we have you, but they will be informed soon," he explained.

Her tears had turned into sobs at the mention of her son's name. "Please don't hurt my son. He didn't do anything. Please!"

PART II
Before

CHAPTER NINETEEN

WHEN HANNA WAS six years old, she began complaining of fatigue. She was in the first grade and the days were sometimes hectic. But Donna Smith was worried when she saw Hanna's face walking toward the car with one of the elementary school volunteers. Her daughter was pale, ghostly with purplish circles under her eyes. She had low energy and put her head down on Donna's lap.

"What's wrong, baby?" Donna asked as she patted her daughter's hair.

"I'm sleepy, Mommy."

She knew something was wrong.

"Okay, baby, let's get you home and into bed and mommy will call the doctor. We need to find out why you're so tired." Hanna didn't answer, and she could hear her daughter's soft breathing. She left her sleeping in her lap and drove home slowly so no one would notice that she wasn't wearing a seatbelt.

It has to be some lingering virus, she thought. *Maybe she needs an antibiotic or some vitamins.* She considered her child's diet, which was mostly made up of grilled cheese and peanut butter sandwiches. But she knew from talking to the other mothers that this was typical for young children. Hanna drank milk and ate yogurt, so she didn't think it was a vitamin D deficiency, but it had to be something.

When they arrived home, Donna had to carry Hanna to her room. She laid her on the bed and tucked her in with her stuffed yellow chicken. She watched her sleeping daughter, sleeping in the middle of the day, with dark circles under eyes, and she was worried. She sent a text to Jason.

"Hanna's not right. Came out of school again with no energy. Slept in the car and sleeping now at home. I am calling the pediatrician." A few minutes later he replied.

"K, let me know when and I will try to get out of here. We are really backed up. I may even have to stay late."

She wasn't happy with his response. He had been working a ridiculous number of hours, and the work sounded awful, tedious and boring. She didn't understand why a doctor would choose that field of work. "Why don't you go into practice?" she asked him. He would nod his head and say that he didn't want to be around sick people. It made no sense to her. Why did he become a doctor? She understood that many doctors worked behind the scenes, but still, she suggested he do a fellowship in something interesting. He refused, telling her that although he was overworked, he liked the work and it was a good fit for their lifestyle. She didn't agree, especially when he started working weekends.

Donna was able to get an appointment with the pediatrician the next morning, but Jason didn't attend. He told her to call him when they were done.

They had first met Dr. Rachel Jamison before Hanna was born to be sure that she was a good match for their child-raising philosophies.

Some of the doctors they met had a more 'naturalistic' approach.

"Just let your child be sick, and they will grow up with stronger immunities." A young pediatrician had told them.

They giggled in the elevator after on the way to the car. There were others with even stranger ideas about raising a child, but when they met Dr. Jamison, they had an instant connection. She was about their age and had two children of her own. She was practical and had just the right amount of concern when it was necessary, and once Hanna was born, she was genuine with their daughter. They hoped she had no plans to leave her practice and would stay with Hanna throughout her childhood.

When she arrived at Dr. Jamison's office the next morning, Hanna was still exhausted. She held her on her lap and watched a Disney movie on the waiting room TV. By the time the nurse called her name, she was asleep on Donna's shoulder.

She pulled up the heavy child and slung her over her shoulder whispering in her ear. "Hanna, time to see Dr. J. Try to wake up, sweetie." Hanna wiggled in her arms and dug her head in deeper into her neck. They sat in a chair next to the examining table.

Dr. Jamison entered the room with a warm smile and greeted Donna. "What have we here, Hanna? You are growing so big!" Hanna clung to her mother and didn't respond. Donna spoke, "She's been very tired lately, and I don't like the way she looks. She's pale and has no energy. She comes home from school exhausted and just wants to sleep. She is eating, but it seems forced. She chews her food for too long, with a distressed look on her face. I am getting worried. Do you think this is just a virus?" she asked hopefully.

"Well, let me do a quick exam, and we'll see what's happening. After a few minutes of looking in ears, tapping on knees and taking Hanna's temperature, Dr. Jamison sat on the small rolling stool.

"I think we should get some blood work done just to rule out anything more serious than a virus. She turned her back for a moment while she typed something into the small terminal that was anchored low on the wall, then she spun back around.

"One of the nurses will be come in shortly and draw a couple of tubes."

"When will we have results?"

"It shouldn't take more than a day, and I will call you." Try not to worry; this is purely routine. My guess is that she has a virus that's hanging on."

Hanna was wrapped around Donna's neck nearly strangling her.

"She's never given blood before," Donna responded.

"Our nurses are pros. Nothing to worry about." She got up from the stool and leaned over to peek at Hanna's face. "Don't worry, little chick . . . it's like a tiny mosquito bite, and then it's over. You can sit in Mommy's lap," she added rubbing Hanna's back.

A few moments later a nurse came in, and just as Dr. Jamison said, quickly arranged Hanna in Donna's lap, and while distracting her with talk about Disney princesses, she skillfully drew the blood from her arm filling two colored tubes.

"All done!" the nurse announced sticking a colorful bandage on Hanna's arm.

Jason worked until eleven that night and was only responding to texts with one-word answers. Donna tried to sleep, but she tossed and turned, worried about what the blood tests would reveal. She thought she saw the concern on Dr. Jamison's face as well, but maybe she was over analyzing. She tended to panic at even the slightest threat to Hanna's health.

The next morning, Donna decided to keep Hanna home from school again. She was worried about exposing her to other kids and teachers in the classroom. Jason agreed. He entered

Hanna's room watching her sleep for a moment and then closed the door.

"I am heading to work. Call me if you hear anything."

Donna was disappointed and didn't answer him. He left the house without acknowledging her or saying goodbye. She was angry at him. She wanted him to stay with her, comfort her until they heard news.

The phone rang at nine. "Donna?" It was Dr. Jamison's voice.

"Yes, this is Donna," she answered.

"Hi, it's Rachel Jamison." Donna's heart was pounding. In the nearly seven years they had known Dr. Jamison she had never addressed herself by her first name.

"We have Hanna's blood test results and I think we should talk. Would it be possible for you and Jason to come into the office and meet?" Donna froze.

"Um . . . sure, I will call him now. What time should we come in?"

"Whenever you get here is fine. I will make time in my schedule. I will see you soon." She ended the call before Donna could respond.

She set her phone down and tried to stop her racing thoughts. Hanna is fine she told herself. She wants us to come so she can tell us that it's a normal childhood virus that needs some special medication.

She walked outside onto the lanai and admired her pool, forcing the negative thoughts away. Her swimming pool had a calming effect, and she needed strength to get through the day. She climbed the stairs to Hanna's room. She checked on her sleeping child and noticed how pale she was. She touched Hanna's cheek making her flinch, then settle. She didn't feel feverish. She adjusted her blankets and then went back into the kitchen and picked up her phone to call Jason. She got his voicemail.

She texted, "Please call me. Dr. wants us to come to her office today. I am so worried. Please call me ASAP."

An hour went by and there was still no call or text from him. She checked on Hanna again, and she was sound asleep. She decided to try calling his cell one more time, and if he didn't answer, she would call the main office number and try to get through to him on a desk phone. Maybe he had accidentally turned his phone off or forgotten to charge the battery. She called his cell, and again the call went straight to voicemail. She remembered he had a stack of business cards in the drawer next to the bed and went into the bedroom.

Sitting on Jason's side of the bed she opened the top drawer of the night stand; nothing unusual, just pens, notepads and assorted paper clips. She shifted the contents of the drawer searching for his business cards and didn't find any. She pulled the lower drawer open and noticed a locked metal box. She took it out of the drawer examining it from all sides, and then shook it, hearing the contents rattle. She didn't remember seeing this box before. Could this be a gun? But why wouldn't he have told her if he bought a gun? It didn't feel heavy enough for it to be a gun. She shook it again. It sounded like a book or papers. She heard her cell phone ring and shoved the metal box back into the drawer and ran down the stairs to the kitchen.

"Jason! What took you so long? I'm freaking out here." She was breathless from her run down the stairs.

"Calm down!" He raised his voice into the phone. "What did she say?" he asked.

"She wants us to come in . . . to talk. She said that she had some concerns about the blood test results. She said she would see us whenever we got there . . . she'd make time even though we don't have an appointment. I don't like the sound of this. Hanna is still sleeping. Can you come home?" she pleaded.

"I will meet you there. It's closer for me just to meet you."

"Jason! Can you not think about work for one minute? I'm scared!"

He ignored her plea.

"Get Hanna up, and I will meet you at Dr. Jamison's office in forty-five minutes."

He ended the call. Donna threw the phone into her bag and went to Hanna's room.

The drive to Dr. Jamison's office took longer than she anticipated. The seasonal traffic was heavy and hitting every red light didn't help.

Hanna was awake and sitting in her booster sit in the back, and she found herself checking her in the rear-view mirror every few seconds. She was flipping through a book and talking to herself, busy and content. Donna tried to find joy in the sight of her, but she was too worried.

An hour later they were seated in Dr. Jamison's office.

"Good morning. Let's have Hanna stay with one of the nurses while we talk." Dr. Jamison picked up her desk phone and called the front desk. A moment later the office door opened and a smiling nurse with a bright cartoon printed top held out her hand to Hanna.

"Okay, so we have the results, and it shows that Hanna has a very high white cell count." Jason squeezed Donna's hand.

"What does this mean?" asked Donna but Jason interrupted.

"She has leukemia," he answered grimly.

"No, now let's not jump the gun here. Our next step will be to get a bone marrow biopsy. This will give us a definitive diagnosis and then we can develop the most appropriate treatment plan." Donna's face twisted with anguish.

"Is she going to die?"

"Donna, I know this is tough news to hear, but please try not to think ahead. Let's get all the testing done and then make some decisions."

Jason had a blank stare and for a moment the office was silent. Then he turned to Donna.

"I am going to make sure she has the best doctors and the best treatment. I promise you right now . . . no matter what these test results say, our daughter will be alright." Jason's eyes were wet with tears.

Dr. Jamison interjected. "Again, let's not panic. She has a suspiciously high white cell count and appears to be symptomatic. Let's follow the protocol and get the bone marrow biopsy done. My secretary will get it scheduled this week. In the meantime, I would recommend that you keep Hanna home from school until we know for sure. We don't want her to contract any viruses, colds or otherwise."

Everything changed. The Smith's world turned upside down. The next six years invoked an excruciating level of stress that nearly tore them apart. Young Hanna endured test after test, chemotherapy infusions, and multitudes of medication, while Jason and Donna sat by and watched their child suffer more than any child should ever suffer.

They networked and searched endlessly for a stem cell donor but never found a match. They frequently argued about his job, whether or not he would be present at Hanna's next doctor's appointment or treatment, and they spent many nights sleeping apart. Donna would sleep with Hanna, arms wrapped around her warm body, listening to her breathing, and he would come in late, from work she assumed, peek at them through the crack in the door, and then go to their bedroom by himself. Some mornings she would wake up, and he would already be gone.

As the years passed and the joy of Hanna's remission turned to pain as the insidious disease returned three times over, Jason's personality grew dark. He would go days without speaking to her, and sometimes he barely acknowledged Hanna. He developed strange personal habits, like sleeping in his clothes and crossing his arms over his chest, mummy-like. When she asked him if he was alright, he would grunt or ignore her, or say he was tired and needed to lay down.

Once on a Sunday when Hanna was eight and in remission for the second time, she suggested they go to the beach for the day. He agreed to go and was excited to spend the day together. They loaded up the car with the beach chairs, a cooler and umbrella and made the short fifteen-mile trip.

During the ride, Donna commented on how they live right near the beach and never go, and somehow that turned into a fight. Hanna was screaming at them from the back seat, begging them to stop arguing. Donna remembered how they had to circle the parking lot for ten minutes to find a space and Jason continued the argument blaming her for not being ready to leave earlier. And when they finally got out to the sand and set up the chairs, he walked off without saying anything and was gone for two hours. Hanna was exhausted from the hot sun and Donna was livid. It was the last time they went to the beach as a family.

Hanna became sick again just before her twelfth birthday, and it was the same story. She was weak and tired, and her white cell count was through the roof. She had another round of chemo, and the search continued for a stem cell donor.

Donna talked to Jason about getting pregnant again, a new baby that could be a stem cell match for Hanna, but he was against the idea. He told her it was unethical and even said it was nothing more than a science experiment. She thought he was irrational.

"What if the kid isn't a match? Would we resent him?" he asked.

She tried to argue her point. If the child were a match, then they'd have two wonderful children to love, and if the child weren't a match, then they'd still have two wonderful children to love. Jason said no, and the conversation was over.

Fortunately, the third round of chemo put her into remission quickly despite never getting the stem cells. Hanna had bounced back. She was warm and friendly, social and she cared about the people in her life. She was a good girl and a great daughter, and she was growing up fast. She had already lost that little girl look and was nearing puberty.

As Donna approached the front of the pickup line, she could see Hanna talking, animated with a group of girls, smiling and laughing. Donna tooted the horn, and Hanna turned her way and waved. She turned back to her friends saying goodbye and ran to the car. "Hi, Mom!" She grinned leaning over to kiss Donna's cheek.

CHAPTER TWENTY

"MOM? ARE YOU there?" Hanna called down the stairs to her mother.

"Mom! I need help with a project." Donna was in the kitchen making dinner and heard her daughter calling. She smiled and thought, we're going to make it. It's all behind us now, and Hanna is healthy. She will live a long and happy life, maybe go to Harvard!

"Mom!" Hanna was halfway down the stairs.

"I'm in the kitchen," Donna answered.

"Mom, the history teacher, gave us a project, and I need help. It's a group project, with four of us, but only me and Darius and Gia know what we're doing. I'm afraid we won't get a good grade if the other kid doesn't do his part. What do you think we should do?"

When Hanna entered the kitchen, she was texting on her phone.

"Who are you texting?" Donna asked her.

"Gia. She agrees with me!"

"Well, maybe the other boy just needs a little extra help."

"No, Mom! It's not like that. He's at a lower level. I swear the teacher puts the dumb kids in with the smart kids so they can let us teach them."

"Hanna! That's a terrible thing to say!"

"Well, it's true! I'm smart, and Darius and Gia are really smart, but Stevie is clueless."

"Okay, that's enough."

"Mom, trust me." She accentuated the 'trust'.

"Hanna, you have to figure out how to work together on this. I am sure everyone wants to do well, even Stevie. Why not just divvy up the work, and then you can check theirs when it's done?"

"Mom!" Hanna stomped her foot.

"Hanna, go to your room!" Donna turned her back so her daughter wouldn't see her holding in her laughter, but she couldn't help it and let out a giggle. It was normal, healthy behavior for a thirteen-year-old girl. She had been in full remission now for over a year. Her hair was growing long and lush, and her skin glowed, though an occasional blemish could be cause for tears. At her last check up with Dr. Jamison last month, all her labs were within normal range. Hanna and Donna hugged Dr. Jamison, thanking her for all that she had done, and continued to do for them. Dr. Jamison told us that each passing month with normal lab work put Hanna closer and closer to a healthy life filled with happiness and longevity.

Donna heard the garage door open, and she checked the time. It was six-thirty. He's home early, she thought.

Jason entered the kitchen with a quiet hello, avoiding eye contact, and then jogged up the stairs. He barely spoke to her anymore, and her recent joy with Hanna quickly turned to sadness. She continued preparing their dinner, grateful that she had cooked enough for the three of them. On most days, Donna and Hanna ate together, and Jason would eat alone when he eventually came home from work. Donna set the table and then hollered up the stairs.

"Dinner's ready!"

Hanna barreled down the stairs, and Jason followed. The three sat at the table eating, while Hanna talked about her new math project.

"Daddy, one of the kids I have to work with, is in the lower level math class. Me, Gia and Darius are going to have to do all the work because this kid doesn't know how. Do you think that's fair?"

"What does your mother say?"

"She said I should just deal with it. We divvy up the work and then just fix the other kid's work if he gets it wrong."

"I didn't exactly say that," Donna chimed putting a forkful of spaghetti in her mouth.

"Yes, you did!" Hanna whined. "Daddy, I have to get an A on this."

"Honey, why don't you wait and see how the other boy does. Maybe he's smarter than you think. Sometimes people can surprise you."

They ate the rest of their dinner and then Hanna asked to be excused.

"How was your day?" Donna asked Jason.

"Fine. How was yours?"

"It was alright. I got some hours in at the reading program. There are so many kids who need help. I wish I could do more."

A moment passed before Jason spoke.

"I have to go out and run some errands. I'll be back later."

"Where are you going?"

"Just out. As I said, I have some errands."

Donna got up from the table and picked up the dishes, her back to Jason as he left through the kitchen out to the garage. She wanted so bad to confront him about his attitude toward her, but she was afraid. She was certain that he was having an affair, though she had no proof.

It had been nearly six months since they had last made

love, and that last time was different, mechanical. She wanted to say something then, but she couldn't face the prospect of a scene, him packing a bag, explaining to Hanna, so she let it go and hoped he would be the first one to say something. But that hadn't happened. Perhaps he was just as afraid as she was. Donna spent many days imagining what hers and Hanna's life would be like divorced from Jason. Would Hanna resent her or him? Would she ever find love again? What if Hanna got sick again? She couldn't bear the thought.

She finished cleaning up the dishes and went up to her bedroom. She sat on Jason's side of the bed and opened the drawer of the night stand like she had done many times since she became suspicious. Nothing had changed from the last time she inspected the contents. She opened the bottom draw, and the metal box lay in its usual spot. She never did ask him about it. What did it matter?

Donna had tried on several occasions to snoop in Jason's cell phone and laptop but was never successful. He had everything password protected, and she spent hours trying to guess them. When she asked to borrow his phone because hers wasn't charged, he told her no, because there was patient information on the phone and he couldn't allow her access. It was the same answer for his laptop. *Patient information . . . right*, she thought.

She climbed on the bed onto her side and pulled her spare pillow in close against her body. She stuffed one of Jason's pillows behind her back and lay there in a fetal position. The pillows pressed against her body gave her comfort like she was being held, and she thought back to happier days when they were in love, and Jason's career was just getting started. She remembered the struggles he had finding the right fit, and she sometimes wondered if she had pushed him too hard to succeed. Why was he so insecure? She thought of how happy they were when she was pregnant.

Hanna came into the room.

"Mom?"

"I'm awake, honey . . . just resting."

"Will you please tell me why you and Daddy are fighting?"

Donna patted the bed and Hanna jumped on, nearly bouncing her to the other side of the bed. They both laughed, and Donna pulled her in for a cuddle.

"Daddy is very busy at work, and it makes me sad sometimes that he doesn't spend more time at home. We're not really fighting."

"Is he going to get a different job?"

"I've asked him to, but I don't know if he will."

Hanna wrapped her arms around her mother and pulled her close.

"Please don't be sad."

Donna was touched be her concern, and she patted her head, noting how thick her hair had become since she'd been in remission.

"Your hair is beautiful, honey."

They lay together for a while until Donna coaxed her out to her room.

CHAPTER TWENTY-ONE

"HANNA, WAKE UP. Hanna, you have to get ready for school." It had been three months since her last round of blood work, but this was the third day in a row that Donna had to wrestle her daughter out of bed.

"Hanna!" Her voice shook as she raised her volume. Hanna rolled over and opened her eyes.

"Mom, I'm tired," she whined. "I don't want to go to school today. Can I stay home?"

Donna didn't hesitate. "No! Now get up. You only have a half day today because we have an appointment. You need your lab work done."

Hanna rolled up to a sitting position, hair covering her face and she groaned. "I'm so sick of this."

"I know, baby. But your nineteen months out and going strong. You can do it," she said encouragingly.

Over the past month, Donna could see Hanna maturing. Her body was developing curves, and she needed a bra under most of her clothes. Donna was grateful for the changes. To her, it meant that Hanna's body was functioning normally and the nightmare was ending. But at the same time, she worried that a new nightmare with Jason was approaching.

As usual, he had left for work before she had woken up. She

had several opportunities to confront him about his behavior, his aloofness and sometimes total disregard for her feelings, but she still couldn't bring herself to say the words. There were times when her eyes met his, and she opened her mouth to speak. She wanted to ask what was wrong, what had changed, why was he ignoring her, but she was afraid to hear the truth. She knew it would come to a head one way or another, and she hoped it would be soon.

Later that day, Donna arrived at the school to pick up Hanna at her appointment. She parked her car in front of the school and entered the building, stopping at the front office to sign out her daughter. She recognized the secretary from all the other times she had picked up Hanna for her doctor's appointments, and she greeted her warmly.

"Hi, Joanne, I'm here to pick up Hanna. She has a lab appointment today."

"It's great to see you, Donna! How is Hanna doing? She looks well," Joanne commented.

"Yes, she's doing great. Thank you for asking." Joanne picked up the desk phone and dialed a short extension.

"Hi, this is the front office. Will you send Hanna out? Her mother is here. What? When?" Joanne's brow furrowed.

"What's going on?" Donna asked concerned. Joanne hung up the phone.

"Hanna is in the nurse's office. She just got there a few minutes ago complaining that she felt weak and tired. I'll bring you down there."

Donna followed the secretary to a small office nearby. A woman wearing pink scrubs that Donna recognized greeted them.

"Hi, Donna. Hanna's lying down in the back. She came in a few minutes ago complaining of feeling weak and tired."

Donna had a pit in her stomach hearing the nurse's words.

There had been many false alarms when Hanna was in remission, which her doctor said was normal considering the anxiety a child had in knowing they had a serious illness.

Donna moved past the nurse and entered a small darkened room with a long-padded bench. Hanna was lying on her side.

"Hanna, what's wrong?"

Hanna sat up surprised to see her mother. "How did you get here so fast?" she asked.

"Don't you remember, you have a lab appointment today. It's twelve. We need to be there in fifteen minutes."

"Oh, right. I forgot. I felt really sleepy, so the teacher let me come here to lie down." Hanna was off the bench and reaching for her backpack.

Donna noted her daughter's pale face. It was good she was going for labs today. She was worried now. They got into the car, and Donna drove to the lab without talking. Hanna's head was wedged between the seat and the window, and her eyes were closed. When they arrived, Donna sat for a moment and pulled out her phone. She texted Jason.

"Just picked up Hanna at school. She was in nurse's office tired. We are at the lab. I'm worried."

She waited a moment but no reply. She touched her daughter's shoulder and said, "We're here."

CHAPTER TWENTY-TWO

HERE WE GO again, he thought reading his wife's text. Every time Hanna sneezed Donna panicked and sent him a text. Jason was sure that the dark days were behind them. She was the furthest into remission that she had ever been. He decided not to respond, and he set his phone back on his desk. A few minutes later his phone chimed again.

"Will you be here tonight?"

Jason smiled and texted back, "Maybe. Hanna not feeling well. Will let you know."

Jason waited for a response, but none came. He hated to say no, but Hanna always came first.

Jason peeked over his cubicle wall and saw Ron Shay's face down the hall. He stood up and waved, grabbing his attention.

"Hey, buddy, haven't seen you in a while," Jason said as Ron plopped himself down on the chair opposite Jason's desk.

"Yeah, I've been working from home more often. I can get more done . . . fewer interruptions if you know what I mean."

"It doesn't work that way for me. Donna is home most of the time, and Hanna has friends in the house," Jason replied.

"How's she doing? Still in remission, I hope."

"Yes, it's nineteen months."

"Great news! Hope it's forever. What an ordeal. I know

you've been through a lot, buddy, and I'm always here if you need anything."

"You've been a good friend," Jason told him. "So, what are you working on?"

"We've got a slew of new medications coming out of the FDA, and couple of devices that the Chief wants us to look at."

"Cool. Are any of the meds something that I'd want to know about?"

"You'd be the first one I'd tell. But there is something that might be coming down the pike. Have you done any reading about the HSP 90 Inhibitors? They are in late stage trials and getting great results, but it's adults only."

Jason's thoughts flashed to Hanna. If she ever needed chemo again, this drug would not be available for her. In all of his years working as Medical Director, he never gave much thought about these things until it affected his daughter. It was so unfair, but he knew that he would be hard-pressed to find a doctor who would prescribe a medication that wasn't FDA approved for that purpose. And even if he could find someone to prescribe the treatment, his insurance company—Unified, or any other insurance company for that matter, would never cover the cost. Typically, these new drugs cost thousands and thousands of dollars. Fortunately, she was in remission, and he hoped that thinking about new drugs was not in his or Hanna's future.

"No, I hadn't heard about it, but keep me posted," Jason replied.

"How are things going with Donna? Are you still in the dog house?" Ron chuckled.

"I hate to say it, but I don't think we're going to make it. We haven't talked divorce, but I think we both know that the only reason we've stayed together is because of Hanna. It's starting to feel like now is the right time to make a move."

"Wow, sorry, man. I didn't realize things were that bad."

"It's not bad . . . we're just not together if you know what I mean."

"Yeah, I know what you mean."

Ron rose from his chair putting his hands on his hips and leaned back in a stretch. "I gotta get back to work. It's all piled up. These idiots keep appealing every denial as if I'm going to change my mind. We need to have someone in the Whitehouse who isn't so soft on patient rights. If you buy insurance, you get what you pay for. Simple as that."

"Yeah, but you forget . . . without all the denials, you and I don't have jobs," Jason reminded him.

"There are other jobs. Better jobs. I'll catch up with you later."

He thought about Ron's comment—plenty of jobs, better jobs, but he was not sure that he agreed. He recalled his first residency after graduating medical school. He and Donna were already married, and both had high hopes for his budding medical career.

He applied for a surgical residency at a large Miami hospital and was lucky enough to be chosen, despite his less-than-average school performance. Donna was so excited to be the wife of a surgeon, but from very early on he had his doubts. He was honest with himself, brutally honest . . . at least, that's what he called it. Donna said it was insecurity. He was intimidated by the experienced surgeons and had trouble building relationships.

The work was too challenging. He was constantly stressed, and worried that his patients would die. He envisioned himself sitting in a courtroom, sued, blamed for someone's death, or worse . . . floating above himself at the most inopportune moment. It didn't take long for the chief of surgery to realize that Jason didn't have the confidence to do the job.

"Jason, after spending time with you in the OR, the team feels that you might be better suited to work in a different medical service. Have you put any thought into what you'd like to do?"

He still had the distinct memory of not being able to breathe through the entire discussion and watching the scene from a distance, as if it was a TV episode.

He drove home to their tiny apartment nearly in tears at the thought of disappointing his new bride. But he had no choice. They didn't want him, and truthfully, he didn't want to be there.

It took about six months to land his next residency in Primary Care. This time his hospital affiliation was across the state, in Southwest Florida. They moved again into another small apartment.

He spent the next three years in a small practice, under the tutelage of a highly competent and popular physician. He made it through, but knew his place . . . in the shadow, in the background, doctoring the patients who begged for appointments with the lead physician but just couldn't get in. When was nearly finished with the residency, he didn't bother applying for a permanent position and had no intention of taking the necessary certification exams. He knew they didn't want him, and once again he had to face his wife and explain his failure.

Ron Shay was wrong, at least where his job was concerned. This job, as a medical director in an insurance company, was the best job he was ever going to get.

Jason was curious about the new HSP 90 Inhibitor that Ron had mentioned. He opened a new browser and typed into the search menu. He read the research, or as much as he could understand, for nearly thirty minutes, and scribbled some notes on a pad. It appeared that nearly every participant in the study achieved remission. It was practically unheard of. All of the recipients had the same type of leukemia as Hanna, and many lives were saved.

He exited out of his work profile and checked his phone for messages, but nothing new had come in. He read his last message again . . . "Will you be here tonight?"

CHAPTER TWENTY-THREE

TWO DAYS AFTER her blood test, Hanna, still tired, went to school while Jason and Donna sat in Rachel Jamison's office.

"I am so sorry to tell you this, but Hanna's white cell count is high again."

Jason stood up and turned away.

"No!" he yelled. "It's not possible!"

Donna dropped her face into her hands and shook her head. Her heart thundered in her ears.

"I will make a phone call to the pediatric oncology team and get her in for additional testing right away."

Donna instantly burst into tears, and Jason instinctively reached for her hand, which she quickly retracted.

"Test her again. She's in remission. The test is wrong." Jason was pacing now, his anger rising.

"I understand how you feel, Jason, and I can order another CBC, but it's just going to delay the inevitable. She needs to start treatment as soon as possible."

Jason's vision blurred and sweat dripped down his back.

"Just test her again, and I will call the oncologist."

"Please sit down, Jason. Getting angry isn't going to help anyone here." Donna said.

"We have to tell Hanna." Her voice cracked again, and tears started to fall.

"We need to try something different. A new treatment." He thought about his recent conversation with Ron Shay.

"I hear you. But I'm not sure what new options we have. I know you've heard me tell you this, before but we have to stick to the process. Let's get the testing done and then we'll meet with the oncologist."

Just hearing the words 'pediatric oncologist' made Donna shiver.

"Why does this keep happening? We've done everything right for her. She's eating well, exercising and showing signs of puberty." Donna forced the words through her sobs.

"I wish I had answers for you. I know it's devastating, but we have to move forward."

Dr. Jamison got up from behind her desk and wrapped her arm around Donna's shoulders, holding her head against her side.

The couple stayed silent, standing on opposite sides of the elevator as they left Dr. Jamison's office. When the doors opened to the sun-filled lobby, Donna stepped out of the elevator and looked back at Jason.

"Are you coming?" she asked.

Jason didn't answer, and Donna noticed a glazed look in his eyes.

"What's wrong with you?" Again he didn't answer and the elevator doors closed.

Donna's heart quickened, and she turned back to the elevator pushing the button to open the door.

"Jason!" she yelled, her voice bouncing off the mirrored elevator walls.

"What? Why are you yelling?"

"There's something wrong with you, Jason. You need to see a doctor."

Donna turned away again sensing he was following behind her and they stopped at the side of the parking lot. It was at least ninety-degrees, and the humidity was high. The sun was beating on her, and for a second she flashed on her swimming pool. She saw herself submerged in the cool water and just wanted to go home. She walked to the car, Jason still following, and turned.

"She's going to die. Isn't she? Her back slumped against the hot car.

"No! Stop saying that!" Jason shouted.

"I was talking to Ron Shay today at the office, and he mentioned a new drug that was just FDA approved. I will look into it and send an email over to the oncologist. In the meantime, we need to prepare Hanna. We have to keep her strong and positive. Her attitude had a lot to do with her recovery, as she's shown us already. She's a little older now, and she's stronger."

"But she's still just a child. She's barely started puberty. Will these drugs affect how she develops?"

"I don't know. All I know is that we have to stay strong for her." He opened his arms, and Donna leaned against him. He wrapped an arm around her shoulder, but her body stiffened, and distance remained between them.

CHAPTER TWENTY-FOUR

THE NEXT DAY Jason had agreed to leave work early, pick up Hanna at school and meet Donna at the pediatric oncologist's office. The air was thick with humidity, and the sun was hazy behind the building clouds. He turned the car into the parent pick-up lane next to the fence and pulled up to the front door of the school. He left the car running.

Hanna was waiting for him in the lobby, sitting on a wood bench digging through her backpack. Jason caught the secretary's eye and waved, then motioned Hanna to follow. He put his arm around her slender shoulders and asked her, "How are you feeling today?"

"I'm okay, just a little tired. But I don't want to miss school. I have a big project due."

"I know, honey. Let's see what the doctor says, and we'll make some decisions from there."

There were just about at the door to leave the building when Hanna heard a voice calling her.

"Hanna!"

She turned to see Darius Williams approaching.

"Darius! What are you doing out of class?"

"Hi, Dr. Smith," Darius said respectfully.

"Hello, Darius. Good to see you."

"I have to pick up something in the office. Where are you going?"

Hanna's face dropped, and she hesitated, her eyes fixed on the floor.

"I have an appointment for a test," she said quietly.

She lifted her gaze and their eyes met and held for a moment. Darius knew what she was saying. His shoulders slumped.

"Will you let me know what happens?"

"Yeah, I'll send Gia an email, and I will write you a note if I can. I'm not sure if I can come back to school." Hanna studied her father's face, but his expression was blank.

The two kids took a step closer, wanting to hug, but held back.

"See you later," Hanna said.

Darius nodded, "Bye."

CHAPTER TWENTY-FIVE

THE LEE ELEMENTARY school made a big production of welcoming first graders into the school and Darius still remembered his first day, but not because it was a joyful experience.

His mother had driven him to school that day, but only as far as the fence before she told him to get out of the car. He remembered arguing with her, pleading.

"Mom, you have to get in the line with everyone else!"

But she wasn't interested in any parent lines or being a parent at all for that matter.

"You can walk from here. I ain't getting' in no line."

"What should I do about lunch?" he asked.

She opened her wallet spreading it wide for him to see.

"You'll have to borrow off other kids. I ain't have no money. Now git going. I ain't got all day here."

Darius got out of his mother's car and walked along the chain link fence down the long driveway to the school. He saw a crowd of parents, teachers, and kids gathered by the door and tried to pretend he belonged. He remembered the fear. He didn't know where he belonged, where he should go. A moment later a pretty white girl wearing glasses was standing next to him waving into the crowd. She turned to him and said,

"I'm Hanna. What's your name?"

"Darius Williams."

"Where's your mom?"

"She's already gone," he answered, lowering his eyes.

"You can stay with me," she said grabbing his arm.

Hanna was just that way. She was always there for him. She never faltered on their friendship, even when she was sick. He knew he had a crush, maybe more than a crush on her. He knew that he loved her.

As each school year approached, he worried that he would be separated from Hanna, that they would have different teachers and be on opposite ends of the building. He begged Hanna to ask her mom to call the school and make sure they could stay together.

When they were in the fourth grade, Gia Bucci was new to the school, having moved from California for her dad's job. Hanna hugged her and told her not to feel scared on her first day of school.

Hanna and Gia made him feel special. They were all getting straight A's in school and were proud to be labeled as the smart kids in the class.

Hanna's mother was always so nice to him, sending extra food in Hanna's lunch or even sending money so that he could buy his lunch. He didn't know what to say when Hanna gave him money or sandwiches.

She would just play it down and tell him that it was okay. "We always have too much food in the house," she would say. He always said thank you when he was at her house, or at Gia's house when Hanna was sick. He knew his Gramma would want him to be polite.

One rainy day, Hanna's mother offered to drive him home from school so he wouldn't have to ride his bike. When they pulled into his gravel driveway, she asked to meet his mother, but he was too embarrassed and said no. He couldn't imagine what his mother might say or do if she was high, or her boyfriend was with her. She quickly dropped the idea and let him know that he was always welcome at Hanna's home.

Sometime later, when Hanna got sick again, he wrote her a letter and gave it to their teacher to include with her assignments which her mother picked up regularly.

"Hanna, I wish it was me instead of you. Can I give you some blood?" Hanna sent a letter back thanking him, letting him know he would have to ask his mother. He would do anything for Hanna, but he couldn't let his mother or brother find out. They would never understand, and he worried they would do something to take advantage of his friendship.

Now, here they were again, both of them thirteen, and Hanna was sick again. He entered the school office to pick up papers for his teacher, catching the secretary's eyes.

"I was sorry to hear about Hanna too. I know you are close friends," she said.

Darius nodded and headed back to his classroom.

CHAPTER TWENTY-SIX

JASON OPENED THE car door for his daughter, and they drove in silence to the doctor's office.

Donna was waiting in the lobby when they arrived, and she opened her arms hugging Hanna while she studied Jason's face.

"Mommy, why is this happening again? I'm so tired of the needles and the drugs."

"I know, honey. Let's see what we need to do before we get too upset."

Jason reached for his Hanna's hand as they entered the elevator. He avoided Donna's stare. They checked in with the receptionist and Hanna settled into a chair, pulling her knees up and playing on her phone.

Donna noticed Jason's odd behavior. He was pacing the perimeter of the waiting room and appeared to be talking to himself while he rubbed his chest. Then he stuffed both hands in his pockets and shook his head. She heard him sigh and she got up and approached him, touching his shoulder, startling him.

His eyes were wide like she caught him in a lie.

"What?"

"You're walking around the room rubbing your chest. Are you alright?"

"I'm fine. And I wasn't rubbing my chest," he said sarcastically. "I was thinking about that drug I mentioned before. I'm going to ask the oncologist about it."

"Well you were rubbing your chest, and I've seen you do it before." She turned away and sat next to Hanna.

A few moments later the door opened, and the oncologist poked his head into the room. He was a burly man in his sixties, with a warm, ruddy complexion.

"Come in. Come in." He waved them toward the door.

"Hello, Hanna, Mr. & Mrs. Smith, please have a seat. I've reviewed Hanna's recent labs, and as you know, she appears to have slipped out of remission. I'd like to get a chest X-ray and make sure that's clear and that nothing else is going on. Assuming the X-ray is clear, we need to start chemo as quickly as possible."

"What are we going to do differently this time?" Jason asked. "I know we talked about stem cells. We can't give up on finding a donor."

"Jason, we've tapped everyone in the family, and she's already on the recipient list," Donna replied.

"We should ask everyone who said no the first time," Jason answered. "What about clinical trials?"

"I will make some inquiries on that subject," the doctor responded.

Hanna started to cry, and Donna pulled her up from her chair to hug her.

"I heard about a new drug that was just FDA approved . . . Cineth," said Jason.

"Yes, I heard about it too, but it's only for adults. We can't use it on the kids. It's a shame because I heard they are getting good results in the trials," the doctor added.

"There must be some way to get it," Donna replied.

"The manufacturer won't give it to us for off-label use. It's just the way it works with these new drugs. It takes a while before the dust settles. You know it's always about liability," the doctor said.

Jason's head was spinning and the familiar band around his chest tightened. As soon as he got back to the office, he was going to do some research. He wanted to know which pharmaceutical company owned the drug. Maybe he knew someone there and could make an inquiry. He couldn't just do nothing and sit by ✔ watching his daughter's condition continue to deteriorate.

The Smiths left the office and headed to the imaging department for Hanna's chest X-ray. The wait was short, and they were done in less than thirty minutes.

"I'm heading back to the office. I want to do some research on the drug I asked about. I will be home later."

"Why can't you do your research at home?"

"I'll see you later."

He answered curtly with one arm still hugging his daughter.

Jason was behind his desk forty-five minutes later, logging into his profile. He accessed the pharmacy menu and searched Cineth. No results. He opened a web browser outside of his Unified Insurance profile and searched again. He landed on the Weston Pharmaceutical website and began reading. The drug had successfully passed all clinical trials on adult patients with glowing results. Jason picked up the phone and dialed Ron's extension.

"Hey, it's Jason. Are you free to talk?" He hung up the phone and walked to the opposite end of the building where Ron was waiting in his cubicle.

"What's up?" Ron asked.

"Hanna is out of remission again."

"Oh, buddy . . . sorry that hear that. Anything I can do?"

"I asked the oncologist about Cineth, but he said no go. It's for adults only. I checked our pharmacy database, and it hasn't been entered yet. Can you check with the policy team and see if they are working on it?"

"Yeah, but even if they are, it's not approved for pediatric use."

"I know, but there must be some way to get it. I know that I'd be asking a lot, but if I can get the doctor to order it, will you approve it when they call for the pre-service request?"

"Jason, what are you thinking? That's illegal. You know I could lose my license. I know this is a horrible situation, but we can't cut corners like that. It would take about five seconds for the team to see what we were up to."

"Yeah, I know. Sorry, I asked. I feel so out of control."

"I understand." Ron got up from his chair and patted Jason on the back.

He left Ron's office and went back to his desk, then logged back into his profile and typed in his insurance ID number. As expected, he was denied access. Jason knew that health insurance companies block employee access to their profile to avoid the temptation of interfering with the claims process. He was no different. There was no way he could see any pre-service requests for himself, Hanna or Donna, and he had no access to claims information.

He clicked again on the Weston Pharmaceuticals tab and noticed that the company was in Boston. Then he clicked on the 'about' menu and scrolled through the list of executives and medical directors. He didn't recognize any of the names. Jason slammed his laptop shut and left his cubicle, heading toward the parking garage. He pulled his cell phone from his pocket as he walked and texted, "See you at 7."

CHAPTER TWENTY-SEVEN

H E PULLED HIS car into a front row space at the Oncology's imaging center. He could see Donna's car a few spaces down and was glad he wouldn't have to wait for them. He checked his phone for new messages and then paused before getting out of the car. He hated the idea of having to enter this building again. The band was tightening, and the imaginary lump in his throat returned, making it difficult to swallow. He opened the car door and spat a mouthful of saliva on the ground, then pulled the door shut. He closed his eyes and relaxed, thinking back to each time before. Each time Hanna fell out of remission. Each time he looked at his sick daughter, and visualized the abnormal cells circulating in her little body. And now this.

The oncologist had called and ordered a PET scan, which could mean only one thing. Hanna's chest X-ray was positive for swollen lymph nodes, and the PET scan was necessary to see if any tumors had developed. Tumors. How would get the word out of his head? He kept his eyes closed and slowed his breathing, focusing on stretching the imaginary band around his chest. But then he lifted and detached himself from his body. The band faded. He could think and see, but it was from someone else's point of view.

Am I having a heart attack? Am I dying or already dead? He willed himself back and swallowed hard, letting out a rush of air. It was over.

He sat for another minute and then realized that he had to face what was happening. He had to go inside and see it through.

He exited the car and entered the building through the automatic sliding doors. The air conditioning hit him like a polar blast. He spotted his daughter sitting in a chair next to his wife, her knees pulled up watching the TV mounted high on the wall.

"There you are! They haven't called your name I assume." Jason pulled his daughter up from the chair and hugged her. "Are you feeling okay?"

"Yeah, I'm okay. I don't remember having this test before," she said.

"You've had it before. It's just like an X-ray, but they might inject a tiny amount of fluid in your arm. It won't hurt." Jason reassured her though he could see the anxiety at the mention of an injection.

Hanna's eyes moved from her father to her mother who was still sitting. "Aren't you going to say hello to mom?"

Donna was surprised by her daughter's question.

"Of course, honey. I am just concerned about you." Jason sat down next to Donna and covered her hand with his. "How are you doing?" he asked her.

"I'm okay. Just wish . . ."

"I know. We'll get through it."

Donna got up from her chair and motioned Jason to follow her to the other side of the waiting room. Hanna continued watching the TV.

"This feels different this time. What if the cancer is spreading?" Donna's face twisted with worry.

"I'm worried too." Jason hugged her close, feeling Donna

relax into him. A moment later a young woman in blue scrubs came through a door and called Hanna's name.

"I'll go with her," Donna said.

He walked them to the door and then sat down pulling out his phone. He opened a web browser and typed, 'chest lymph node biopsy' into the search bar. He was a medical doctor, but when it came to Hanna, it was like he knew nothing about medicine. He couldn't remove himself personally from Hanna's illness. He couldn't compartmentalize the experience and simply be a doctor to a patient. It was like Hanna's illness or maybe just Hanna, removed his educated self, and left him simple. Just a weak, desperate father with a sick daughter and a failing marriage. His whole body slumped at the thought.

He flipped the screen lengthwise and watched a video of the procedure. *Easy enough, with little risk. Hanna will power through it.* He tapped on Dr. Jamison's name in his favorites menu and typed, "Hanna having PET scan today. Can you follow results and call me?" Jason knew it was unlikely that she would reply, but she would see the message between patients. The oncologist would also call, but he wanted to hear from Rachel first. She had a way of easing his tension.

CHAPTER TWENTY-EIGHT

His phone chimed just before eight am the next morning while he was driving to the office. Jason pulled the car into an empty lot and read a text message from Rachel. "Call me." His heart pounded as he tapped her name on his phone.

"Jason, I'm looking at Hanna's results, and it's not good. She has a mass in her chest that might be pressing on her heart, and she has a small mass in her lower intestine. I'm so sorry. I am sure you will hear today from the oncology team about next steps. I'm guessing that they will want biopsies."

Jason was struggling to breathe.

"I know this is tough, but Hanna is strong. The biopsies will help to guide the treatment, but it's likely that she will need radiation along with the chemo. You also have to keep searching for a stem cell donor. Do you want me to talk to Donna?" Defeat flowed over him, and his voice became quiet.

"No," he answered. "I'll tell her. Thank you, Rachel. I'll talk to you later."

He sat in his car, in the empty lot trying to hold his emotions, but he couldn't. He examined his face in the rear-view mirror. *I am so fucked up. What am I doing?* His face had aged and was dull, drawn, and gray. His daughter, his baby, was facing an uphill battle now. A much steeper climb than the last three times. He lowered his forehead onto the steering wheel, shaking his head, and then let out a deep, visceral moan.

CHAPTER TWENTY-NINE

HANNA STAYED HOME the next day, but Donna made arrangements for her friends to visit after school. The doorbell rang, and Hanna ran down the stairs. "Mom! They're here!"

"Please, Hanna, go back up to your room and give me a few minutes to talk to Gia's mother and explain about the masks." Hanna rolled her eyes at her mother and stomped up the stairs.

Donna opened the door and greeted Angela Bucci, her daughter Gia, and Darius Williams.

"Hi Angela, kids." She nodded toward them. Angela opened her arms to hug her.

"I was so sad to hear that Hanna is sick again. Please let me know if there is anything we can do," Angela offered.

"Thank you; I appreciate that." Donna extracted herself from Angela's strong arms.

"Hanna is very excited about finishing your history project. I'm sorry, guys, but you will have to wear these masks whenever you are near Hanna. We can't risk her catching a virus."

"It's okay, Mrs. Smith," Darius said. "We don't mind." Angela stroked her daughter's hair and bent to kiss her cheek, but she pulled away, embarrassed.

"Teenagers," Angela stated attempting to cover her daughter's behavior.

"Gia, call me when you are ready to come home. I can drive you too Darius."

"K, Mom," Gia said sarcastically. "I'll text you when we're ready."

"Thank you, ma'am," Darius added.

Angela gave her daughter a look of disapproval, then smiled at Darius and left.

"Come into the kitchen, and I'll get you the masks. No snacks today because you'd have to take the masks off to eat. I'm very sorry."

"That's okay, Mrs. Smith," Darius said.

"I'm not hungry anyway," said Gia.

Donna helped the kids put the masks on and then called Hanna to come down.

Hanna flew down the stairs and seeing her two best friends, with masks on their faces, started to laugh. She pulled out her phone, squeezed her head between theirs and took a selfie.

"It's hard to breathe in here," Gia complained.

"Shut up, Gia." Darius's barked.

"Come up to my room, and we can finish the project."

Hanna had a large poster board laid out on the floor with a variety of magazines and three pairs of scissors. As they settled into work, Darius asked, "Is the cancer really bad this time?"

"I don't know. I'm pretty sure that my parents aren't telling me everything. I had special kind of X-ray yesterday so they could see inside me. I don't know if they found anything."

"Are you scared?" Gia asked.

"Yeah, I know I could die," Hanna replied in a matter of fact way.

"You better not die!" Darius's eyes were bulging above his mask.

"If I die, you guys can have all my stuff. Darius, you take my iPad and phone since Gia already has one. Gia, you can have all my clothes and stuff."

"Can we stop talking about this?" Gia's eyes were tearing up. "You're scaring me! I don't want your stuff! You need all your stuff!"

"I'm just saying that it could happen. That's all."

They worked in silence for several minutes before Darius asked to turn on some music. Hanna reached for her iPad and tapped on a music app, and within seconds, their three heads were bobbing to the beat as they finished their work.

"Done!" said Gia, standing up to take in their completed poster board.

"It's good! We'll get an A for sure. I'm glad that other kid got moved to a different class and it's just us. Hanna, do you like it?" Darius asked.

Hanna didn't answer his question.

"I don't . . . feel . . . so good. I . . . can't . . . catch my breath."

Darius and Gia's eyes grew wide with fear. Darius instinctively ran to the bedroom door while Gia took Hanna's hand.

"Mrs. Smith come quick!" Darius yelled.

Donna was up the stairs in seconds yelling, "What's wrong?"

"Hanna can't breathe! Call 911!" Gia yelled. Her young voice was shaking with fear. Donna's eyes widened, viewing her daughter's pale face and watching how hard she worked to catch her breath.

"Hanna! I'm calling an ambulance." Donna pulled her cell phone from her back pocket and sat on the floor cradling her daughter. Her hands shook as she dialed 911.

"Gia, call your mother to come get you and Darius."

She tried to stay calm through the rise of hysteria, but it wasn't working. Her voice shook, and she asked them to wait downstairs for the medics to arrive.

"Just leave the door open and then tell them to come upstairs."

Gia was crying, and Darius took her hand. "Come on, let's go let them in. It will be okay." He tried to comfort his friend but his voice was shaking too, and he was ready to cry.

Moments later the medics arrived, and as instructed, Darius and Gia pointed them to the stairs to Hanna's bedroom. Darius told the medic that they were working on a school project, and then suddenly Hanna was struggling to breathe. He told him that Hanna had cancer and they needed to wear masks. The two kids sat on Hanna's couch holding hands, tears streaming down their masked faces, waiting for Gia's mother to come . . . waiting for Hanna to go by them, on a gurney, to the hospital.

CHAPTER THIRTY

THE TWO MEDICS worked in sync, efficiently, placing the oxygen mask over Hanna's nose and mouth, and inserting an intravenous line into her slender arm.

"Shouldn't we be on our way to the hospital?" Donna questioned, alarmed by the delay.

"Ma'am, it's easier to stabilize her while we are parked than when the truck is moving," the medic answered keeping his eyes on Hanna. Then finally, one of the men climbed from the back, slamming the door shut, and took the driver's seat. The sirens went on, and the truck lurched forward. Donna grabbed her cell phone from her purse and tapped Jason's number. The call went to voicemail, and she didn't leave a message. She decided not to text him either. She was angry and scared, and as usual, he wasn't answering. He wasn't there for her, or their daughter.

The ambulance ride took less than ten minutes, and by the time the hospital attendants were opening the doors, Donna could see that the color in Hanna's cheeks was returning. She took a deep breath, climbed out of the ambulance, and followed Hanna's gurney inside. Within minutes, her daughter was surrounded by a medical team.

"Mommy?" Hanna called to her.

"I'm right here, honey. Just let them do their job."

"I'm feeling better already. I can breathe now."

"That's great, honey. Just hang in there. We need to find out why this happened."

"Is Daddy coming?"

"I'm trying to reach him. I'm sure he'll be here soon."

A technician approached from behind her pushing a cart with a small monitor. "Excuse me, Mrs. Smith? I need to do an ultrasound of your daughter's heart. We have a portable X-ray on her now, so the doctor will have some information for you very quickly.

"Thank you," Donna replied. "I'd like to stay with her if that's okay."

"Sure, no problem."

The test took just a few minutes, and then the small room cleared out. Donna sat next to Hanna's bed, took her hand, and started to cry.

"I'm sorry, honey. I got scared. I know you are scared too."

"Mom, I'm better now."

The nurse replaced the oxygen mask with a cannula that plugged her nostrils.

A few minutes passed, and then a tall, thin, older man in a white coat entered the room introducing himself as the emergency room doctor.

"Mrs. Smith, do you want to step outside so we can talk?"

"No!" insisted Hanna. "I want to hear what's wrong with me! It's my body!"

Donna froze at hearing her daughter's passionate request, and then finally shook her head in agreement.

"We can talk here," she replied.

"Hanna," the doctor addressed her directly, "you have a lump in your chest that is putting some pressure on your heart. This means that your heart can't pump as well as it did before."

"But what does that have to do with my breathing?" Hanna asked.

"When your heart isn't pumping effectively, your lungs aren't getting enough oxygen. Does that make sense?" The doctor met Hanna and then Donna's gaze.

"Yes, I guess so," Hanna said. "But why am I feeling better now if the lump is still there?"

"Well, we gave you some oxygen, and we also gave you some medication to reduce the amount of fluid in your lungs. Sometimes when the heart isn't pumping well, fluid can build up, and that also causes you to have trouble breathing."

"Does this mean that her condition can be treated with medication?" Donna asked.

"Yes, for now, we can control it. I understand from Hanna's medical record that this is new, so the best thing to do is to speak to her oncologist and get her treatment started as soon as possible."

"She just had the PET scan yesterday . . . so this lump is what they found?"

"I'm afraid so. She has a smaller one in her lower intestine as well," the doctor answered.

"Does this mean that the cancer has spread?" Donna already knew the answer but needed to hear it out loud. She caught her daughter's eyes filled with fear.

The doctor's eyes moved from Hanna and then to Donna. "Unfortunately, this is indeed a sign that the cancer has spread. It's critical that you speak with your oncologist as soon as possible. We will keep Hanna here for a few hours just to make sure she remains stable and then she can go home."

Donna thanked him and walked with him out of Hanna's room. "Is she going to be okay?" she asked.

"She's stable, and I think the medication will keep her that way. Hopefully, once she starts the chemo and radiation the tumor will shrink. I will send a note over to her oncologist and let him know that she was here."

Donna thanked him again, holding back her tears and then went back to Hanna's bedside.

"Mom, where's my phone? I want to call Daddy."

"I tried to call him. I will send him a text."

Donna took out her phone and typed, "At the ER. Hanna couldn't breathe. She's doing better now. Going home soon. She has a lump in her chest and her intestine."

A few seconds later he texted back, "On my way to you now. Be there in ten minutes."

"Daddy is on his way," she told Hanna.

CHAPTER THIRTY-ONE

WHEN HE READ the text he was surprised, but then not surprised. After all, Hanna had a mass in her chest. No wonder she couldn't breathe. His stomach turned when he thought of the havoc the cancer could cause in her body. He tapped on Rachel's name and typed, "Hanna in ER, short of breath. They are going to discharge her. Heading there now." *Better to keep her in the loop,* he thought. His office was just a few blocks from the hospital, and he luckily made all of the lights, driving just slightly over the speed limit. He parked the car in the emergency room spots and walked quickly inside, approaching the information desk.

"My daughter, Hanna Smith, was brought in by ambulance," he said anxiously.

The receptionist typed some information on her computer and then wrote a number on a sticker.

"This is her room number," she said handing him the sticker. "Through the doors and then turn right."

Jason pushed through the double doors marked 'Employees Only', and turned right down the hallway. He burst through the door to Hanna's assigned room.

"Hi, Daddy!" Hanna reached out her hand for his as he entered the room.

"Hi, honey, are you doing okay?"

"Yes, I'm feeling better. All of a sudden, I couldn't breathe. The doctor told me that I have a lump in my chest." Jason's eyes welled up, and his head turned to Donna. Her expression was blank, or angry. He wasn't sure.

"Yes, I heard, honey. You're going to start treatment tomorrow. Now let's get you home. I'll check on your discharge paperwork." He motioned Donna to follow him out of the room.

"Rachel called me earlier and gave me the news," he said. "Did you hear from the oncologist?"

"No one called. Why didn't you call me?"

"I was going to tell you at home. What happened to her?" He asked deliberately changing the subject.

"Darius and Gia were at the house, and they were working on their project. Then suddenly she couldn't breathe, so I called 911. I called you too . . . but as usual . . . ." Donna didn't finish her sentence.

"You did the right thing. She has fluid around her lungs and heart. I will call the oncologist and get the ball rolling for tomorrow. She's going to need radiation too."

He spoke in a matter-of-fact tone, but inside he was losing it again. His gut was twisted, and he was ready to vomit, but he fought it . . . for Hanna.

He took Hanna in his car and Donna followed behind. When they arrived at the house, Jason helped Hanna out of the car and walked her up the stairs into her room, tucking her into bed. He stayed with her, sitting on the edge of the bed, patting her hair.

"I promise you, Hanna, you will get better." He kissed her on the forehead and then left the room. Donna was waiting for him at the bottom of the stairs.

"We need to talk," she said.

"I know. I'm sorry I didn't call you after Rachel called me. I'm sorry I didn't answer the phone when you called."

"I'm really tired of your sorries, Jason. I'm tired of being ignored, and I'm tired of all of this." Donna started to cry, but he didn't move to comfort her.

"I told you I'm sorry that I didn't call." It was the best he could do. He was busy, worrying about Hanna and trying to figure out a way to save her. Commiserating with Donna accomplished nothing. He needed to take action, and whatever that action was, it needed to happen fast. He walked past Donna into the study and closed the door. He sat behind his desk, opened his laptop and typed 'Weston Pharmaceuticals' into the browser. There had to be a way to get that drug. He pulled out his phone and sent a text to Rachel. "Look up Cineth. A new AML drug for adults. Would oncologist order it if I was willing to pay cash?" Jason already knew the answer. No doctor or clinic was going to order a new drug for off-label use. He closed his laptop and went back upstairs to check on Hanna. Donna sat on her bed watching her sleep.

He whispered, "I'm going out for a while. Call me if anything changes. I will answer the phone. I promise."

Donna nodded and continued to watch her sleeping daughter.

He backed the car out of the driveway, then stopped to take in his beautiful home and landscaping before putting the car in drive. It had been their dream house. They had four large bedrooms, a large home office, plenty of living room space and a beautiful, fully enclosed pool. It was the ideal Florida family home, but it was expensive, and since Hanna got sick, they were living on a single income. Insurance companies didn't pay nearly what a practicing medical doctor could make, and although he had never discussed their financial status with Donna, they were living from paycheck to paycheck. Every time Hanna got sick, the medical bills rolled in. He was able to stay on top of them, but just barely. And now they were facing another round. A more intense round with more expensive treatment.

Guilt at just having these thoughts made him queasy, but he couldn't help it. In the end, they would likely be financially ruined. But if saved Hanna's life it was well worth it. The money didn't matter, and the house certainly didn't. It was just a place to live, and they could find another house. A smaller, less expensive house.

He drove slowly . . . thinking. *How can I get money, pay the bills and save Hanna? How can I make this go away? Why won't Unified help us?* He slammed his hands on the steering wheel in frustration.

The business of health insurance was complex, layered with rules and regulation. He was employed by a Health Insurance company that also insured his, and his family's health. He learned quickly what most people don't know, which is that signing up for health insurance is like signing an iron-clad contract. The insured agrees to pay a monthly premium, co-payments, deductibles, and co-insurance. In exchange, the insurance company agrees to pay their share of the bill if the insured gets sick. It was simple. But before Hanna got sick, before there ever was a Hanna, he always thought that there was some flexibility on what the insurance company would cover. But it just wasn't true.

When Hanna was first diagnosed with Acute Myeloid Leukemia, he wanted to make sure that her doctors were within his insurance plan's network. He found out the hard way that asking the doctor's office didn't always get him the correct answer. He made an appointment for Hanna to get a second opinion from an oncologist in Atlanta, and asked the office if they would accept his insurance. The answer was yes. But it never occurred to him that accepting insurance could mean that the provider was willing to bill the insurance company. The amount the insurance company would pay was another subject, an unanswered question, until the final bill arrived, which was too late.

The cost of that visit, including all of the lab work that he had insisted be repeated, was over $4,000. He didn't panic when he got the bill because he thought that being an employee might allow him some special consideration. But that wasn't true either. Being an employee was no different than being like any insured member of Unified. There were no added benefits, no special treatment, no additional access. Just an iron-clad contract.

Maybe it's time to sell the house, he thought. He did some mental math and figured there was plenty of equity to cover all of their debt and leave a few dollars to start fresh. But then he considered Donna and Hanna's reaction. They would be so upset. He began to dismiss the idea. But then no, perhaps he'd make a couple of inquiries with a local realtor just to see how much he could get and how quickly he could sell. Nothing to lose by just making a call. The other option was to refinance the house and pull out some cash. Maybe that would be the best option. He took a deep breath and continued his drive.

CHAPTER THIRTY-TWO

I CAN'T BELIEVE HE *left the house. Our baby is laying here with a lump in her chest, a big mass pressed between her heart and lungs, and another mass in her belly. He's a coward!* Her eyes were tearing up, and she didn't want to wake Hanna, so she left the room, leaving the door cracked open just in case Hanna called out during the night.

Her body felt heavy with melancholy, and exhaustion made it hard just to lift her feet and walk. She stripped off her clothes and stood in the shower and tried to wash the horrible day off her skin, out of her thoughts, but it wasn't working. It took all of her effort to shut the water off and wrap a towel around herself. She caught sight of herself in the mirror and was shocked. *What happened to me? I used to be pretty and strong.* But instead, she saw a wrinkled, old woman with the corners of her mouth turned down. Her shoulders dropped, and she hunched forward, dragging her feet toward the bed. And like before, she lay down, this time with the towel still wrapped around her. She pulled the pillows in, one behind her back and one to hold onto, and curled into them. She cried softly for a while and then fell asleep.

Sometime later she was startled awake, confused, cold from the wet towel and her still-damp hair. *Was Jason home?* Her joints were stiff, and the heaviness of her exhaustion made it harder to get out of the bed. She sat up and pulled on a T-shirt and pajama bottoms then shivered for a minute before going to Hanna's room. She was still sleeping. Donna waited a moment listening to her breathing and then went downstairs. She opened the door to the garage and saw that Jason's car was still gone. *Bastard!* she thought. It sickened her to imagine him rolling around another woman's bed, holding another woman close, when she was here in their house, watching their precious daughter struggle to breathe. She wanted to scream, stomp her feet, cry and break something, but what would be the point?

Donna opened the sliders to the pool area and turned on the pool light. The water glowed an ethereal blue and sparkled in the moonlight. She rolled up the bottom of her pajamas and stepped down into the water, then sat on the edge, hypnotized by the ripples. *How did all this happen?* she thought. The heaviness of her fatigue pushed her down again. Deep in her heart, she knew she was going to lose Hanna. It was more than just negativity; it was real. They were doomed. Hanna was doomed. She was doomed. She twisted herself back and glanced at Hanna's window. The lights were off. She hoped Hanna would sleep through the night without any trouble. She hoped, but inside, there was only hopelessness.

CHAPTER THIRTY-THREE

As Jason had predicted, the oncologist wanted a biopsy of the mass in Hanna's chest, and the results would determine the most appropriate treatment. A best-case scenario was a non-Hodgkin's Lymphoma, and a worst case was Hodgkin's Lymphoma. Jason couldn't imagine what other cancers could be looming inside of her.

On the day of her biopsy, Hanna insisted on keeping her iPad in the bed.

"Gia would want to know what's going on and then she could tell Darius."

"I understand, honey," Jason said. "But her mother might not want her to know every detail. You have to remember that they have not been exposed to all this medical stuff. They need to ask their parent's permission." He tried to keep his tone calm as his stomach churned. It was an awful time to say no to her.

"I will call Angela and let her know what's going on. It's up to her what she wants to tell her daughter," Donna said.

"Fine, but at least keep my iPad with you . . . just in case."

"I will keep it right here in my bag."

Within a few minutes, two nurses wearing scrubs and face masks arrived saying it was time for Hanna to go. Jason and

Donna kissed their daughter and watched the nurses wheel her away.

The biopsy procedure was quick, lasting under an hour when the nurse reported that Hanna had been moved to the recovery room. The Smiths paced anxiously in the waiting room waiting for the surgical oncologist to deliver the news. What felt like hours to Jason was only fifteen minutes. The same young doctor they spoke with before Hanna's procedure pushed through the double doors and suggested they all sit down.

"Hanna did very well during the procedure and should be ready to go home in a couple of hours. We sent the specimen to the pathology lab for an early look, and it appears to be Hodgkin's Lymphoma."

Donna covered her face with her hands and started to cry. "No, no, no."

"Please keep in mind that this is an early result. We won't have the final report for a few days. The pathologist needs to go through his process."

Jason sank into his chair shaking his head. "This can't be happening."

"I'm very sorry. I'll call over to pediatric oncology and give them a heads up so they can get her treatment plan ready. I expect she will have the first dose of chemo tomorrow and radiation the next day. I know this is a lot to absorb," he said sympathetically. The surgeon sat with them for a moment and then got up from his chair.

"Best of luck to you and Hanna," he said softly and then left through the same double doors.

"What are we going to do, Jason? What are we going to do?" Donna leaned on his shoulder sobbing.

"We're going to bring her tomorrow for the chemo and then for the radiation. That's what we're going to do. One day at a time." Jason was trying hard to hold himself together, but that familiar tightness in his chest was gripping him, threatening to steal his breath and detach him from reality. He stood up without warning, catching Donna off guard, her head jerking, and said, "I have to make a phone call. I'll be right back."

Donna got up and followed behind him into the hallway beyond the waiting room.

"Who are you calling?" she yelled after him. "What's so important that you have to leave your sick daughter?"

Her hands gripped her hips, and her body leaned forward.

"Are you calling your girlfriend, Jason? Is she the one you NEED to call?"

Jason spun around and glared at her.

"You don't know what you are talking about. Go back in the waiting room and pull yourself together." Jason continued to stare her down until she finally turned and went back into the waiting room, and then he headed to his car.

It was another ninety-degree day, as most of them were, but the sun was hiding behind the storm clouds that were rapidly approaching. As the 'snowbird' season was coming to an end, the rainy season was just gearing up. Jason heard thunder as he pulled the car door shut. He took out his phone and once again searched 'Weston Pharmaceuticals' on his browser. He spotted the phone number in the contact menu and tapped it.

"Weston Pharmaceuticals," a woman stated in a sing song voice. "How may I assist you?"

"Ah, yes, this is Doctor Jones calling from pediatric oncology associates, and I wanted to get some information about one of your drugs. Is there someone I can speak with?" Jason asked.

"One moment, Doctor, and I will transfer you to one of our sales reps."

"No wait, this drug hasn't been released yet. Is there someone in the R&D area?"

"Oh, um . . . yes, I can transfer you to Ken Blake. He's our lead in this field. Just a minute please." Jason's heart was pounding. He wasn't sure why he lied and gave a fake name, but anxiety interrupted his thoughts, and his name wasn't an option. Music was playing in his ear, and he cocked his head spotting a flash of lightning in the distance. He hoped he could get back into the building before the rain started.

"This is Ken Blake." Jason hesitated to hear the man's voice, waited too long, and then disconnected the call.

"Fuck!" he yelled. "What's wrong with me?" He slammed his fists on the steering wheel. "Coward!" He got out of the car and jogged back to the building just as a loud boom of thunder announced the downpour of rain.

CHAPTER THIRTY-FOUR

J ASON WALKED BACK to the waiting area where Donna sat reading something on her phone. She had stopped crying, but he could see the anger had not left her face. She had assumed that he had been unfaithful, but that was the least of their problems now.

He caught her eye and said firmly, "The call was about Hanna. I don't want to talk about anything else but Hanna."

She glared at him and said, "Fuck you, Jason. Just stay away from me."

Jason wasn't expecting that response, but he decided it was better to let her stew than to keep the conversation going.

An hour later, one of the operating room staff was pushing Hanna in a wheelchair to the front entrance. Jason had pulled the car to the curb, and Donna helped her daughter get settled. Thankfully the storm had passed quickly, and Jason noticed a rainbow over the building.

"Look, honey!" He pointed up to the sky.

Hanna opened her window and stuck her head out to see.

"A double rainbow. It's pretty," she answered emotionlessly.

"Are you doing okay, honey? Jason asked sympathetically.

"It's not bad, Daddy, just a little sore on my chest. They just used a tiny bandage," she explained.

"Good, you probably won't even notice anything happened by tomorrow. Today you should just rest.

"I still have some school work to finish. There's only a few weeks left of school. I think I can do it today."

"We'll see in a couple of hours if you're up to it. I can always call the school and let them know you'll have it done tomorrow." Donna said.

Donna was grateful that the school year was nearly over and she wouldn't have to deal with the back and forth with the teachers. She was also grateful she wouldn't have to constantly be asked about Hanna's health. She knew they all meant well, but she had trouble keeping her emotions in check, and it was so awkward and uncomfortable to cry in front of them.

When they arrived home, Donna helped Hanna up to her room and Jason went into the study.

Jason opened his laptop and typed 'Ken Blake' into his browser. There were several Ken Blake's with Facebook pages and LinkedIn pages, and he spotted one link referencing a research paper that also had Weston Pharmaceuticals in the short description. He clicked on it and read. It was a white paper on the HSP 90 Inhibitors. The outcomes of the adult clinical trials were incredible, making the FDA approval a slam dunk. It also included a picture of him, a young man probably still in his twenties. Jason opened his Facebook page, which he had not posted anything to in months, and typed Ken's name into the search tool.

He scrolled through several Ken Blake profiles and then spotted the same profile picture that he used for the white paper. He clicked on it. The profile was mostly locked. However, he was able to see that Ken was married to Laurie Blake, lived in Boston, was twenty-six years old and worked in R&D at Weston.

He clicked on Laurie's page and could see that she also worked at Weston Pharmaceuticals. Her title was 'Biologist'.

Smart couple, Jason thought. He went back to Ken's profile and clicked onto his friend's list and started scrolling, and then stopped on a picture of Lindsey Blake. He stared at the picture for a moment thinking she looked familiar, and then he clicked on it. Lindsey Blake was Ken Blake's mother, and she worked at Unified Health Care in Fort Myers, Florida. Jason sat back in his chair, amazed at the coincidence. He sat up again and continued reading her profile, which was also mostly locked, but he could see that she was forty-six, single and her cover page was a picture of Fort Myers Beach at sunset. He recognized it from all the Friday nights that he and Donna had taken Hanna to play in the sand while they watched the incredible sunsets.

He selected a new tab and opened LinkedIn. He typed Ken Blake into the search menu and spotted his picture. But then he hesitated. If he clicked on his profile, Ken would know that Jason had read it. He decided not to go any further, and he closed the tab. He sat thinking for a minute, and then he clicked on his Unified Health shortcut. He logged into his profile, and then searched for Lindsey Blake. He couldn't believe what he was reading. She was the nurse manager for the Pre-service approval team. Her team reviewed all of the special requests from doctors and hospitals to make sure they met the medical criteria for coverage.

Jason was so excited that he stood up. But then it occurred to him that he and Ron Shay were the medical directors for that division, and he already approached Ron about approving the use of Cineth for Hanna. Ron was firm in his ethics, but there had to be a way around this. "Think!" he said out loud.

He sat down again and logged into Unified's medical pharmacy application and typed, 'Cineth'. The drug wasn't listed. It was too new. Weston was probably just setting the price and negotiating with the insurance companies what they would accept for payment. Until this was completed, the drug wouldn't be added to the formulary. One thing was for sure, no matter what price was set, the use of the drug would need pre-authorization, which meant that Lindsey Blake's team would be the first to see the request. Jason logged off his profile and then closed his laptop. He jogged up the stairs to Hanna's room.

"Everything okay?" Hanna was sitting up on the bed, her pillow behind her back and her legs out with her iPad in her lap. She held her gaze on the iPad.

"Yeah, I was facetiming with Gia." Hanna held up the iPad to Jason showing Gia's face.

"Hi, Gia." Jason waved at her. Gia flipped the iPad around and told her friend goodbye, disconnecting the call.

"Move over, honey." Jason sat on the bed with his arm around his daughter and his legs stretched next to hers.

"Hanna, the biopsy you had tells us that the cancer has spread. I know this sounds really scary, and your mother and I are scared too, but we all have to be strong. Tomorrow you start chemo, and then the next day you will have a radiation treatment."

"What will the radiation do? Will it hurt?"

"No, honey, it won't hurt, but you might have some side effects afterward, like being tired. The doctors will put some marks on your chest and belly and then aim the machine at those marks. You might feel sore in those areas afterward also. They just send a beam of radiation right to the lumps, and they should start shrinking pretty quickly. You might have to do the radiation every day or every other day for a week or two. We'll have to wait and see what they say. The chemo will be two or three rounds over the next few weeks." Hanna sunk into Jason's side.

"I know this sucks, honey, but it's the only way to get you better.

"My hair." Hanna held out a fistful.

"I know, honey...I feel terrible. You know I would do anything to make all this go away if I could. I love you so much, Hanna." He squeezed her.

"Daddy, do you think I'm going to die?"

Jason's heart sank, and the band around his chest instantly reappeared.

"No, honey, I don't think you're going to die."

"I read on the Internet that the more times the cancer comes back, the harder it is to recover. Is this true?"

"I suppose in some cases it is, but not in your case. We have excellent doctors, and this is just a setback. We'll get through it. I promise."

"But, Daddy, it's spreading." She turned on her side moving even closer under his arm and pulled up her knees. She was suddenly a little girl again.

"I know, honey, but you can beat it. You're a little older now and much stronger."

They stayed quiet for a few minutes, and Jason could see the sun was setting. He started to move off the bed, but Hanna grabbed his shirt.

"Daddy, don't go," she whined.

"I'm just turning off the lights. I'm not going anywhere."

He got off the bed and turned off the lights, then climbed back into her bed, where he spent the night in a restless sleep, listening to Hanna breathing and his thoughts circulating in a continuous loop. How was he going to save his daughter?

CHAPTER THIRTY-FIVE

THE NEXT MORNING the Smiths arrived on the pediatric Oncology floor of the hospital at seven-forty-five am. Donna held Hanna's hand as they walked the long, sterile hallway passing one closed door after the next. Donna couldn't help but wonder how many other mothers were behind those doors, suffering the way she was, the way their daughters or sons were. When they approached the check-in desk, they found the pediatric oncologist waiting for them.

"Morning, folks. Hi, Hanna. I am sorry you have to be back here, hon, but we need to get you started as soon as possible. Come this way and the nurses will get you comfortable." The doctor turned to Donna and Jason and added, "We may keep her overnight tonight and give her the first radiation treatment first thing tomorrow. We'll see how the day goes."

"Are you concerned that she won't tolerate the chemo well?" Donna asked. "She did well in the past with few side effects."

"I lost my hair mom!" Hanna blurted.

"I know, honey, but I was talking about sickness. You really didn't have much nausea. Just fatigue."

Jason put his arm around Hanna and bent to speak into her ear.

"You won't have to stay here alone. I can sleep in the chair."

"I am more concerned about Hanna's recent episode with her breathing. I'd rather play it safe and keep her here."

"I agree with you. We shouldn't take any chances." Jason said, his eyes fixed on his wife.

Within an hour, Hanna was lying in the hospital bed, an IV line placed in her arm and a strong chemotherapeutic agent was coursing into her child-sized vein. Jason bent over the bed and kissed his daughter's forehead.

"I'll be right back, honey. Just going to talk to the doctor."

Jason left the room, this time avoiding his wife's stare.

"Mom, are you and dad fighting?"

"No, honey, not really," Donna lied.

"I think we all are stressed. We hate that you are going through this again."

"I know, Mom, but I don't want you and daddy to fight about me."

"We're not fighting about you!"

Hanna shrugged. "If you say so."

"Yes, I say so."

"School gets out in a few weeks. I won't get to say goodbye to everyone for the summer."

"I know, hon. You could send an email to your teachers though. I'm sure you will see Gia and Darius soon."

"I hope so. I want to see them before I lose my hair."

Donna's heart dropped at the thought. Now that Hanna was a teenager, and more mature, she was far more sensitive to her appearance than she was when she was younger.

"I think that's an awesome idea, honey. I will call Gia's mother and see if we can plan to have her come over. I'm not sure how we can get word to Darius once school is over."

"I will send him an email through his school account, and hopefully he will see it before the last day."

"Good idea," Donna replied.

Hanna was typing fast on her iPad while Donna was catching up on the news on her phone. A few minutes later, Hanna set the iPad down and laid back on her pillow. She was asleep in seconds.

Donna took her iPad off the bed and opened her daughter's email account. She didn't like to think of herself as spying, but she was curious as to how Hanna was dealing with the situation, and how her friends were responding. She opened the sent email to Darius and read.

"D, I'm in the hospital getting chemo. They put a needle in my arm, and it drips in slowly. It doesn't hurt but it will take all day, and I have to stay overnight cuz of my breathing. I don't know what's going to happen, but I wanna see you and Gia before I lose my hair or die. If I die, please take my iPad and cell phone. Hide it if you have to but you need it to go to college someday. My mom is calling Gia's mom to set up a time to see me. Ask her if you can come too. I wish I were at school. Let me know if we got an A on our project. H-out."

Donna held back her tears and opened the second email to Gia.

"Gia, I'm in the hospital getting chemo. I just sent an email to D. My mom is calling your mom to see if she will bring you to see me when I get home. But I might not go home. I don't know what's going to happen. The cancer spread. I might die. It's okay though. I don't feel scared. Just want to see you before I lose my hair . . . and my eyebrows . . . and my eyelashes. It really sucks. I get so cold without my hair. Mom will get me some hats I guess. I meant what I said before about you taking my clothes and stuff. I want you to have them . . . we wear the same size, so it's okay."

Donna was crying full on now but continued to read her daughter's message.

"I want you to tell the kids at school that I will miss everyone.

Sounds like I'm going on a trip . . . but it's not a trip . . . well maybe a trip to heaven . . . If there is a heaven. I'm sorry, Gia. I don't want you to cry so don't. You're my best friend. Hanna."

Donna set the iPad back on the bed and got up from her chair. She gazed out the window at the sky, half-filled with storm clouds, and worried for a moment about how the hospital operated when it lost power from a storm. She shrugged off the thought. Would she really die? Donna couldn't bear the thought. But did Hanna know something that she didn't? She remembered hearing about how people knew when the end was near. Were those emails Hanna's way of telling her friends that she knew, or was it a cry for sympathy? Hanna was not known to be attention seeking, but these were new and different circumstances.

Donna pulled a tissue from her purse and dried her eyes, then went into the bathroom and washed her hands, studying her face. Once again, she was shocked again at how her appearance had changed. No wonder Jason had found someone else. How could things possibly be any worse? Her daughter could be dying, or maybe already was dying, and her husband had checked out of their marriage, and she was old and fading. How could things be any worse?

Jason pushed the door open a few minutes later, and Donna put her finger to her lips motioning him to be quiet. He looked at Hanna sleeping and then studied the IV bag hanging next to her bed. It had a long way to go. He sat in the chair on the opposite side of the bed from her and took out his phone. He was texting someone . . . someone he was hiding from her. What did it matter, she thought? Nothing mattered without Hanna.

CHAPTER THIRTY-SIX

WHEN THE BELL rang signaling the end of the first period, Darius pulled Gia's arm guiding her out of the classroom into the hallway.

"Have you heard from her?" he asked.

"No, but I haven't checked my email. Let's go to the computer lab." She checked her watch.

"We have to go quickly. We only have ten minutes before the bell rings."

Darius followed Gia down a long hallway and then made a left turn down another long hallway to the last door on the right labeled, 'Computer Room'. The door was left unlocked during the day, which gave the kids who didn't have home computers or Internet an opportunity to send and receive email. The computers were restricted to certain websites and email access, but allowed enough flexibility for communication and learning. They each sat at a terminal and accessed their email, then their eyes met.

"Did you get one?" Darius asked.

"Yeah, you?"

"Yeah."

There were both quiet as they read Hanna's email and then logged off the terminal. Darius asked,

"What did she say in yours?"

Gia started to cry. He turned his face away so Gia wouldn't notice that his own eyes were filled with tears.

"Are you okay?" he asked.

"She's going to die," Gia said sobbing.

"Maybe she just thinks she's going to die. She just started the chemo today. She can't know that she's going to die." Darius tried to rationalize, but Gia's crying grew louder.

"I don't want her to die!" Gia hollered.

"Me either! What are you going to do when her mom calls your mom?"

"I don't know. I'm scared."

"I'm scared too, but she wants us to come."

"I'm scared to see her if she's going to die."

Darius checked his watch.

"Come on. We gotta get to class. I'll see you after school. Let me know if she texts you or calls. I wish I had a phone!"

They left the computer room, jogging down the hall to their next class.

CHAPTER THIRTY-SEVEN

I T WAS AFTER nine, and Hanna's room was dark. Only a sliver of light from the monitors over the bed shined on Jason, asleep in the reclining chair next to Hanna's bed. Donna sat on the window sill, knees pulled in and leaned against the window. She stretched her neck, following the windows down the side of the building to the dimly lit parking lot and wondered how many other parent's cars were parked out there, while they sat or slept in their children's hospital rooms, waiting and wondering if they would ever have a normal day again.

Hanna tolerated the infusion well, sleeping through most of it, and when she did wake up, she asked for a peanut butter sandwich. All good signs. But she knew that tomorrow might not bring the same tolerance. The radiation appointment was scheduled for 7:30 am, and they were all anxious. Donna noticed how Jason's hand moved to his chest every time a nurse came in the room, and especially when they learned the time of the appointment. She wanted to ask him if he was feeling alright, but she didn't want to give him the satisfaction of knowing that she cared enough to ask.

She was angry, and thoughts of revenge crept in. She hoped he was suffering at least as much as she was. She hoped he felt guilty. But she also knew that it didn't matter. If he was in love with someone else, there was no turning back. No matter what happened with Hanna, their marriage was over. Donna sighed out loud and swallowed back the desire to cry. She leaned her head against the window, feeling the cold glass pressed against her face, and wished the hours away until the radiation treatment was over, and she could take her daughter home.

A few hours later, Jason awoke startled, confused and stiff as he wrangled himself out of the reclining hospital chair. He hadn't realized just how tired he was. He checked his watch, surprised at the unexpected passing of time and was jolted fully awake. Donna was perched on the window sill and appeared to be asleep, and Hanna lay sleeping under the glowing monitors. He had to piss, and the combination of hunger and thirst bordered on nausea. He quietly closed the bathroom door behind him, relieved himself and then splashed water on his face. He knew he looked like shit, but he didn't care.

He walked toward the nurse's station, but no one was there. He figured they must be with patients. He continued past the desk and noticed bright lights coming from a room near the end of the hall.

The waiting room was in fact brightly lit with colorful furniture and children's play areas in all corners. The sofas were low to the floor and long, and at the end sat a young man who Jason guessed was thirtyish.

"Hey, didn't mean to disturb you, man," Jason said.

"You're not. Have a seat if you want."

Jason sat on the bright orange sofa and stuck out his hand. "I'm Jason. My daughter is here, sleeping down the hall."

The man had a strong grip.

"Jonathan . . . my, son, is here too."

"Yeah, sorry. It's tough. How's he doing?"

"Not so good."

"Oh, sorry. My daughter has AML . . . Leukemia. This is her

fourth go 'round with the chemo, and now it's spread, so she's having radiation tomorrow."

"That's tough . . . we've been there, done that. It didn't work. There's nothing left to do for my son."

The blood rushed from Jason's face, and the familiar tightness in his chest distracted him. He placed his right hand on his left shoulder as if to mask his hidden discomfort.

"Wow. I don't know what to say. I'm so sorry." Jason replied.

"Nothing anyone can do now. We just wait, and then say goodbye."

Jason was shocked at how nonchalant he was with his words, or maybe he was just defeated.

"Are you married?

"Yeah, she's in the room sleeping with him. He's eight."

"My daughter is thirteen."

The two men sat there not saying anything for a moment, and then Jason got up from the couch, not sure what to say. "I gotta get back . . . sorry about your son."

"Thanks."

Jason could barely breathe as he walked down the hall back to his daughter's room. He noted each of the closed doors that he passed and wondered which one Jonathan's dying son lay behind. *Never*, he thought. *That will never be my daughter.* He pulled himself straight, sucking in a deep breath and took his hand away from his chest. *That will never be my Hanna.*

He quietly pushed the door open and climbed back into the reclining chair.

"Daddy?"

"Hi, Honey, it's late; you should sleep."

Hanna didn't answer, but Jason could hear her breathing softly. He focused on his wife's jack-knifed body against the window and wished he could just will it all away. But that wasn't possible, so he had to dig deeper, think smarter.

CHAPTER THIRTY-EIGHT

ON A COOL Saturday Florida winter morning, a few months before Hanna slipped out of remission, Jason slept in, lying in bed, though he was not sleeping. He was avoiding a conversation or physical contact with Donna. If he stayed in his sleeping position, on his right side, arm up and over the side of his face, she would leave him alone. It's not that he didn't love his wife, he just wasn't in love with her. She had become Hanna's mother and care-taker of their home. He didn't necessarily feel bad about it, but he also didn't feel good about where it left their sinking marriage.

At his last doctor's appointment, a routine physical, Jason talked to his friend and primary care physician about his history of panic attacks. It was the first time he went into detail, telling him about the period tightness in his chest, and his disorganized thinking when the attack was imminent. He purposefully didn't mention the episodes of detachment that he'd experienced. At first, his doctor was concerned that Jason could have a legitimate heart problem. He ordered an EKG and stress test just to rule out any underlying cause of his chest discomfort. Jason wove the appointments into his workday, never sharing with Donna what was happening and he was relieved when the tests came back negative.

At his follow up visit, his doctor told him that his symptoms were, in fact, a physical response to anxiety, but he never made Jason feel bad about it.

"Lots of people have General Anxiety Disorder," he said casually.

"Look at all you've been through with Hanna. Poor kid so young, being so sick . . ." Jason was relieved that he understood, and although he still felt physically and emotionally defective, at least his doctor didn't make him feel any worse. He offered him Xanax, and an anti-depressant to take the edge off. Jason took the prescription for the Xanax but turned down the anti-depressant. He recalled all the times at work when he reviewed medication requests for multiple antidepressants, and even as a doctor, with advanced knowledge and training, he still attached a stigma. Fucking crazy people who think they can fix their miserable lives with drugs, well it doesn't work that way. He, Dr. Jason Smith, would not be one of them. The Xanax was for emergency use only. He kept the bottle in his car, out of Donna's sight, and the thirty-day prescription lasted for months.

The doctor also recommended massage therapy and gave him a card for a local woman who had a studio or would travel to the person's home. He told Jason that he'd been having regular massages for months and felt much more relaxed and more productive at work. Jason accepted the suggestion and later that day called the number to make an appointment.

The first time he met Nathalie Serbo, she was not at all what he expected. She was in her early thirties, with dark African glowing skin and a full head of braided hair that she pulled back in a thick bunch, and tied with a colorful scarf. Her nose and lips were full, and she had a full, white tooth smile that was contagious. His first thought was Rastafarian, perhaps because of her hair and fashion, but that didn't apply to Nathalie. She had a British accent and an almost musical tone to her voice, like a perfectly tuned instrument. Sade, the singer, came to mind. He wanted to hear her talk, listen to her melodic voice. What she said didn't matter.

Her massage studio was her small condo in a gated community not far from Jason's house. She was up on the third floor, and the building did not have an elevator. When they first spoke on the phone, she offered to come to his house or office, and now as he fidgeted uncomfortably in her living room, he wondered how she was able to get the full-sized massage table and bag of towels and oils, safely down three flights of stairs.

"Please try to relax, Mr. Smith," she said as she hurried around the room lighting candles and adjusting the light. "In a few minutes, you will feel much better, I promise." The room had a small two-person sofa pushed against the wall under the windows. A bookcase stood on the opposite wall filled with family photos and assorted colorful candles and knick-knacks. "Please, Mr. Smith, go to the bathroom and get undressed. You'll find a robe hanging on the bathroom door." She pointed to the door down the hall. Jason followed her directions and emerged a few minutes later in a clean, white robe.

"Come," she said patting the massage table. He approached the table, and she held up a large towel, screening his body from her view.

"Just slip out of the robe and lay on the table and you will feel better." Jason was hooked on her voice. He would have done anything she asked. He had left his boxer briefs on, unsure of the appropriate protocol for a private massage, and she did not comment as she covered the lower half of his body with the towel. Soft music was playing, and a sweet smell filled the room that reminded him of the incense he used to burn in his bedroom as a teenager.

She worked his neck with both hands, pressing her fingers in deep, rounding muscle and tendons with her thumbs. He tried to imagine the experience from outside of his body, watching this exotic black woman massage him, and he pushed away sexual thoughts. His doctor was right. She was an expert. She moved down his shoulders and back, pressing and massaging. Her touch was strong where it needed to be and soft in more sensitive places. She bypassed his buttocks and worked over each leg, starting from his upper thigh just below his briefs and then ended with his feet. He had never experienced anything so intense, yet unbelievably relaxing.

When the session was over, Nathalie helped Jason sit upright. His body slouched. He wondered if he'd be able to stand and walk.

"Did you enjoy that?" she asked. He couldn't stop grinning.

"I'm so relaxed; I don't think I can make it to the bathroom to put on my clothes!"

"I'm glad you are happy," she replied in her perfectly accented tone and perfect smile.

She held up the towel again offering him privacy while he put the robe back on, but he waved her off. By the time he finished getting dressed, she had folded the massage table, slid it against the wall and was blowing out the candles.

"That was great," Jason told her still grinning. "I haven't felt this good in such a long time." He opened his wallet and handed her a one-hundred-dollar bill.

She accepted the payment, thanking him and then asked if he'd like to book another appointment.

"Yes!" he answered enthusiastically. "Of course! How long have you been doing massage?" he asked.

"Around five years," she answered. "I started in London and then followed my brother when he moved here for a new job. It's hot here in the summer, but I like it," she added.

"Yeah, me too," he answered.

"Can we set a regular weekly time?" The words came out of his mouth at the same time his brain was adding up the four-hundred-dollar monthly expense. He dismissed the thought and continued, "Do you work nights?"

"Sure, I can see you in the evening. How about Thursdays?"

Every week Jason kept his Thursday evening appointment, and with every hour he spent with Nathalie, he learned a little bit more about her. Raised by their grandparents, she and her brother grew up in London. Her brother worked for an environmental research company and lived nearby. She said he was her best friend and they looked out for each other. Jason asked her about her parents, but she gave a vague answer about them traveling in Africa. He didn't push. Neither she nor her brother was in a relationship, but both were open to dating and settling down, having a family. He told her about Donna and Hanna, confiding about his marriage and Hanna's illness. Nathalie passed no judgment and was genuinely sympathetic about everything he shared.

Three weeks ago, when Jason arrived for his appointment, Nathalie could see that something had changed. "What's wrong?" she asked in her sweet tone.

"Hanna is sick again." Jason held back tears.

Nathalie opened her arms, and he leaned on her, breathing in her exotic scent. He wanted to kiss her and touch her hair, but he resisted the urge. He knew he was vulnerable and he needed her to make him feel better, and not in a sexual way. As much as he wanted it, he knew he couldn't add another layer of secrecy and stress to his life. He pulled back from her embrace and went into the bathroom to change.

He laid on the massage table and allowed himself to sink into the moment while she worked his upper body. Then she broke the silence and asked, "Jason, what else can I do for you? I feel so bad that your daughter is sick. I could visit your wife and daughter in the hospital and teach them some breathing techniques for relaxation?" she offered.

Jason remained still as her hands continued their magic.

"I appreciate the offer, Nathalie, but I still haven't told my wife about my visits here, and I prefer to keep it that way. Right now, what I need is someone who knows how to hack a computer," he said jokingly.

"I know someone who can do that," She replied.

Jason pulled himself up on one elbow and faced her.

"Seriously?"

"Yes, seriously." Her eyes widened mischievously. "There's a guy I knew at the gym up in Georgia, before my brother and I moved down here. We went on a couple of dates, and he hinted that he makes money doing that kind of work. He seemed like a nice guy, so I was surprised when he told me. I didn't go out with him again, but I still have his number. I'll text it to you," she offered.

"Thanks! I'm not going to doing anything bad or illegal. I'd never jeopardize my career. I just want to see something." He attempted to play down his motives.

"I know," she answered, her voice unconcerned. His muscles stiffened after their conversation, and she pressed her fingers and palms in deeper and harder.

"Ouch!"

"Sorry . . . you are extra tense tonight. But it's understandable. Let yourself go, Jason. Let me take care of you."

"I don't know how I survived before you, Nathalie."

CHAPTER THIRTY-NINE

NATHALIE KEPT HER word and texted Jason Ben's phone number, but it took Jason another twenty-four hours before he got up the courage to send the text.

He sat alone in a small booth at his favorite local diner. The snow-bird crowd packed the restaurant and loud voices carried over the booths. Thunder rumbled in the distance, and he heard the folks in the booth next to his comment about how it was time for them to head north. *Good idea*, Jason thought. He hated the way traffic was constantly snarled, and how long he had to wait to get a restaurant table.

He ordered himself a bowl of chicken soup and a grilled cheese and tomato sandwich, then set his phone on the table opening a new text.

"Got your name from someone. I need some information that I don't have access to. Can you help?"

Ten minutes later, the waitress set his meal on the table and asked if he needed anything else.

"I'm fine. Thanks," he answered and continued to stare at his phone. Finally, it chimed.

"Send an email to this address with the details." Jason read the message, and the band around his chest instantly appeared. He had a mouth full of grilled cheese but had to keep chewing because his pounding heart wouldn't allow him to swallow. He turned the phone over and scanned the restaurant crowd to distract himself. Finally, he was able to swallow. The Xanax bottle flashed in his mind, and he decided to take one as soon as he got into the car. He finished his dinner and paid the check, buying a water bottle from the cooler at the entrance.

He arrived home a short time later and found Hanna and Donna sitting at the kitchen table doing her homework. He nodded at Donna and kissed his daughter's forehead.

"How was your day, honey?"

"It was okay. I had a radiation treatment this morning. My chest is sore," she answered pointing to the middle of her chest.

Donna chimed in, "The doctor said that was normal and recommended we put ointment on the area."

"I know this is tough, honey, but we have to stay on track with this. Hopefully not for too long. I know the doctor will order another scan soon to see if the lump is going away."

Hanna blinked at him but didn't respond. Her face was pale, and she had dark circles under her eyes. She appeared exhausted.

"I'll be in my office," he said to Donna as he left the kitchen.

Jason opened his laptop and thought about how to word his email. He had a plan. It was far-fetched, but he needed to at least explore the possibility. He would begin by convincing Hanna's oncologist to order the Cineth knowing that the pre-service request would be reviewed at Unified and denied by one of the Medical Directors. His question to this mysterious hacker would be . . . can he hack into the system and overturn the denial? If this were possible, then Hanna would get her medication. He tried to think about any consequence to this happening. He supposed it was possible that someone would notice the chain of events and then do an audit. In which case, the Medical Director whose name was attached to the record could be called to explain, but that was unlikely. The sheer volume of claims being processed was enormous. Why would this particular claim even be seen? Another possibility would be if Hanna's name triggered on a high-risk list because of her medical expenses. One of the pediatric case managers could review her entire record and note the medication. If the case manager did her job, she would research the medication and know that it was meant for adults. She might ask the Medical Director about it. He was certain there were other ways he could be exposed, but did it matter? He sat back in his chair and rubbed his chest.

The Xanax was working on the band around his chest, but not on the lump in his throat and the butterflies that had taken up permanent residency in his gut. He opened a web browser and created a new email address. Then he started to type.

"I need someone to hack into the Unified Insurance claim system and pay a claim. If this is something, you think you can do I will send more specifics."

He decided to keep it brief. No point in giving any details unless the hack was even possible. He closed his laptop and went back into the kitchen. Maybe Hanna would let him help with her math homework.

The next morning Jason had a reply in his new email account. It simply said, "Send me your access info and claim number. Wire $1000 to IBAN 2502020689."

Jason stared at the screen and then realized that the guy didn't read his request carefully. He wrote back. "I just want to know if it's possible."

A few minutes later a new reply came. It was one word. "Maybe." He slammed the laptop shut.

"Maybe? What the fuck?" he mumbled. He opened the laptop again and logged into his work profile, and then logged into the claims system. He would find a small dollar claim, something for less than fifty dollars that was recently denied. He would send Ben the info and then see if he could reverse it. But no way was he paying a thousand dollars to reverse a fifty-dollar claim. He typed Ben an email.

"Need to test it first. Will wire $100." He included his login information and the claim number and then hit the send button. Then he logged into his bank account and sent the money.

Jason made it to work in less than thirty minutes, hitting every green light on the way. He couldn't wait to log in and see if the claim had been reversed, though it also occurred to him that this guy, Ben, might have just ripped him off. He checked the claim over and over again throughout the day, but nothing had changed. He sent him an email.

"Did you try?"

Almost immediately he received a reply.

"Firewall air tight. Can't do it."

"Fuck!" Jason jumped up from his chair and circled his cubicle. He needed a new plan. He sat down again and searched Lindsey Blake's name. She was online. Then he opened a window to her boss, Lisa Simmons. Her indicator was on red. She was busy or in a meeting. Lisa wrote the policies that included the terms and medical necessity for the drug. Maybe he could bribe her to include pediatric use in the policy. Too risky . . . she would call the police, and he'd be done for. What about the son, the one at Weston? There had to be a way.

Conceptually it was so simple! Cineth was the answer they had been waiting for. It had a near one-hundred percent remission rate over five years. There was no logical reason why his daughter shouldn't have it. The common link was Lindsey. If he could convince Lindsey, then she could talk to her son and boss, and maybe they could help him, help Hanna. But how long would that take and what would motivate her to try? If he failed, then he was done, there would be no other options.

He threw his pen across the cubicle bouncing it off the fabric-covered wall.

He was up again, pacing, circling the office. He leaned over his computer and opened the email window with Ben's response and then hit the reply button. "Can we meet? Give me a time and place and make it soon."

CHAPTER FORTY

ASON WALKED INTO the old, train car diner in a less desirable area of Orlando. It was the true definition of a greasy spoon. The air was thick with old cooking smells and the patrons were blue collar, red neck and tough. A row of booths lined the window side of the car, and round, wooden bar stools dotted the length of the counter. It was apparently a halfway point from wherever Ben was driving from. He spotted him immediately, being the only black man in the place. He sat across from him in the booth and nodded, skipping a handshake.

"I need someone held for a couple of days. Is that something you can do?" Jason asked.

"Maybe. Is that it?"

"Well, no. Once she's secured, then I will need you to have contact with her son and her boss. They will need instructions to complete a task. It's a simple task so I don't anticipate it would take more than forty-eight hours. I'd need you to find a safe place to keep her, and I don't want her hurt. I am firm on that."

Ben thought for a minute and then said, "I'll need fifty grand, plus any additional expenses that might come up. When do you want this done?"

"Sooner rather than later. Within the next two weeks."

"Use the email address I gave you and make sure you are

deleting your email address after every exchange we have. Just keep creating new ones. Send me the specifics today on who you want to be held, and I will need you to wire twenty-five thousand to the same account I gave you before. I will notify you when I have a plan in place. I also recommend you get yourself a burner phone. Don't ever contact me on your personal phone. Also, if you change your mind . . . I keep the money."

Jason nodded in agreement.

The meeting left him shaken and uneasy, but the Xanax helped. He made it back to Fort Myers in record time. Thankfully it was Thursday, and he would see Nathalie for his weekly massage. "Things are looking up," he said out loud.

PART III
Now

CHAPTER FORTY-ONE

I N TIMES OF extreme stress, the brain's limbic system bursts into action directing the fight or flight response. In Lindsey's case, this included the inconvenient side effect of a rapidly filling bladder. She sat stiffly in the hard chair, knees squeezed together, hands shaking, her eyes fixed on the two monitors that displayed her son in his living room and her boss in her home office.

"What do you want from me? This is insane! Why are you watching my son?"

Lindsey got up from the chair, but Cliff blocked her path.

"I have to go to the bathroom again."

"Jesus, lady," Cliff lisped. "What's your fucking problem?"

"Let her go," Ben insisted.

She returned quickly, eyes opened wider, though the throbbing pain in her forehead continued to blur her focus.

"What the hell do you want from me?" she demanded.

"Sit down," Ben instructed.

Lindsey sat on the edge of the chair, her eyes creeping over the room. She spotted the front entrance and noticed the over-sized dead bolt.

"Until your son and boss finish this job, you're not going anywhere so don't bother looking at the door," Ben said.

"What job?" Lindsey's face was throbbing so intensely that she could hardly see.

"Your son works for a company that makes a drug that was just released by the FDA. Weston has just started contracting with the insurance companies. We need your son and your boss to work together to make sure that the drug is covered for kids."

"You're crazy! My son has nothing to do with how insurance companies cover drugs!"

"We're not crazy, and you're not going anywhere until we get what we need."

"I am not going to ask my son to do anything illegal!"

"Listen, bitch. You don't have to ask your son to do anything. We're going to do that, and you're going to watch. So sit the fuck down and shut the fuck up." Cliff had moved in close, and she could smell his rotten beer-laced breath and sweat stink. If it weren't for his formidable size, and the way he leered at her, she would have a hard time taking him seriously with his ridiculous lisp.

Lindsey couldn't imagine how this would play out. She knew her son had no influence with an insurance company, and what could Lisa do?

"Look, whatever you think you're doing here . . . it's not going to work. This is asinine!"

Ben moved in close crouching in front of her chair, so they were face to face.

"Here's what's going to happen. In a few minutes, I am going to send a text message to your son and to your boss and instruct them to turn on their TVs. They will both be able to see you . . . here . . . locked in this house, with your messed-up face. They will be told not to call the police or get anyone else involved. We are watching them and will know immediately if they call the police. What we are asking them to do is simple. In fact, it shouldn't take more than a couple of days. If they do what we ask, we will let you go. If they don't do what we ask, well then . . . you won't ever see them again."

Lindsey was shaking again, and she needed to pee.

"I have to go to the bathroom again. This happens when I'm scared." She flinched, preparing herself. *Would he hit her again?*

Ben rolled his eyes.

"Go."

"She's fucked up," Cliff announced. "Are you gonna call the son now?"

"Yeah, when she comes back. I'm gonna send a text."

"Ha, ha . . . he's gonna freak when he sees her."

"Is everything a joke to you? This is serious business. We need to get this done and get the fuck outta here before something happens."

Ben remembered the night at the bar when they agreed to work together, and how crazy Cliff behaved with even the slightest provocation.

He'd drank at least six beers, each followed by a shot of whiskey. Another severely intoxicated man, scrawny, with at least three days of growth on his chin, came up behind him, nudging him, just as he threw his head back in a whole swallow of whiskey. Cliff turned his head to see who had touched him and the man looked him straight in the eye and slurred, "You're a faaat fuck."

Cliff spun his chair around to face him full on, but the man continued, "You ought to lose some weight, faaat man. You take up two bar stools."

Cliff's face was bright red, and through the haze of whiskey and beer, he had morphed into a raging bull.

There was no verbal warning, no finger poke to the chest, no shoving the man back. Cliff just lifted himself off the bar stool, rising like a cartoonish figure as his belly rolls jiggled, then settled. Then he raised both arms with elbows bent and chopped the man on the shoulders. The guy went down like a crumpled piece of paper.

Ben shook off the memory and watched Cliff head into the kitchen.

"We need food," Cliff announced.

"Then go get some!"

Cliff pulled out his wallet and held it open, showing Ben.

"I ain't have any money left. I spent it on the clothes for the bitch."

"Jesus Christ!" Ben took out his wallet and handed Cliff a hundred-dollar bill.

"Get us enough food to last a few days. Do you think you can do that without fucking up?"

Cliff took the money without answering and left the house.

Once again Lindsey returned from the bathroom just as Ben was keying the lock shut on the front door.

"My buddy went to get us some food since we're going to be here for a while."

"I'm not staying here! Whoever came up with this idea is insane. It's not going to work!" Lindsey insisted.

"You don't have a choice. There's no way out and your son will figure it out, unless he doesn't care what happens to you."

His words stung and Lindsey started to cry again, but then quickly stopped when the pain in her forehead worsened. She was quiet for a moment and then asked, "What's your name?"

"John," Ben answered.

"I doubt that."

"You don't need to know my name. Your job is to behave, follow instructions and hope that your son and your boss get this done quickly."

Lindsey looked back at the monitor that displayed her son's living room. She had been there just a few weeks ago and everything was exactly as she remembered it. Their condo was small, seven-hundred square feet at the most. But real estate in Boston was expensive and they were lucky to have found something affordable. Eventually, they could sell it or rent it for a large profit and move into a larger home when they were ready to start a family.

A moment later, her son entered the living room from the kitchen holding a beer.

"Your son likes his beer. This is his third one today. Maybe he's got a problem."

"Fuck you," Lindsey sniped.

"Watch your fucking mouth, lady, or I'll land another punch and mess you up for good. I aimed high last time but next time I won't."

Lindsey recoiled. Her instincts were right.

She watched her son sit on the living room couch, set the bottle on the floor and open his laptop.

"He also likes to play video games. In fact, we played a game of League of Legends this morning. He's really good at it. Better than me. I used to play all the time, but I'm out of practice, so he beat me in no time. Then I got him to duo with me, and we kicked some ass together."

Lindsey's head was spinning. She knew nothing about video gaming and couldn't understand how they could be playing a game together while she was unconscious after being punched by the guy Ken was playing with! She decided not to respond.

"Watch," Ben instructed as he typed a string of commands on the computer. Lindsey watched the monitor split into two screens. On one side, she could see her son sitting on the couch, his eyes intensely focused on his laptop, on the other side she saw what appeared to be a video game screen. Then he typed into a small chat window next to the game screen. "Bagels17: What up?" Lindsey immediately recognized his screen name as a reference to his childhood. Every Sunday morning, they went out to breakfast at a small bagel shop in Brookline. Although the shop grew into a large cafe, they still went there when she visited. She watched as 'John' continued to type. "I see you're searching for a game. You wanna duo again?"

Bagel7 responded, "Sure."

Ben grinned at Lindsey.

It took everything she had inside not to throw herself at him and scratch his eyes out.

For the next thirty minutes, Lindsey watched a screen full of small, colorful and oddly shaped cartoon characters running around a mountainous terrain shooting at each other. She pulled her eyes away wishing that her smart son wasn't wasting his time on video games.

"Check this out. We are just about to take the Nexus." Lindsey still had no idea what she was looking at or what a Nexus was. She assumed they were winning the game.

"We did it again. He's good. We're good partners!" She watched as he typed into the chat window, "GGWP." Then he explained, "This means Good Game Well Played." Then he typed, "Signing off. Catch you next time", and closed the game window. "You see, your boy Ken hasn't got a clue, but he will soon. When my buddy comes back, it's time for the big reveal. You better hope that your son thinks you were a good mother and that your boss believes you do a good enough job at work."

Lindsey stood up and started to turn away, but Ben grabbed her arm.

"Just remember what I said. If you try anything, the next punch will be square in the face."

She pulled her arm from his grip and with balled up fists went into the bathroom. She examined her face closely in the mirror and could see that the deep red circles around her eyes were already turning black. Her body was absorbing the blood from the burst vessels quickly, and hopefully, they would be turning to purple then yellow in the next few days . . . that was if she lived to see the next few days. She would ask John, or whatever his name was, for some ice to help with the pain. Maybe he would take pity on her, though so far, the best she could get was being allowed to use the bathroom.

She sat on the closed toilet, nervously fidgeting with the fitness band on her wrist, and considered how Ken would respond to learning that she had been kidnapped. He would be horrified, scared for her, and want to do anything to get her out of this mess, but she couldn't imagine how Lisa would react. She would be shocked, and would surely tell Dan. After all, he was a retired cop, and there was no way she would keep a secret like this. And what about Laurie? Could her son keep a secret like this? Not likely. And if Ken tried to manipulate data at work, Laurie would probably learn about it anyway. This was a no-win situation. People were going to find out, and people would eventually know that she was missing.

She wondered again what happened to her cell phone. *Did they have it?* She assumed they did and she assumed they were smart enough to disable the GPS. She was able to track Ken's phone with her phone, and she thought he could do the same. She was sure that Ken would remember that. They were connected in other ways as well. She checked the battery on her fitness tracker. If he logged into his account, he could see that she been walking earlier that day. He could also see how many steps she took before her phone was taken. Before she was taken. Ken was smart. He would think of these things.

She got up from the seat and checked her face one more time, cupped some water in her hands to hydrate herself, then opened the door. John was sitting at the computer watching her son play another game. Her boss had apparently left her office.

"Go in bedroom if you want. It may be a while before my buddy gets back."

"Can I have some ice for my face?"

Ben swung around and glowered at her. He considered her request for a moment and then shook his head no.

"Just go in the bedroom," he said dismissively.

Lindsey followed his instructions, closing the bedroom door and lying on the bed. Her eyes fixed on the camera in the corner and she raised her middle finger.

CHAPTER FORTY-TWO

JASON SAT IN his office with his hands positioned on his keyboard ready to send a reply to an email, but his hands were shaking. He gave up and cradled his head, putting his elbows on the desk. "What am I doing? What have I done?" he said out loud. It was after five o'clock, and the office was nearly empty. He could hear the heavy rain pounding against the building. He sat up forward again, straight, forcing determination back into his posture, and then he logged into the shared drive where Lisa Simmons stored the policy templates. He could see that she had started working on Cineth earlier that day, and had copied over the FDA approved research. If all went according to plan, she would have the template finished tomorrow, and it would be approved by the committee on Friday. Now he just had to wait and hope that Ben and his idiot friend didn't do anything stupid.

"Hey, buddy." Jason's body jerked.

"Oh, hey, Ron . . . what you are still doing here? You startled me."

"Just wrapping up for the day. How about you? How's Hanna doing?"

"Not too good. Not too good," Jason repeated.

"Oh, wow, what's going on?"

"She's had three rounds of chemo and nine radiation treatments. The tumor isn't responding, and she hasn't been able to eat. They put a feeding tube in. This is such a fucking disaster, Ron."

"What is the oncologist telling you?"

"It's the same old bullshit. Hopefully, she'll rebound. But I'm not seeing any signs of her doing that. She's getting weaker by the day."

"Shit, I don't know what to say."

"We need a miracle here. Something has to break soon."

"I hope so, man. I really hope so. Let me know if there is anything you need. I can cover whatever work you have."

"Thanks for offering but it helps to be here ... takes my mind off things. I've been running over to the hospital during the day and then catching up on work when Hanna is sleeping."

"Okay, well I'm here if you need me."

"Thanks again. I'll see you soon."

Jason wondered what Ron would think if he knew what he'd done. What he was doing. Ron didn't have any kids. He couldn't possibly understand what it would be like to watch your daughter fighting cancer for the fourth time. *Fuck it,* Jason thought, *who cares what he thinks. I gotta do whatever it takes.* "Focus," he reminded himself out loud. He spotted his phone on the desk, and it read five-thirty. He pulled out the burner phone and texted, "What's happening?" A few seconds later a text came back. "We'll make the calls after we eat. Everything is under control." Then he opened a text on his phone to Donna and typed, "Are you home yet?"

She replied almost immediately, "No, they want to keep her."

"Fuck!" he yelled. Then he typed back, "I'll be right there."

He logged out of his computer and grabbed the large black umbrella leaning in the corner of his cubicle. He heard a loud boom of thunder outside and figured it would take him an extra ten minutes to get there due to the poor visibility. *Why can't anything go my way?* he thought.

CHAPTER FORTY-THREE

B EN TURNED HIS key in the deadbolt and yelled at Cliff to stop hollering.

"You're going to draw attention to us, dumb ass!"

"Why you have to call me names? Here's the food." Cliff handed Ben two large bags filled with Chinese take-out.

"Smells good. I'm starving," said Ben.

"Where's the woman?" Cliff rubber-necked around Ben.

"She's in the bedroom. She'll come out when she's hungry enough."

The two men sat at the small kitchen table tearing open the bags and lining up the small food boxes.

"When you gonna contact the kid?" Cliff asked shoving his mouth full of lo mien.

"Soon. I need to think it through one more time. I have to scare the shit out of him so that he does what we tell him to do."

"What if we tie the bitch to the chair and gag her? The kid will go nuts if we do that."

Ben raised his eyes from his food.

"That's not a bad idea," Ben replied grasping an egg roll with his chopsticks.

"How do you do that?" Cliff asked.

"What?"

"Use those sticks?"

"You never used chop sticks?"

"Naw. Never learned how."

"Jesus, Cliff . . . were you living under a rock? They don't have Chinese food near the farm?"

"Yeah, they did," he replied defensively. "I just ain't never learned to use them. That's all."

"Well, I'm not gonna teach you. But it sure tastes better with chopsticks." Ben was grinning as he expertly clicked the chopsticks together.

Cliff jammed his fork into the lo mien box and twirled it like pasta.

"What are we gonna do if the kid won't cooperate?"

"He will," Ben answered.

"But what if he won't?"

"He will! He's close with his mom. He's not gonna let anything happen to her cuz he wants to stay true to his job. I'm more worried about the boss. Her husband is a retired cop. Don't know what might happen if she freaks out and tells him."

"Bet she does tell him." Cliff nodded his head up and down.

"Even if she does tell him, he isn't going to find us. There's nothing he can do. We can't be traced. He'll tell her to fix the paperwork as we ask and then he'll report us, but we'll be long gone. It won't matter then."

"Glad you got it all figured out, man."

The men finished their meal and put the leftovers in the refrigerator. Ben was considering Cliff's idea of tying her up for show, but he didn't want to get violent with her again. He felt mildly guilty about the punch, but at the same time, he smiled at the thought of his perfect aim. Though she had raccoon eyes and the lump on her forehead, she wasn't hurt that badly and would heal in a few days. If everything went according to plan, it would only take a couple of days to get the job done, and then they could let her go.

"I'm keeping my eye on the prize," Ben answered.

"Yeah? And what's that?"

"Freedom."

"You're already free."

"Not like you think, dumb ass."

Cliff pushed his chair away from the table and went into the living room. He sat in the chair watching the monitors and saw that the woman was sitting on the edge of the bed. Then he saw the woman's son sitting on his couch staring intently at his laptop. The woman's boss had left her office, but her dog was curled up under the desk.

Cliff hollered into the kitchen, "The boss isn't in her office!"

Ben didn't reply, but he noticed that he'd caught the woman's attention and she was off the bed walking toward the door. Cliff stood up to greet her and grinned. Then his mouth hung open as his eyes surveyed her body.

"Got some Chinese food in there if you want some. Bet this cougar bitch knows how to use those sticks!" he shouted toward Ben.

She was hungry and thirsty, but didn't want to give him the satisfaction of hearing her admit it. She walked toward the kitchen taking as wide a path as possible around the fat man.

Ben pulled out a chair and said, "Sit. Eat. The food is good." He set some chopsticks on the table along with a stack of paper napkins.

Lindsey sat in the chair adjacent to his and inspected the food.

"Go ahead. Eat. There's plenty here."

Lindsey picked up the chopsticks and expertly snared an egg roll.

"After you eat, I am going to tie you to the chair in front of the computer." Ben noticed Lindsey had stopped chewing.

"I'm not going to hurt you. It's just for show . . . so your son, and your boss will know we mean business. The instructions are simple, and if all goes well, we'll be out of here in a couple of days."

Lindsey swallowed hard and set her chopsticks down.

"Why are you doing this? You must realize how insane this is. Someone will find me, and you will go to jail. Just let me go now, and I won't tell anyone about this. I will find my way home and pretend this never happened."

Ben kept eating, ignoring her plea.

"Like I said, I'll tie you to the chair just tight enough to keep you still, and I'm going to put a gag in your mouth. As soon as your son and your boss agree to cooperate, I will cut the video and untie you." Then all we have to do is wait.

"And how will you know that they did what you want? How will you know that whatever medication this is all about it suddenly going to be available for kids?"

"We'll know. Trust me. Now finish eating and let's get this show on the road. I'm already sick of this place."

Lindsey forced down a few bites of Moo Shu chicken and then opened a water bottle and drank. Ben left her alone at the table and went into the living room to check the monitors. The woman's boss had returned, but he could tell that she was wrapping things up for the day. It was almost 5:00 pm and Ben wanted to get his message out before the son's wife, and the boss's husband came home.

"Let's do this now." He aimed his voice to the kitchen.

Lindsey pushed back from the kitchen table, setting down the water bottle, and entered the living room.

"Ready?" Ben asked.

"I have to use the bathroom."

"There's something wrong with this bitch," Cliff announced.

"I told you . . . I have to go when I get scared!" Lindsey shouted at Cliff. He raised his arm aiming threatening her with the back of his hand.

"You watch how you talk to me, bitch, or I'll teach you a lesson you'll never forget."

"Never mind him. Go to the bathroom and then let's get this done," Ben instructed.

Lindsey took her time again in the bathroom . . . peeing, washing her hands and splashing water on her face. She sat on the edge of the tub hugging herself and rocked back and forth . . . wishing, hoping that she'd catch a break. Her son would come through for her somehow, and Lisa would too. Her thoughts were broken by a boom against the door.

"Let's go, bitch!" the fat man hollered.

"I'm counting to three, and then I'm coming in to drag your ass out."

Lindsey was standing behind the door. She put her hand on the doorknob and slowly turned it, opening the door. He grabbed her upper arm and pulled her hard, her feet nearly lifting off the floor.

"I got her," Cliff announced. "Sit down right here, bitch."

He put his mitt-sized hand on her slender shoulder and pushed her down onto the chair.

"Now don't move." Cliff reached down and pulled Lindsey's wrists behind her and Ben wrapped what felt like a torn-up sheet around her wrists.

"Ouch! That's tight!"

Cliff laughed. "Shut up, bitch. Put the gag on her."

She heard the sound of more sheet tearing and then he came around to face her.

"I'll wait until the last minute to put this in your mouth. Just remember what I said. The sooner they agree to do the job, the sooner we get out of here."

Ben took out his phone and typed with his thumbs. Lindsey watched the screen in horror as she saw her son pick up his phone that lay next to him on the couch. He studied it for a minute and then set it back down. On the other monitor, Lisa picked her phone up from the desk and read the message. Her head lifted, toward the TV Lindsey assumed, and then back at her phone again, an expression of confusion covering her face.

CHAPTER FORTY-FOUR

THE DAY WAS long, full of mundane meetings, and Lisa was glad to be winding it down. Dan would be home soon from his part-time job, and she wanted to get Missy out for a walk before she started dinner. She stood up from her desk chair, stretched, then picked up her phone. A second later a text message came in. She swiped to read it. "Turn on your TV to channel 227." Lisa studied the message. It came from a 5-digit number, a format that she didn't recognize. She looked at her TV in the corner, and CNN was streaming the latest headlines. The TV was on all day, keeping her company, but it was on mute most of the time. Channel 227? It didn't mean anything to her. It wasn't one of the regular news channels or movie channels but she was curious. She picked up the remote and punched 227 with her thumb. At first, the image was frozen and blurred, but then it cleared. Lisa took a step forward and squinted, and then reality struck. But it was impossible. She couldn't be seeing what she thought she was seeing. But she was. She was seeing Lindsey. Her dear friend and colleague, tied to a chair, her eyes were sunken and bruised, and something white was stuffed in her mouth. Was this some kind of joke? Her hands started shaking, and she froze, locked in her stance. Then the phone rang in her hand, the same number appearing on the screen. It took a second before her brain registered that this must be the same person who told her to turn on the TV.

Lisa held the phone to her ear, and without saying anything, she listened.

"You'll be receiving a phone call shortly from Ken Blake, Lindsey's son. He works at Weston Pharmaceuticals. You and Ken need to ensure that Unified Health approves Cineth for kids. I repeat, Cineth must be available for kids. It's that simple. If you do this, then we will let your friend go. If you refuse or tell anyone, including your husband, Dan, then we kill her. Do you understand? All you need to do is nod your head. We can see you. Lindsey can see you, just like you can see her. Now put the phone down. Leave the TV on, take your dog for a walk like usual and then get back to work."

The call ended, but Lisa's arm remained frozen, still holding the phone to her ear. She was shaking all over now and couldn't think. *Was this really happening? Did the voice say that they were watching me? Was that really Lindsey?* Lisa snapped back into the moment, and her head swung around the room. Her security camera was pointing out the window so that couldn't be watching her. She moved around to behind her desk and studied her computer screen. The camera. Was it possible? Missy's tail was wagging. Could whoever these people see Missy from the monitor? Dan! She had to tell him . . . but, what if she did? What if they killed Lindsey because she told Dan? Her heart was pounding out of her chest.

Missy put her paws up Lisa's leg. She had to go out. Lisa walked to the back of her house and opened her sliding doors. "Go on . . ." she told the dog. Missy cocked her head and let out a quiet whine. "Go on!" she snapped at the dog. Lisa put the instep of her shoe on the dog's backside and pushed her out the door. She checked the time again. Dan! He would know what to do. Then she went back to her office and shook her mouse. The screen popped up displaying the document she had been working on all day. The policy template . . . for Cineth.

She sat in her chair searching the room. The TV was still on, and the screen was black. Then she realized . . . the smart TV. He hacked my TV! Dan's old Xbox! She rushed from behind her desk to examine it more closely, but then worried . . . if she disconnected it then what about Lindsey? She backed away and picked up the remote. She considered powering it down but decided to wait. He said to leave the TV on. She thought about the rest of the house. Her office was the only room that had a smart TV, but what if there were cameras?

Missy was barking. "Jesus Christ!" She went to the back of the house and opened the sliders letting the dog in, and then she heard the garage door open. Lisa went into the kitchen, then out of the kitchen into the bedroom. She was lost in her own house. Nothing made sense. What were the instructions? She would wait for Lindsey's son to contact her. Dan was in the garage. Lisa started texting, "Lindsey Blake has been kidnapped. I saw her! On the TV! They are watching my office! They hacked the TV and said to keep it turned on! They said if I told you they would kill her so, please pretend that you don't know anything. I'm so scared. They want me and her son to fix some new medication for kids. Lindsey was tied up and beaten!" She hit the send button.

A moment later, Dan rushed through the door into the kitchen. Lisa was crying, and Dan pulled her into his arms. She whispered in his ear, "I think they hacked the smart TV in my office. I'm so scared. What if they kill her? I didn't check the rest of the house. What if there are cameras watching us?" Dan pushed Lisa back and opened the refrigerator, reaching in with both hands.

He was texting, "Let's not panic. Get Missy and let's go for a walk. Now say it out loud that you want to take Missy for a walk."

"Missy hasn't gone for a walk yet. Do you want to go with us?" Lisa asked.

"Sure."

Lisa pulled Missy's leash from the hook next to the door to the garage, and the dog appeared at her feet wagging her tail. They went out through the garage to the street and Lisa immediately burst into tears.

"Okay, calm down and tell me exactly what happened."

"I texted you earlier . . . Lindsey didn't show up for work today. I texted and called, but she didn't answer. I was worried, but I figured she had taken PTO and forgot to let me know. Then I got a text." She handed Dan her phone showing him the text from the strange number.

"So I turned on the TV . . . and there she was." Lisa sniffled deeply.

"She was sitting in a chair with her hands tied behind her and a gag in her mouth. A gag! Oh my God, Dan. Her eyes were black and blue. They hurt her!"

"Okay, hon, what did they say? Try to be exact. What did they say, exactly?"

"It was one voice, and he told me that I would be hearing from Lindsey's son and that we needed to get Cineth—that's a new drug—approved for kids. He said that once we do that he will let Lindsey go. Then the call dropped, and the TV went black, but they told me to keep it turned on."

"Okay, let's walk and figure this out. What is this new drug?"

"It's a cancer drug. I just started working on the policy today! It was approved by the FDA for adults, but not for kids!"

"Then why would someone want to use it on a kid?"

"The phase III testing was really good. They had almost full remission on all of the patients. Lots of these drugs work the same on kids, but the drug companies don't typically test on kids. They wait until the drug is used for a while on the adults and then they will allow use for kids. It's just the way it's done."

"Well someone has a sick kid, and they are desperate. Can you think of anyone that has a kid with cancer?"

"No, I don't know anyone with a sick kid."

"How easy or hard is it to do what this guy wants?"

"I need the research to back up the policy. Lindsey's son works at the pharmaceutical company. He will have to forge or doctor up some research to make it look like kids were tested. Then I would have to write the policy and get it approved by a committee! They could ask a million questions and then what would I say?"

Dan hugged her again. "I need time to think about what we're going to do," he said.

Lisa's phone chimed, and she pulled it out of her back pocket.

"It's Ken Blake. He just sent me an IM on Facebook."

"Okay, let's keep walking for a few minutes, and we'll figure out what to do, but when we get back to the house, you stay in the kitchen and give me a chance to look around."

CHAPTER FORTY-FIVE

KEN CHECKED THE digital clock on his laptop, and it read five o'clock. Laurie would be home in about a half hour, and he hadn't thought about dinner. He would order take out, but first, he would send her a text and ask what she wanted. He checked the clock again. It was five-o-one. He had just enough time for one more game. He quickly sent her text and then dropped the phone on the couch.

A few seconds later a text came in. He kept his eyes on the screen, having just started a new game and picked up the phone glancing. The text read, "Turn your TV to channel 227."

Ken didn't recognize the five-digit number. He tossed the phone back on the couch and continued his game. Another text chimed, and he picked it up again. It was from Laurie. She wanted pizza. Good. He wanted Pizza too. He split his laptop screen, still playing the game with one hand and ordered a cheese pizza from the shop on the corner. Laurie would pick it up on the way home. Perfect. He would have a few extra minutes of game time before he had to shut it down for the night. Again, another text. He picked up the phone again and read, "Channel 227 now or your mother dies."

Ken read the message again, and the hairs stood up on his arms. He hadn't heard from his mother all day, well not since about six that morning. He had texted her back and called, but she hadn't called back. It wasn't like her. She always took his calls or sent him a text if she was too busy at work and couldn't talk.

Ever since she moved to Florida, they had some contact at least daily. Usually, it was a text, but sometimes a quick call or chat on Facebook. He hated that she lived so far away. He stared at the phone, unsure of what to do. He went back to the game screen and minimized it, then typed the five-digit phone number into the browser. Maybe other people reported this type of crank call or text. No hits. He stood up and looked at his phone again and tapped the 'Mom' icon. It rang a couple of times and went to voicemail. He picked up the remote from the ottoman and turned on the TV, changing the channel to 227. The picture flickered but then cleared. It was his mother, but wait, she didn't look like herself. He stepped closer to the big screen TV and bent lower. "Mom?" The blood drained from his face, and his grip tightened on the remote. "Mom!" His mother was tied to a chair with something stuffed in her mouth. She had two black eyes and a swollen forehead. His phone rang, startling him and a shiver went down his spine. He set down the remote and picked up the phone. It was the same number as the text. He swiped to answer.

"Ken, I know this looks bad, but your mother is fine. Here's what we need you to do. First, if you tell anyone about this, including your wife, Laurie, you will never see your mother again. I can see you standing in front of the TV, so don't think you can sneak anything past us. You need to call Lisa Simmons at Unified. She's your mother's boss, and the two of you need to figure out how to get Cineth approved for kids. It's that simple. Once you do that, your mother goes free like nothing ever happened. If you call the police or don't follow the instructions, she's gone. Do you understand?" Ken stood staring at his mother on the TV screen. She was crying, and his eyes welled up. He took in a breath, thinking, and quickly figured out that whoever this was, had hacked his smart TV or his game console. "Ken!" Do you understand?"

"I . . . I don't know how to do what you want."

"Yes, Ken, you do. Just remember what I said. If you tell anyone, including Laurie, your mother dies. I'll be watching, and I will know when you succeed . . . and you will succeed because I know how close you are to your mother. She has been a good mother to you, so don't let her down."

The call ended, and the TV screen went black.

Ken shuffled backward and sat on the ottoman.

"What the fuck?" He covered his face with his hands and shook his head. He picked up the phone again, his sweaty hand making it slick. Laurie would be home in twenty minutes. Lisa Simmons? How would he even get her number? Facebook! Ken grabbed his laptop and opened his Facebook clicking on his mother's profile. Then she searched her friend's list and found Lisa's name. Her profile located her in Sarasota. He opened up a chat window. "Lisa, this is Ken Blake. I need to talk to you right now." He entered his phone number in the window and waited. His heart raced, and he checked the time again. How would ever keep this from Laurie? She would know by just looking at him that something was wrong. His eyes stuck to the TV and hairs stood up on his neck. *Were they watching?* His stomach churned.

He went into the bedroom, then remembered that the bedroom TV was also connected to the Internet. *Should he disconnect it? Would they hurt her if he did something they didn't like? She had two black eyes!* He couldn't risk it. The vomit was coming. He ran into the bathroom just in time and heaved. His stomach was empty.

Laurie was coming with pizza. *This can't be happening!* He

would write a note and leave it in the bathroom for her to read. There was no way they could see in the bathroom. He searched the room for something to write with but couldn't find anything, but then remembered Laurie's pile of makeup in the bathroom. He opened Laurie's draw in the vanity and found an eye pencil. Then he opened the linen closet and found an unopened box of tissues. He wrote in small print on the bottom of the box.

"Mom was kidnapped, and they want me to forge some documents at work, or they will kill her. They are watching us through the TVs. You can't let on that anything is wrong. Please, for mom." He set the box on the toilet seat and left the bathroom. He checked his phone again, and no message had come back from Lisa. He sat on the edge of the bed gripping the phone, and then he heard Laurie come in the front door.

"I'm home. Pizza!"

Ken sucked in his breath and pulled himself up. His legs wobbled like he could topple to the floor at any moment.

"I'm in here."

A moment later Laurie entered the bedroom smelling like pizza and wrapped her arms around him. "Are you hungry?"

"Actually, no. I might eat it later."

She pulled back and studied his face.

"Are you alright? You look sick."

"Yeah, my stomach is off, and I made a mess in the bathroom. Sorry."

"I hope it's not a virus. I'll clean it up. You should lay down."

Ken sat down on the edge of the bed and watched her enter the bathroom. His heart was exploding from his chest. His ears pounded and the vision of his mother, with her beaten and swollen face, was stamped in his mind.

Laurie took her time in the bathroom and then finally came out. Her face was drained, and her eyes glistened.

"I don't feel so good either. Maybe it was cleaning up your puke."

Ken put his arm around her and glanced at the TV.

"Let's skip the pizza tonight," he said.

"Good idea. I need some air. Come out on the balcony."

Ken took Laurie's hand and led her outside to the balcony and then hugged her close. He whispered in her ear. "Did you see what I wrote?"

"Yes, what are we going to do?"

"Whoever this is wants me to contact Lisa Simmons, Mom's boss. I sent her an IM on Facebook, but she hasn't responded yet. I don't know how else to reach her. I saw her . . . mom . . . tied to a chair. Her face was all beat up." Ken started to cry, and Laurie squeezed him tighter.

"We should call the police," she said.

"No! No police! I will do what they want me to do. I don't care. I'm not taking any chances with my mother's life."

"Okay, okay." They were still holding on to each other.

An instant later, his phone chimed. He pushed Laurie back, and looked at the phone.

"It's her. It's Lisa. I'm going to call her."

CHAPTER FORTY-SIX

IT WAS AFTER six o'clock and Lisa heard thunder off in the distance.

"We have to get back to the house before the storm comes."

Dan checked his weather app.

"We have a few minutes. Let's call him now."

Missy was making a circle around their legs, twisting her leash. Her anxiety was increasing as the storm got closer.

Lisa squatted down and patted her dog's head, speaking in baby talk trying to calm her.

"We can't stay out here much longer with Missy freaking out."

She opened the message from Ken and tapped in her phone number and then hit send.

"I hope he calls me right back," she stated.

The couple continued walking slowly back to their house.

"What if they have people watching us outside of the house?" Lisa asked.

"Not likely. This sounds like a small job. Probably two guys hired by a third." Dan felt confident in his assessment.

"How can you be so calm?"

"I was trained to be calm. Getting excited doesn't solve

anything, and we were more likely to make mistakes. I still think we should get the police involved. Doesn't matter that I'm retired . . . they'll step up to help."

"No! Not yet. Let's see what Ken says." Then her phone rang. "Lisa?"

"Hi, Ken. What did they say to you? Did you see her? I'm so sorry this happened. I can't . . ." Ken cut her off.

"Lisa, I need to know what you do at work. They want us to somehow get this drug approved for pediatric use. All of the testing was done on adults. I don't know what they think we can do."

"They said the same thing to me! And I was working on the drug today!"

"Working how?" Ken asked. "What does that mean?"

"I write the medical policy for the use of the drug based on the pharmaceutical company's FDA approval. I just copy and paste the information into a template and suggest some appropriate medical criteria. For example, with this drug Cineth, it's for Acute Myeloid Leukemia. I write the policy for the insurance company to pay claims when the drug is approved after passing through the medical necessity review. The patient must have the diagnosis and have tried other less expensive drugs that failed. Whoever orders the drug has to send in all kinds of clinical documentation for the insurance company to approve it and pay. Because all of the testing was done on adults, the policy would also state that the patient has to be an adult."

Lightening lit up the sky and a thunder boom shook the ground.

"We're outside, Ken. We have to get indoors. There's a storm right over us." Dan bent down and scooped up the dog, and they started to jog back to the house.

"Lisa, can you just leave out the part about adults in the policy?"

"Ken, I have to call you back. We have to get inside."

"Wait!" Ken yelled into the phone, but Lisa was gone.

The sky opened dumping heavy, cool rain on them just before they reached their driveway. Dan pointed to the garage. Once inside Lisa threw herself into Dan's arms, whispering in his ear.

"Do you think they bugged the house? I'm so scared. What if they find out that you know?"

"These guys aren't stupid. They know you told me. No wife can keep a secret like this," he whispered back. "We have to assume that they have eyes on us and we'll keep our conversations outdoors. At least they won't be able to hear what we're up to."

"I should call him back. Poor guy." She tapped the phone button to redial his number, and he answered immediately.

"Sorry about that," Lisa said.

"I asked if you could just leave out the part about adults when you write the policy," Ken reminded her.

"No, said Lisa. Once I have the template complete, it goes to a committee of medical directors for approval. They would notice right away that the policy doesn't identify the population that the drug is intended for. Plus, I attached the research and outcomes that are provided by the pharmaceutical company. That's where you must come in." She heard Ken groan.

"How am I supposed to change research that was already FDA approved? This is fucking ridiculous! These people have no idea what they are asking. It's impossible." Lisa could hear his anger.

"Let me talk to him," Dan said.

"Ken, it's Dan. Lisa's husband. I'm a retired Sarasota County cop."

"No cops!" Ken yelled into the phone. "Oh my God. They are going to kill my mother!" As Ken's words raced into Lisa's ear, lightening flashed in the yard across the street. The thunder crack was deafening, and Lisa felt the hairs on her arms stand up. She flew a scared look at Dan.

"Jesus, it's like the Apocalypse out here." He put the phone back to his ear and watched as Lisa let their terrified dog into the house.

"Ken, try to calm down. I know this is bad. I'm not going to get anyone involved, but there was no way Lisa could keep this from me. We can work together to get your mother out of this. We can figure out a way to give them what they want and then worry about the consequences later. Let's think about this. They want this drug approved for kids because someone with money and power has a sick kid. Right? Maybe we can work this backward while you and Lisa try to figure out how to give them what they want."

"What do you mean work it backward?" Ken asked.

"If we can find out who is orchestrating this, then maybe we can trace where they are holding your mother and at that point get the cops involved."

"No cops! What the fuck is wrong with you? I am not putting my mother's life at risk. It's not worth it. I don't care about catching these people; I just want my mother back alive!"

"Okay, Okay." Dan gave in. Lisa motioned him to hand her back the phone.

"Ken, what can you do about the research? I can email you what I would normally enter into the template. Maybe if you can somehow change it and get it posted on the FDA site, then I can copy it into my template. If it looks legit, the committee won't question it. I doubt any of the medical directors have even heard about this medication."

"How long does it take to get approved once it goes to committee?" Ken asked.

"It's usually pretty quick. The committee meets this Friday."

"Fuck! She'll be tied up with these assholes for two more days. Who knows what they are doing to her! We don't even know if there is more than one of them! We're just assuming! We only heard one voice." His words skipped a beat as held back tears. "Oh God, I'm sick to my stomach."

"Ken . . . I'm so sorry."

Lisa paused giving him time to pull himself together.

"If I try to call a committee meeting sooner they would surely get suspicious and would likely say no anyway. We'd be safer going through the routine process and not drawing any extra attention to it."

"Fine. I will log on tonight and read through everything on my side. But even if I have the option to change the research, it won't take long before someone notices it. The company has invested millions on this drug. They know everything about it . . . especially the sales team. Oh shit, I just thought of that. They are already out contracting with pharmacies and insurance companies. This is a fucking disaster. How can a drug now being marketed for adults suddenly be available for kids? No fucking way."

"Ken, let's just go one step at a time. Text me your email address, and I will send you the template so you can see what I will be presenting to the committee. Then let's talk again in the morning. Maybe they will contact us again, so we know your mom is okay. They seem determined to have us do this, so I don't think they will harm her again."

"Okay," he answered.

There was a moment of silence between them, and then Lisa said, "Ken, we're going to get her back. I know we don't want to involve the police, but Dan can at least offer us some guidance. Did you tell your wife?"

"Yeah, she knows. Nothing she can do either. She works at

the same company in a different department. Even if I didn't tell her, she'd eventually find out when they discover the research was changed."

"Good, I'm glad you told her. You need the support. We'll get her out of this. Try not to worry. I know it's hard. I'll talk to you in the morning."

"Okay," he answered, and then ended the call.

The storm was moving West over the gulf, and Lisa thought about Lindsey and where they might be keeping her. Did she hear the same storm? It was dinner time. Were they feeding her? The image of Lindsey tied up, her face black and blue, was overwhelming, and she started to cry.

Dan opened the door to the kitchen and Lisa followed, her eyes darting around the room wondering if someone was watching them. She pulled a tissue from the box on the counter and wiped her eyes, then blew her nose. Her stomach growled. Somehow hunger managed to supersede her fear. Dan was one step ahead, his head in the refrigerator.

"Let's go out for dinner," she suggested.

"Good idea. How about the Bistro?"

"Fine. Hopefully, the traffic won't be bad."

What would normally be a ten-minute drive took just under a half an hour. Though the tourist season in Sarasota was nearing the end, the roads and restaurants were still crowded with northerners. They were mostly quiet on the ride. Dan noticed Lisa wringing her hands and shifting in the seat. He hoped she wouldn't cry again. The quiet also gave him time to think about the time line. He would need more information from Ken, but he would have to extract it carefully. He didn't want to alarm him or make him think that he was getting the police involved. Mentally he compiled a list of questions. He wanted to know. When he had last heard from his mother, and what her daily routine was. Maybe Lisa would know some of this too.

Dan pulled the car into the restaurant parking lot and grabbed Lisa's hand.

"Try not to worry. We'll get her back."

Lisa leaned over and laid her head on Dan's shoulder.

"I can't believe this is happening," she said.

CHAPTER FORTY-SEVEN

ARIUS LEFT HIS room only once that night to sneak into the kitchen and grab a box of cereal from the pantry. He could hear his mother's voice coming from her bedroom and assumed she was in there with her boyfriend doing drugs. He quickly wiped the image from his mind and tiptoed back to his room, pushing the bookcase into its blockade position. He sat up on his bed stuffing fistfuls of Fruit Loops in his mouth while he continued listening to the audiobook.

He was still firm on the decision to return the phone to where he had found it, but in the meantime, he had one more night to enjoy it. As the narrator plodded along, Darius began swiping and tapping the apps as he had done earlier in the day, thinking he might discover something new. He swiped through the pictures again and studied the ones from Boston more closely. They were tagged to Faneuil Hall, The Boston Common, The North End, and at the New England Aquarium. It would be so awesome to go there he thought. He opened the map app and tapped in 'New England Aquarium', then tapped the directions button. The result was a thick blue line up the east coast that read '1464 mi'. It was a world away.

He pressed the home button on the phone and opened

the fitness app. This time he swiped through the history and could see that the woman who owned the phone used the app nearly every day. Darius was impressed. He wondered what the app would show for his usage considering all the days he rode his bike to school, and all around the neighborhood. Then he noticed a map icon in the fitness display and tapped it. He waited while the app clocked, and then a flashing red dot appeared.

The narrator's voice was still telling the story, but since his concentration had moved to the phone, he had lost track of what was happening. He pushed the home button, went back to the audiobook app and tapped the pause button. Then he returned to the fitness app. The same flashing dot appeared. This time he pinched it open, making it large enough to see where the dot was originating from. It was North of Fort Myers, South of Sarasota, up the coast, flashing on the edge of the water. Was this the person who owned the phone? He stared at it again and thought it must be her. Then a red symbol flashed on the phone indicating the battery was down to ten percent. He powered off the phone and stuffed it into his backpack along with the earbuds. He would bring it to school tomorrow and somehow try to find a way to charge it on one of the school's iPad stations without being noticed.

Back on his bed, he opened a notebook and started writing a letter to Hanna. It had been about three weeks since he had heard any news and he was worried about how she was doing. He hoped that her mother was still picking up her school work and she would get his letter tomorrow.

"Hanna, I haven't heard about how you are doing. I hope you are feeling better and can come back to school. We only have another week left. I found a cell phone in the grass in front of the school. I think I figured out who it belongs to. I am not sure what I am going to do with it, but right now I got to listen to

'Cujo' on it. Did you ever see the movie? Hanna, I am sorry that you are sick again. I miss you. Darius."

He folded up the letter, wrote Hanna's name on the outside, and then put it in his backpack. He took out his math book and settled back in to do his homework.

CHAPTER FORTY-EIGHT

THEY SAT ON either side of the bed where Hanna lay sleeping. Jason claimed the reclining chair and Donna was once again perched on the window sill. The monitors attached to Hanna's chest sounded soft, rhythmic beeps, letting them know that their daughter was peaceful, sleeping like the angel that she was.

When he arrived at the hospital the evening before, Donna had met him in the hallway outside of Hanna's room.

"The oncologist came by after reading her labs and said he was concerned about organ failure. She's dying, Jason."

His brain didn't register what she said, though he stared at his wife trying to listen, he couldn't keep his focus. He was aware of his heavy breathing, but the sensation of moving air in and out of his lungs was gone.

"What?" he asked.

"Jason, did you hear me? The doctor said he was concerned she was going into organ failure."

"No! Where is he? Is he still here?" He snapped his head left and right down the hallways.

"I don't know. He had just left the room when you texted me."

"I'm going to find one of the nurses and see if she can page him."

Jason checked his phone and wondered if Ben had made contact with Lisa and Ken, then he realized he wouldn't see anything from Ben on his personal phone. He was unraveling, disconnecting. He wished he hadn't waited so long to execute his plan. *What if I'm too late*, he thought?

"Excuse me," he called out to get the nurse's attention. "Is the oncologist still here? I want to talk to him about Hanna."

"One sec," The young woman replied picking up the phone. "He'll be right up. I'll send him to Hanna's room." He thanked her and went back to the room to wait.

"Do you think he's going to tell you something different?" Donna asked him.

"Just shut the fuck up, Donna. I'm so sick of you," he snapped. You give up on her so easily. She's not gonna die, so I don't want to hear it again."

Donna had no words. She didn't recognize her husband anymore. She turned her back and went back into Hanna's room without acknowledging his outburst. He paced up and down the hall until he saw the doctor get off the elevator, and he walked to meet him. The doctor put his arm around his shoulder and spoke softly, sympathetically.

"Hey, Jason, I'm sure Donna told you that Hanna's labs are not looking good. Her LFTs are showing signs of failure."

Jason pulled away from him.

"Just because her LFTs are abnormal doesn't necessarily mean that she's going into liver failure. It could just be a response to the chemo. We've been here before, and she bounced right back."

"I know. I know," the doctor repeated. "I just wanted you to have a full understanding of where she is right now. We'll keep her here and watch her closely."

"Thanks, doc. Hey listen, I know I mentioned this before but what about a trial of that new medication, Cineth. If it does get approved for kids, would you order it?"

At this point, he didn't care if he was exposing himself. He just needed to know if there was even the slightest chance.

"Well yeah, but I think it might be too late for that. I'll have to check, but the last literature that I read about it said it was just for adults, but I will look into it again."

"Thanks, I would appreciate it," Jason replied.

He watched the doctor get back on the elevator and then he walked in the opposite direction to the waiting room where he had met the young father a few weeks before.

He resisted thinking about their conversation, not wanting to visualize their poor son's last moments. He sat in the corner of the room on a bright yellow easy chair and took out the flip phone and texted, "We are running out of time. Did you get them started?"

He stared at his phone willing it to chime with a response. It finally came. "Yes. They know what needs to be done. Everything is fine." Jason stared at Ben's response. Everything was not fine. He started thinking about all the ways he could get caught.

He had just given the oncologist a clue by bringing up the drug again. He also had a conversation with Ron Shay about the drug, but that time Ron was the one who brought it up. Ron and his secretary knew he had a daughter with Leukemia. Lindsey and Lisa worked together at the same company he worked for, and calls could be traced from his cell phone to the pharmaceutical company where Ken Blake worked. It was all so out of control. Getting caught before Hanna got the drug would be a disaster. Getting caught after Hanna got better . . . well, he was prepared to live with that. Maybe a jury would be sympathetic.

He rubbed his hand over the top of his head and then made a fist. He wanted to punch the tightness out of his chest. He opened a browser on his personal phone and tapped, 'How much prison time for kidnapping in FL?'.

CHAPTER FORTY-NINE

S HE SLEPT THROUGH the night; she assumed her exhaustion and the remnants of the sedative helped her stay asleep. When she finally woke up, she could hear her two captors rustling around in the kitchen. Were they seriously going to cook breakfast? She had already figured out that the fat one was only there for his size and muscle, but she couldn't quite get a handle on what was motivating the black guy. He seemed smart and certainly had advanced computer skills. Couldn't he get a real job instead of kidnapping and hitting innocent women?

She glanced up at the camera and, knowing they couldn't see her if they were in the kitchen, she quickly checked out the closet. It was empty except for the wooden closet rod, but there was an attic access door in the ceiling. She scanned the entire bedroom trying to think of any way she could get herself up high enough to climb into the attic. Nothing in the room was useful. It would take too long to drag the mattress into the closet and try to climb it, and they would surely hear her or see her on the camera.

She left the bedroom and went into the bathroom, closing the door behind her. She remembered there was a plywood-covered small window in the shower and she climbed into the tub to investigate. She pulled on the side of the board, but it didn't budge. She could see the nails all around the perimeter. This wasn't going to work either.

She climbed out of the tub and splashed water on her face. She looked like a scared raccoon, but the pain was now less, and the color was already starting to turn to a brownish yellow. She rubbed her teeth with her index finger and then examined her clothes. She cringed at the thought of that disgusting fat man buying her clothes. Her original shorts, which were torn but still wearable, hung over the dirty tub, but wearing them would leave her with too much skin exposed. She picked up the shorts and noticed her underpants were gone. He took them . . . she was sure the fat one took them. She slammed the shorts into the tub and pulled the curtain closed.

She tapped the display on her fitness tracker and saw that it was ten after nine. Her stomach growled, and she wondered what their plan was for eating. She relieved herself, and then washed her hands again and left the bathroom.

The black guy was sitting in the living room in front of the monitor, watching Lisa at her computer, and the fat one was sat on a folding chair against the wall. He gawked at her and then licked his lips.

Lindsey glared at him, twisting her face in disgust.

"My man here is going to go out and get us some breakfast."

"I'm going to McDonald's," Cliff announced accentuating the 'Mac'. "What do you want, Princess Bitch?" 'Princess' sounded more like 'printheth'.

"Whatever," Lindsey answered. "I don't care. Coffee."

Cliff rolled his eyes and went to the front door. Ben followed behind him with the keys. Lindsey watched as Ben turned the key and opened the door. Even if she ran . . . flew at the door, she would never make it out the door without one of them grabbing her. She turned her eyes away from the front door and back at the monitor while Ben turned the lock.

"Can she see me?"

"No. I don't have that channel open. But she knows we can see her."

"Why are you doing this? You seem like a smart guy. Good with technology. Why don't you just get a real job? They pay good money for people with skills like yours."

Ben started to respond, but then paused and moved in close to her. Too close. Lindsey held her position.

"It's none of your fucking business what I do, or don't do. You're here until your son and boss do what they're told. That's all you need to know."

She broke his glare and walked into the kitchen.

She eyed the door that led to the backyard, but it was covered with thick plywood, and she could see the perimeter filled with nails. There had to be some way out of here.

She left the kitchen and walked back down the hallway to see the bedroom at the end of the hall. The room was dark, but she could make out a mattress on the floor. She guessed they took turns sleeping. There was no way out. She was here for the duration.

She went back to the kitchen and leaned with her back against the counter. "Are you still watching my son?"

"No. I assume that your son is at work, fixing that research so your boss can do her part."

Ben was sat on the middle chair at the long table and watched Lisa sitting at her desk, working on her computer.

"How can you see her? Where's the camera?"

"I hacked her Smart TV. Same as your son."

"Look, I can get you more money than whoever is paying you. Just tell me how much and I'll get it. My son can get the money for you."

Ben turned to her again, and this time he reached out to grab her arm, but she pulled back just as his fingers brushed by.

"If you don't shut up I'm going to tie you up and gag you for real. My buddy will be back soon. Just go relax."

Lindsey held her position just a second too long, and Ben lunged from the chair forcing her to take a step back.

"I told you to go relax!" His tone was a low, threatening growl.

Lindsey took another step back and saw past him, watching Lisa get up from behind her computer. She wondered if Lisa knew she was being watched. She must know. This was all so horrible, and for what? She had already figured that there was a sick kid involved, but whose kid? It had to be someone closely related to the insurance company else how would they have discovered the connection between her and Ken.

Lindsey thought about Ken's health. What would she do if he got sick? She'd be devastated of course . . . but kidnapping? Never. Whoever was responsible, whoever was giving the orders, was a deranged coward. She had no sympathy.

CHAPTER FIFTY

CLIFF BACKED THE Mercury out of the dirt driveway and then made a three-point turn aiming the car back to the main road. His stomach churned with hunger, and the skin on his arms was beet red. He reached into the back seat and pulled his cap up from the floor. It was old and torn in places, but he pulled it down on his head to absorb the sweat before it ran into his eyes.

The nearest McDonald's was a couple of miles away, just around the corner from the convenience store where he stopped for gas and beer yesterday morning. He thought about the chubby lady that led him to the storage room, and how she held firm on the ridiculous price she charged for the beer. Big, strong women appealed to him, and suddenly he was aroused. He decided to stop and get some beer before picking up breakfast.

Cliff pulled the car into the gas station and noticed that the parking lot was empty. Yeah, he thought . . . I'll have her full attention. He parked on the side of the building, away from the main road and then lumbered toward the entrance.

The cold air was an instant relief. Cliff looked around the store but didn't see the woman. Maybe she wasn't working today. Now that he thought about it, he didn't see any cars in the parking lot. Well, maybe she had parked out back. He didn't think to look there. He made his way to the back of the store and stopped to listen at the stockroom door. For a second he heard some shuffling footsteps, and then the door opened.

"Oh, sorry, ma'am. Didn't meant to startle you. Howya doin today?"

She hesitated a moment and then said, "Hi, Mister. You done scared me at the door."

"I'm sorry. I didn't mean to."

"That's alright," she replied studying his face.

"Your the guy that came in yesterday for the Bud."

"Yeah, that's right. I was hoping you had some more back there." Cliff aimed his chin in the direction of the door."

"I got some more. How much you want?"

"I'll take a couple of sixes."

"Wait right here, and I'll be right back."

Cliff obeyed, his eyes meeting the dirty floor. She wasn't interested in anything he had in mind. A moment later the door opened and a bald man with a handle bar mustache, at least a head taller than Cliff, walked past him carrying the two six packs of Bud. He wasn't sure if this was another customer or what.

"You want the beer or what?" the man yelled.

"Uh . . . yeah." Cliff pulled his wallet out and approached. The man was wearing a leather vest, and when he bent slightly forward, Cliff could see he had a gun. The man caught his glance.

"You need something else?" he asked sarcastically.

"Uh, no. Juth the beer," he lisped.

"I know you came around here gawking at my wife yesterday. The beer will cost you twenty dollars today, and if you come back tomorrow, it will cost you thirty. You git my meaning?"

"Uh, yeah . . . I git it." Cliff handed him a twenty-dollar bill without making eye contact, took the beer, and walked quickly out of the store.

He gunned the old Mercury's engine, then shifted the car into drive cutting his wheel hard to turn on the main road. His cap was soaked, and sweat stung his eyes.

He thought about telling Ben what happened but then decided not to say anything. Ben would just call him stupid for even thinking that the store clerk would be interested in him. He rounded the corner onto the Tamiami Trail and could see the golden arches up ahead. Eggs, pancakes, and coffee for three, well four. Two orders for himself. There was just one car ahead of him in the drive through, and he sat tapping his fingers on the steering wheel. His phone vibrated on the seat, and he flipped it open.

"You on your way?"

"Yep In 10", he texted, then snapped the phone shut. He shifted his weight in the seat, attempting to unstick himself from his sweaty pants and thought about Ben. The guy was so bossy and called him names all the time, even in front of the woman. He wanted to punch him. Prick. *This shit better be over with tomorrow cuz I ain't hanging around. He don't need me for nuthin anyway.* He wondered what Ben would say if he asked him for his share of the money now. Maybe Ben was sick of him too and would pay him off . . . let him leave, or maybe he would tell him to give him the money or else he'd rat him out.

Cliff loaded the food into the front seat and drove back to the cottage. He would wait for the right moment and demand the money. *Fuck it,* he thought. *Ain't got nuttin to lose.*

CHAPTER FIFTY-ONE

WHEN HANNA WOKE up the next morning, she appeared brighter, less pale and more energetic.

"You should go home, Daddy. I'm okay, really."

Jason considered the idea. He needed a shower and wanted to change his clothes. But more importantly, he wanted to know if everything was okay at the cottage.

"Are you going home?" he asked Donna.

"I think one of us should stay here until the doctor comes in," she answered curtly.

"Fine. I'll run home and take a quick shower. Text me if there's anything I should know. If everything is good, I may stop at the office for a couple of hours."

He leaned over to kiss Hanna, but she popped up and grabbed him around the neck.

"You've got some energy today! That's great, honey!" Maybe he was right. Maybe the labs yesterday were just a reflection of the chemo, and she was bouncing back.

"I'll be back a little later," he said to Donna, but she ignored him, her eyes focused on Hanna.

He had barely slept, unable to reposition himself in the small reclining chair next to Hanna's bed. His arm was sore from having kept his hand in his pocket the entire night, just in case

Ben texted him, which thankfully he didn't. As soon as he got outside, he took out the burner phone and sent a text. "What's happening? Did you check on Simmons?"

He wanted to skip the shower and go straight to the office, but then he remembered he could log in from home and see if anything was happening. He got into the car and started the engine. It was seven o'clock and already in the upper eighties. The rain would come early today, he thought. He drove faster than he should have, but he couldn't wait to get online. The cell phone vibrated and he flipped it open with his thumb.

"She's online working."

He tossed the phone onto the passenger seat and weaved his way through traffic.

Jason was glad the house was quiet. He needed to think, and he needed to calm himself down. The tightness in his chest was a constant now, and he knew it could get out of control at any time. A shower would help.

He stayed under the water longer than usual and thought about Hanna. She looked good today. It was a good sign. She just needed to hang on a while longer until he could get her the new treatment. Just a few more days. He toweled off and dressed. He sat and opened his laptop, but had trouble logging in. The screen was clocking. "Fucking server!" He didn't want to call the IT help desk and get placed in the hold queue. He slammed the laptop shut and then logged into his work email account on his phone. There was nothing of interest. Why would there be? The vice-like grip on his chest was back and creeping up his neck. He heard the garage door open. Donna? He pulled the curtain back seeing the back end of her car enter the garage.

"Changed your mind?" he hollered toward the kitchen.

Donna came down the hall into his office.

"I wanted to get cleaned up and go to the school. They have some letters for Hanna from some of her friends. The doctor stopped and said she looked good this morning. They drew more blood, so they'll let us know later if anything is new. Hanna was playing on her iPad, and I told her I'd be back a little later."

"Good," he answered. "You need some time too."

She turned away and went up the stairs. Jason followed. His heart beat in his throat, but he needed to say something, somehow reassure her that he was going to fix everything.

"I'm working on getting that new drug for her. The one with the near perfect cure rate," he announced.

Donna turned and faced him.

"Really . . . I thought the doctor said it wasn't for pediatric use."

"Well, sometimes they make acceptations."

"How do they make exceptions, Jason? I never heard of such a thing. We talked about clinical trials for her, and there were no exceptions. You're grasping at straws."

"Jesus fucking Christ, Donna. You're always so negative, ready to put her in a coffin." He regretted the words before he spoke the last syllable.

"I'm sorry. I didn't mean that." But he knew it was too late to be sorry.

Donna started to cry. He stood there for a moment with his head down and then turned and left the room. "Fuck me!" he mumbled on his way down the stairs. He grabbed his keys and drove to the office.

Thirty minutes later he was online, studying Lisa Simmons' picture in a chat window. Her indicator was on green, which meant she was not in a meeting. He didn't dare type anything, but he was satisfied that she was working on solving his most important problem. He closed the chat window and then opened the shared drive. He right clicked on the Cineth template and could see that she had checked it out. If he tried to open the document, she would know that an attempt was being made by someone else to read it. He pulled his cursor away. Now if only he had a way to learn what was going on at Weston Pharmaceuticals. He sat back in his chair and thought about it, then took out the burner phone and dialed the number.

"Ken Blake, please," he said to the receptionist. A moment later Ken answered, "This is Ken." Jason closed the phone. He was there, at work. Good sign. There was no way he would let his mother get hurt. Jason opened the phone again and sent a text to Ben. "I need this to happen today. Put some pressure on." He put the phone back in his pocket and sat up straight. *I'm in control*, he thought. *I'm in control.*

*   *   *

The house was empty, and Donna stood at the end of Hanna's bed looking around her daughter's room. Just a month ago she was spreading her school work out, listening to her music and playing on her iPad. Donna sat on the bed and pulled Hanna's pillow in, embracing it, letting Hanna's sweet aroma fill her. She cried into the pillow, shaking her head. "Why?" she sobbed. She laid back on the bed for a while quieting herself and then remembered her task. She wanted Hanna to have her friends' cards and notes.

She left the house and drove to the school. It was almost midday, and the road along the chain link fence was empty. It would be at least three hours before the parent pick-up line would start to form. She wished she would be in that line. It was all so unfair.

The school secretary had a package ready, and Donna thanked her.

"I'm going to try and come back later, after Hanna has some time to read and answer the letters. She's having a good day today, so I want to be sure that she makes the best of it."

"I'll be waiting for you," the secretary replied. "Hug Hanna from me."

The hospital was only two blocks away from the school, and by the time Donna entered Hanna's room they had already served her lunch. Jason had talked to the oncologist about holding off on the feeding tube for another day to see if Hanna would rebound. She was pleased with the decision and hoped that Hanna would be able to eat something on her own.

"I'm back!" Donna announced cheerfully.

"Did they have anything for me?" Hanna asked?

"Sure did. Look!" Donna handed her the envelope. "You need to eat your lunch, honey."

"I can't." Hanna lowered her eyes.

"Why not?"

"I've got nausea. The nurse was here while you were gone and I told her. She said she was going to tell the doctor."

Donna sat on the bed and put her hand on Hanna's blanketed leg.

"I'm sure it's all the medication they are giving you. Can you try and drink some water?" Donna held up a cup with a straw.

"In a little while. I want to read the cards."

"Okay, honey, but I'm going to keep reminding you. Did the nurse say anything else?"

"She asked if I had to go to the bathroom. She said I wasn't making enough pee."

Donna swallowed hard.

"It's probably because you're not drinking enough. Just take one sip and then you can open the envelope."

Hanna took the cup and put the straw in her mouth, but when she handed the cup back, Donna wasn't convinced that she had taken in any fluid.

Hanna spread the cards across the rolling cart over her bed

examining the writing on each one until she spotted the folded note with her name.

"This one is from Darius," she announced.

She laid back on her pillow and opened the note.

"What does he say?" Donna asked.

Hanna hesitated and then said, "Nothing."

"Nothing? He must have said something." Donna insisted.

Hanna hesitated again.

"What is it, honey? Show me the note."

"He found some woman's cell phone yesterday by the fence . . . outside the school. He figured out who it belongs to, but he hasn't returned it yet. I think he wants to keep it, but he knows he has to give it back."

"I see," Donna replied. "What will you tell him?"

"I'll tell him that he has to return it. I feel bad that he doesn't have a phone or an iPad. But he can't keep the phone."

"Darius is a good boy, honey. He'll give back the phone."

Hanna nodded and started writing on the bottom of the page under his note.

"Darius, I miss you too. I wish I were at school with everyone, but I'm still sick. I'm still in the hospital. I don't know if and when I will go home. I never saw the movie Cujo, but you have to give the phone back. Please write me more notes. I got lots from other kids too. Say hi to everyone from me. I hope I will see you soon. Hanna."

Hanna handed the note to her mom.

"I told him to give it back."

Donna hugged her daughter.

"You're such a good girl. I love you so much."

"Mom! Stop!" Hanna pushed her off, and Donna smiled. For a second, Hanna was back to her normal self.

"Finish up with the rest of the notes, and then I want you to take at least two bites of that sandwich. I'll run the notes back to the school before the buses come."

Hanna took another half an hour to write her notes and then followed Donna's instruction, taking two bites of her turkey sandwich.

"I don't feel so good, Mommy."

Hanna reached for the kidney shaped pink container and held it under her chin.

Donna grabbed what was left of her daughter's thinning hair and patted her back. A moment later Hanna regurgitated the two bites she had taken and then laid back on the pillow.

"I'll stay with you, honey. I can bring the notes back later or tomorrow."

"No! Go now. It's just around the corner. I'm fine now. Please go. I want everyone to have my notes."

"Okay, I'll go. But I'll be right back. I'll let the nurse know that you're having a hard time holding down food. Maybe she can give you something."

Donna stuffed the notes into the envelope and grabbed her purse. By the time she reached the hallway, Hanna had curled herself up in the blankets and had closed her eyes.

CHAPTER FIFTY-TWO

KEN AND LAURA sat on Storrow Drive for nearly an hour on Thursday morning. The traffic was unpredictable, and sometimes they took the T and a bus out to work, and other times they took their chances in the car. Today it was gridlock.

"It never fails. The one day I need to get to work in a hurry some douchebag gets his truck stuck under the bridge." Ken squeezed Laurie's hand hard, and she pulled away.

"We'll get there. I can see the tow truck up ahead."

Ken slumped back in the seat and took out his phone.

"Do you think he'll contact us again?"

"I don't know what to think," Laurie answered.

"This is un-fucking-believable." He huffed again.

They were on the road another forty-five minutes before they finally pulled into Weston's parking lot.

"Have you figured out what you're going to do?"

"I have an idea, but I have to re-read everything before I can say for sure that it will work."

"I'm probably going to get caught. But I can't worry about that now," Ken added.

They entered the building, and Ken hugged Laurie at the elevator.

"Everything is going to work out . . . you'll see," she whispered in his ear.

Ken got on the elevator and headed to the fifth floor.

He had two work spaces at Weston. One was a small desk in the corner of the lab, and the other was a small office with a door near the other senior research staff on the side of the building that faced Boston. On a clear day, he could see the Prudential Center building nearly ten miles away. He stood gazing out the window but only saw the image of his mother, black and blue, tied up and gagged. Nausea rose inside him again. He was startled when his desk phone rang.

"This is Ken," he answered, but the caller hung up. It was him. He knew it was him, checking on him, reminding him that his mother's life was on the line. His heart sank.

He sat behind his desk and logged into his computer, then brought up the white paper on Cineth. It stated, "Adult use over 41 Kilograms." He wondered how much the kid weighed. Was it an infant? A teenager? He might be able to do something if he knew how much the kid weighed. A teenager could easily weigh 41 Kilograms. Removing the word "adult" might work long enough for the doctor to put in the order. He still couldn't rationalize just how insane this plan was, how dangerous it was. Ken sent a text to Lisa.

"Have an idea. If we can find out how much the kid weighs, and it's at least 41 Kilograms, then maybe the word adult can be removed from the criteria for ordering the medication." He waited for a response.

"I think he's watching me in my office. I will make a sign and hold it up," she replied.

Ken read her response. A shiver ran down his spine. Did they bug his office too? He sat at his desk and scanned the room. His company issued laptop did not have a camera, and there were no CCTV units in the area. He relaxed his shoulders and dismissed the idea, but felt sympathy for Lisa. He couldn't imagine having to work under those circumstances, with some sick, twisted criminal watching her every move.

He opened a web browser and searched the FDA website for any information on the off-label use of new drugs. *Maybe these idiots didn't have all the facts,* he thought. He read through several websites, and all of them said the same thing. A doctor can order a drug for off-label use if he or she feels it's the best course of treatment for the patient. He guessed that whoever was the treating doctor was not willing to order it, and even if that doctor did order it, the insurance company wasn't going to pay. He also read several paragraphs about emergency use of drugs that were considered 'Investigational.' Cineth didn't fall into that category either since it was already approved by the FDA. He closed his laptop, left his office and took the elevator back down to the first floor.

Laurie had a workstation in the Biology lab, and he could see her working at her computer as he approached the glass wall enclosure. She caught his eye, pressed a button to release the door and waved him in. He sat on the raised counter chair and leaned into her.

"I sent Lisa a text asking if we can find out how old the kid is. Maybe she can leave off the word adult from the policy if the kid is over 41 Kilos." She put her arm around his shoulder and moved closer to his ear.

"If there is any way that Lisa can keep you out of it . . ." Ken pulled back and shook his head.

"This isn't about me!" he grumbled in a low voice.

"I know, but if there's a way . . ."

"She's my mother. I don't care about getting into trouble. I can fix that later. I just need her home . . . alive."

"I know. I'm sorry."

Ken got up and left his wife without saying goodbye. He

was annoyed at her attitude, but he supposed that if it were her mother, she would feel differently. He knew she was just protective of his career, but that didn't matter now. Once this was over, his boss would understand, and regardless, he was ready to deal with any consequences.

He took the elevator to the third floor where the marketing team's offices were located and stood on his toes eyeing the rows of cubicles. He spotted the top of a man's head in the end cubicle and approached, knocking on the wall to avoid startling him. A name plate designated the cubicle as Charles Benson's.

"Hey, Charles, I'm Ken Blake from the Chem team." Charles stood up and stepped out of his cubicle, putting his hand forward. Ken shook his hand.

"Hi, Ken. What can I do for you?"

"I worked on the Cineth project, and I was wondering where you guys are with marketing."

"Oh, well that was recently approved. It's going to be a while before we start pushing that one out to the oncology groups. Why are you asking?"

Ken avoided his question.

"But if a doc ordered the drug they would be able to get it, right?"

"Well, I suppose. Is there a doc you want me to talk to?"

"No, thanks. I was just curious about the process."

"Sure, no problem."

"One more question," Ken continued.

"Do Weston ever give the medication for free? You know . . . for people that can't afford it?" He thought of all the commercials he saw on TV hinting that the pharmaceutical company would help pay for medications if the patient can't afford it.

"I can't imagine they would do it for something like this. The insurance company would cover it anyway," he replied.

"Thanks for the info. I gotta get back to my office." Charles nodded and turned back to his cubicle.

Ken returned to his office on the fifth floor and closed his door. He logged back into his computer, clicked on the Human Resources site, and then opened the benefits section. He clicked on his health insurance policy, which he had jointly with Laura, and started reading. He spotted a link to the formulary, and a large PDF file opened.

The manual was broken down into tiers, and each tier had a copay and a percentage attached. The lower the tier, the lower the cost. Ken scrolled through page after page but didn't see any cancer drugs. Would they be kept in a different place? He searched the company directory and found the name of a human resources rep, and then opened a chat window and typed.

"Hello, where would I find cancer drugs in the formulary?" He waited a moment for the rep to respond.

"Are you asking about drugs that are infused?"

Ken thought for a moment, realizing he should have known that infusion drugs were different than routine medications.

"Yes, where would I find a list of infusion type drugs?"

"Those are under the medical pharmacy benefit. You have to look in the benefit brochure. There should be a tab for medical pharmacy."

"Great, thanks." Ken closed the chat window and the formulary PDF and searched the benefit tabs. He huffed.

"Where the hell is it?" he mumbled to himself.

He spotted a search tool on the site and typed in, "Medical Pharmacy." A list of links appeared in less than a second. It took him another few minutes to drill down to the information he was looking for. Medications that were infused fell under a different type of benefit, and the specific criteria had to exist before the insurance company paid for the medication. He should have known this after seeing all of the paperwork that came in the mail for Laurie's Botox treatments for her migraines. He recalled that she had to hold off on making the first appointment until the Neurologist sent her medical record to the insurance company for a pre-approval.

He understood the problem now. Cineth was not approved for kids, and it even if it were, it would require specific criteria before the insurance company would pay for it. He sent Lisa another text. "Any response?"

She replied almost immediately. "Nothing yet."

CHAPTER FIFTY-THREE

D<small>AN STAYED HOME</small> from work the next day, but he avoided Lisa's office going on the assumption that the kidnapper had hacked her smart TV and was watching her. He sat at the kitchen table with his laptop open and started a word document with notes on every detail of what they knew so far:

- Lindsey kidnapped early in the morning
- Lindsey walks around her neighborhood every morning
- Likely two men
- Assume they are still in FL
- They want her son to fix some documents so that a cancer drug can be ordered
- They want Lisa to change the policy, so the insurance company approves the drug order
- The drug was FDA approved for adults, not kids
- The drug must be ordered by a doctor
- The perp must have knowledge of how the FDA process works

- The perp must have knowledge of how insurance companies pay for drug claims
- The kidnapper is violent
- The kidnapper has advanced computer skills
- They communicate through burner phones
- Someone has a kid with Leukemia

Dan studied his list and then opened a text message to Lisa.

"Who is the person or persons who know how an insurance company pays for drug claims?"

Lisa texted back, "Could be anyone that works in the claims area, pharmacy, nurses in the pre-service area, case managers. It could be hundreds of people."

Then Dan asked, "Can you think of anyone mentioned that they had a kid with cancer?"

She responded, "No, I was thinking about it all night."

Dan texted again. "It's more likely a man than a woman with a sick child. Women aren't likely to arrange for a violent kidnapping. Try to think."

"I don't know anyone. Just got a text from Ken. He said we need to find out how old the kid is and how much the kid weighs. He thinks he has a way to give them what they want. I'm going to hold up a sign in front of the TV and see if they contact me."

Dan studied Lisa's text thinking that what she was about to do was a bad idea, but on the other hand, if she got a response then they would know for sure that the TV was hacked, and maybe the kidnappers would reveal more than what she asked. Maybe they would get to see Lindsey again and know she was alright.

"OK, do it," he replied.

Lisa dug through her desk drawer and found a thick black

marker. She tore the cardboard off the back of her note pad and wrote, "We need to know how old the kid is and the kid's weight. This will help me write the medical policy." She stayed behind her desk and held up the sign until her arms got tired, then she texted Dan.

"I did it, but I don't know if they are watching me."

"Just wait and see what happens," he answered.

"I don't know how I'm going to work like this."

"I know. Just hang in there. Something is going to break soon."

Dan thought about Mark O'Brien, his former partner at the county sheriff's office. Maybe Mark would be willing to do a little investigating without asking too many questions. He sent Lisa a text.

"What is Lindsey's cell phone number?"

"Why?" she asked.

"Just doing a little research. Give me the number."

Lisa texted back the ten-digit number, and Dan went out into the garage.

"Mark? Yeah, hi, how ya doing? Great, I'm doing great. Hey listen, I need a favor. Is there any way you can track a cell phone for me? Aww, thanks, man. I really appreciate it."

Dan gave Mark the number, thanked him and ended the call. He knew it was a long shot, but it was worth a try.

He added a note about the cell phone to his list and then sent another text to Lisa.

"Anything new?"

"No," she replied.

"They may not know. They might need to ask."

Lisa read Dan's text and then sat the phone down. Assuming they were watching her, she expected to hear something soon. In the meantime, she was having trouble concentrating, getting up and down from her desk, patting and talking to Missy, and getting no real work done. A chat beep caught her attention, and she opened the window. It was Dr. Shay. Lisa groaned.

"I'm stepping in for Dr. Richardson tomorrow. He has another commitment." The guy didn't even have the manners to say hello before starting a conversation. Lisa made it a point to say hello back regardless.

"Hi, Dr. Shay. That's no problem. I will forward you the meeting invite. Have a great day!" She added the exclamation point for final affect.

Her face dropped for a moment thinking of all the time she and Lindsey talked about the staff that had poor email and chat message etiquette. She hoped this would be over soon and they could get back to work as usual.

She opened the invite and read the committee members' names on the list, thinking back if she knew any of them on a personal level. She didn't. Well, she knew Dr. Shay and was pretty sure he was single but didn't know if he had any kids. She couldn't think of a time when he covered for anyone in the approval committee meetings before, but she had only been facilitating them for a couple of years. Was it just a coincidence that Shay would have a say in the one committee meeting that mattered most? Lisa sent Dan a text.

"Dr. Shay just sent me an IM. He's covering for Richardson tomorrow in the approval committee meeting."

"So?" Dan answered.

"It's odd. I don't remember him attending any of these meetings before."

"Does he have any kids?"

"IDK. IDK Richardson either."

"See if Richardson is online."

"He is . . . on DND."

"What's DND?" Dan asked.

"Do not disturb."

"Not sure if it means anything."

Lisa set the phone down and searched the template file until she found the most recent medical policy approved for a new cancer drug. Her initials were on the bottom. They had all become so routine to her that she didn't always take the time to learn about the drugs.

She thought about the committee meetings. Most of the Medical Directors attended in person on the main campus, but several participates worked remotely, like Lisa. The meetings were routine, sometimes only lasting fifteen or twenty minutes— if there was only one or two drugs or devices to approve. Could she just write whatever she wanted and get it approved? All of the Medical Directors on the committee had worked for Unified for years. Were these meetings just as mundane for them as they were for her? She would have to explain the process in detail to Dan and see if he thought it was worth taking the risk. If she failed, and the drug wasn't approved, it would take a rewrite and then another committee meeting in two weeks to get it through. She doubted that Lindsey had two weeks, and she wondered if the sick child was also running out of time.

Lisa shivered at the thought. Though she and Dan had no children together, he had three kids from a previous marriage and couldn't imagine having to go through watching your child die. But on the other hand, she couldn't image kidnapping someone either. The whole thing sucked.

CHAPTER FIFTY-FOUR

FAST FOOD ALWAYS smelled better than it tasted, but Ben was hungry.

"Gimme the bag. What took you so fuckin' long?"

Cliff was halfway through the door as he passed off the bag of food, and then nearly dropped the cardboard tray with the three cups of coffee.

"Get your fat ass in here and put the coffee down . . . and not near the computer!" Ben moved in behind him and locked the bolt.

Cliff set the coffee on the edge of the table away from the monitors and moved in close to Ben.

"You think I'm that fuckin' stupid? I ain't stupid, and I'm getting sick and fuckin' tired of you thinking I'm stupid."

Ben held his position. "Get the fuck outta my way."

Cliff pointed a finger toward Ben's face.

"I ain't moving, bitch. You want that coffee, you gonna have to go through me."

Cliff pulled his finger back and pushed out his chest.

"Fuck you," Ben answered.

"No, fuck you," Cliff replied, then stepped back and walked behind the table.

Ben could see the sweat pouring down Cliff's face.

"Fuckin loser," he mumbled toward him and then went into the kitchen. He tore open the bag, set the Styrofoam food trays on the table, and then went down the hall to Lindsey's room. She had shut the door, not that it mattered since he could watch her on the camera, and there was no lock, but he knocked anyway, banging the bottom of his fist against the door.

"Food's here. Coffee too . . ." and then went back to the kitchen to eat.

Lindsey came out of the room and brushed past him without making eye contact. She spotted the coffee cups on the table in the living room and helped herself. Then she hesitated when she saw Lisa on the monitor sat at her desk. She appeared to be writing something with a large marker. She watched for another second, but the smell of food caught her attention, and she wanted to eat. She needed strength to get through whatever this day would bring.

She sat at the small table and opened the tray. Eggs and pancakes.

"I need a fork," she announced.

Ben dug in the bag and groaned.

"Hey, dickhead. You didn't get any forks," Ben's voice barreled through the small cottage.

The two waited a moment for a response, but none came. Ben stood up, "Where is that idiot?"

"Why is he even here?" Lindsey asked thinking she might be able to increase the tension between them, which would take the attention away from her.

Ben raised his eyebrows.

"What's it to you?"

"I'm just saying . . . he's just here, doing nothing, and you obviously don't like the guy. So, what's he doing here?"

Ben considered her question for a moment and then said, "Just eat your food and let me worry about Cl . . . him."

Lindsey realized that he almost slipped out the fat man's name. What names began with CL or KL? Her brain went to work.

Ben rose from the table, pushing his chair back with more force than necessary, and went into the living room. He glanced down the hall and could see the bathroom door shut, and the shower was running. Ben decided that it wasn't a bad thing that the fat fuck was cleaning himself up. He'd come in the door nearly out-stinking the food and coffee. The woman was right about Cliff, he had no purpose here, and he questioned why he ever got him involved. But he knew the answer. He had never kidnapped anyone before. He needed a 'someone' to help. Someone big and strong, just in case things got out of control. But now that they were here, everything was fine. But then again, that could quickly change. They had a loose plan for letting her go. They were going to just tie her to the chair and leave. She'd get out on her own eventually, and they would be long gone. But in the meantime, he had to find some way to tolerate Cliff.

Cliff burst through the bathroom door and gave Ben a hard stare. He was naked from the waist up, and Ben noted the considerable size of his gut.

"You got something to say to me?"

"Yeah, where are the forks? There's no forks in the bag." Ben could see Cliff start to boil again. His face and upper chest quickly flushed bright red and looked ready to explode. But instead, he just turned and went into the bedroom at the end of the hall and closed the door.

Ben went back to the kitchen and opened his food carton. He scooped a handful of eggs with his fingers and plopped them on a pancake and then held it to his mouth like a taco, stuffing the entire combination in all at once.

When Cliff reappeared, his demeanor was back to his usual

obnoxious self. He sat at the table and ate, using the same method as Ben, shoving one egg-filled pancake after the next into his mouth. It was disgusting to watch, and Lindsay left the table. Lisa was on the monitor when she entered the living room, standing in front of the camera, holding a sign that read, "HOW OLD IS THE KID AND HOW MUCH DOES THE KID WEIGH?" Lindsey called out to her captors.

"Hey, get in here and look at the monitor."

Ben rounded the corner and stared at the screen. He thought about his conversations and emails with Jason, but he didn't mention the kid. He would have to ask Jason. Cliff stood behind him and asked, "Wuth up?"

"The boss woman wants to know about the kid."

"You gonna call the boss?"

"Yeah. I'm going outside."

Ben took the keys out of his pocket and turned the lock. He checked to see that Lindsey was far enough back and then opened the door. Cliff moved toward the door.

"You stay here, with her."

"She ain't going anywhere. Princeth Bitch gotta have her coffee." Cliff's voice was firm, and Ben didn't want to get into it with him now. He wanted just wanted to make the call.

The two men went through the door, and Lindsey heard him turn the bolt from the outside.

She was alone in the cottage. First, she thought about Lisa's image on the monitor and wished she knew how to contact her, but she didn't, and if she started messing with the computers, it might make them angry enough to hurt her again. The kitchen! It was the only place she hadn't searched.

She started at the end closest to the living room, opening all the drawers first. Empty. She pulled open the cabinets below the sink; it was too dark to see, so she pulled open all the upper cabinets. All empty. She dropped to her knees, nearly crawling inside the cabinet under the sink. She moved her hand across the floor of the cabinet, feeling soft pebbles along the left side. She pulled back. Rat droppings or something. She nearly gagged. She put her hand back in and scanned the right side. She felt an object, a round handle. She pulled it out. A screwdriver! It had a yellow rubber grip, dirty and worn, a six-inch shank and a flat tip. She stuffed it down deep into her sweat pants and then scanned the cabinet one more time. She stood up and peeked around the corner. They were still outside. She heard the key in the front door and flew back into her chair. She reached for her coffee cup but then resisted, thinking of the rat droppings she had touched in the cabinet. She could hear them talking at the front door. She got up from the table and walked casually into the living room, letting them see her, then went to the bathroom to wash her hands. She felt the screwdriver in her pocket scrape against her leg, and she smiled, victorious, though she had no idea what she would do with it. She washed her hands a second time, then sat on the toilet and peed.

When she opened the door, Ben was waiting.

"You didn't eat much," he commented.

"I'm not finished. Just needed to wash my hands. It's disgusting in here." Her eyes pierced his as she spoke, and then she moved past him, toward the kitchen, her hands deep in her pockets.

* * *

The McDonald's food took the edge off her hunger and the screwdriver tucked in her pocket gave her some semblance of control. She tried to imagine how she could use it, and the image of her stabbing at her captors kept coming to mind. *Am I capable of doing that?* She supposed that she would do whatever she needed to do. She walked past the living room seeing Ben at the computer and noted Lisa was sitting at her desk. She wondered what Lisa was thinking, what she was doing. As if sensing her question, Ben turned.

"She's fixing it so that the medication will be approved. We should all be outta here tomorrow afternoon."

"If she already fixed it then why not just leave now? This is so stupid. You're going to get caught!"

"Shut up and go back in the bedroom," he answered, his back turned.

Lindsey followed his instructions and went back into the bedroom. She faced the camera and again stuck up her middle finger, then laid down on the bed facing the wall. She could feel the screwdriver digging into her thigh and thought about hiding it under the mattress. But then what good would it be if her opportunity came when she was in a different part of the house? She adjusted her position on the bed, so it didn't hurt, and then threw an arm over her face. "Fuck you," she said out loud. She had no idea if the camera had a microphone, but she hoped that it did.

She slept through most of the day, periodically gaining consciousness when she heard the two men bickering in the living room. She wondered how they ever found each other. They had nothing in common other than their propensity for crime. She knew they would eventually get what they deserved and she looked forward to the day when she would face them again in a courtroom. She laughed to herself at what the fat one would look like in an orange jumpsuit . . . like a big parachute. Pig. Anger quickly replaced her humorous thoughts and her temples throbbed again.

She pulled herself out of bed, checking the time on her fitness tracker and went into the bathroom. She was pleased the battery lasted as long as it did. She washed her face and hands and peed, taking her time to think. She closed the toilet seat and sat, examining the screwdriver. She held it in her fist and made a stabbing motion. She imagined herself in one of those silly Lifetime movies that she watched on Sunday afternoons, fending off her crazed captors and running out the door. Were these guys really planning to let her go? How would that work? They had to know that she would run straight to the police and describe them. Both were so unique in appearance and stature. They would surely be easy for the police to locate. But they must have a plan, something they would not discuss openly in front of her.

She put the screwdriver back in her pocket, and the stood in front of the mirror. Her hair was dirty, and she needed a shower. She glanced back at the filthy tub and decided against the idea. Instead, she took her hair down and put her head in the sink, letting the water run over it. She rubbed the soap in her hands and then massaged her fingers into her scalp. She rinsed her hair for an extra-long time and then squeezed out the water. She fingered out the tangles and then wrapped her hair up in a high bun. *Better*, she thought.

She exited the bathroom and stood in the hall. The two men glanced up.

"Check out the bitch!" Cliff commented with a lascivious grin.

"Fuck you," Lindsey shot back.

"Oooo, you better watch your mouth, bitch, or I'm gonna put somethin' in it that you're gonna love."

Ben punched Cliff hard in the upper arm.

"What the fuck?" Cliff stood up and towered over Ben. "I'm sick of you tellin' me what to do. If you dun like me here, just give me my fuckin' money, and I'll be gone."

Ben got up from his chair and faced him.

"You're not going anywhere cuz I don't have your money until this is done. So sit down and shut the fuck up."

Cliff turned his back and went into the kitchen.

"There's leftover Chinese from last night if you're hungry," Ben offered.

"I think I'll wait till your friend is out of the kitchen," Lindsey answered sarcastically. She turned back to the bedroom putting her hand in her pocket.

The rest of the night was quiet, the three of them avoiding each other. She turned off the bedroom light at eight o'clock but lay awake until well into the night. Sleep evaded her as thoughts of son filled her mind. She wondered where he was, and how worried he must be. She gripped the screwdriver in her pocket reminding herself that she had power and drifted off to sleep thinking of him as a boy, playing street hockey in their old Boston neighborhood.

CHAPTER FIFTY-FIVE

"WHAT'S GOING ON there?" Jason asked Ben. "The woman's boss, Lisa, held up a sign asking for the kid's age and weight. What do you want me to do?"

Jason thought for a minute and then realized that they were trying to figure out a way to get the drug approved based on weight instead of age. They were on the right track. Hanna's last weight was ninety-two pounds. She had lost some weight since the chemo and radiation, but she was still within normal limits for her age.

"Tell them ninety-two pounds. That's it. How's the woman doing?"

"Fine, no problems."

"Let me know if anything else happens."

Jason snapped the phone shut. It was nearly eleven now and the day was flying by.

He thought about leaving the office and going back to the hospital, but he worried that Ben might call and he couldn't take a chance on letting Hanna or Donna see the burner phone, or his added anxiety. He stood up from behind his desk and looked around. Ron Shay was heading his way waving.

"Fuck," Jason murmured.

"Hi, Ron, what's going on?"

"Not much. Just checking in on you. I'm in the office today and tomorrow. I'm covering for Richardson."

"Oh? Where's he at?" Jason asked.

"He went to Miami. Not sure if it was business or pleasure."

"Okay, well I'm in and out . . . checking on Hanna, but if you need anything let me know."

"How is she doing?"

"Better today. I'm hoping they discharge her a little later."

"Great. I hope so. Hey, by the way, I will see you tomorrow in Lisa's approval committee meeting at noon. I'm covering for Richardson.

The color drained from his face, and the pressure in his chest stifled his thoughts. He hesitated and then answered.

"Oh, really? You know, I'll be here tomorrow. I can do the meeting. There'll be enough of us for a quorum. No reason for you to sit in all the traffic just for that."

"Really? That would be great! But wait, what if Hanna needs you?"

"If anything comes up, I'll give you plenty of warning, but it will be fine. I'll cover it."

"Great! Thanks, buddy. I will forward you the meeting invite."

"Thanks. I'll catch up with you later. I'm heading back to the hospital."

By the time Ron was out of sight, Jason was in a full-blown panic attack. He turned to face the back wall and put both arms across his chest holding the opposite shoulder. He bent forward clenching his eyes shut. He pushed the air out of his lungs and then pulled it back in and tried to will the squeezing sensation away. He mentally counted slowly and tried to match the count to his breathing, all the while forcing the doom-filled question, 'Am I having a real heart attack?' out of his thoughts. He prayed no one could see him to witness his bizarre behavior. His knees were weak, and he wanted more than anything to lay on the floor, but instead, he fell back into his chair and bent forward, as if he were tying his shoes. One . . . two . . . three . . . four. He kept counting. He let his arms dangle to the side. It was passing, and his shoulders started to relax. The grip on his chest loosened. He pulled himself up and sat facing the wall. His clothes stuck to him drenched in sweat, but he shivered.

"I'm a fucking mess," he huffed. He sat still in the same position, trying to stay relaxed for another ten minutes, and then stood up to see if anyone was around. He logged out of his computer and went to the men's room, hoping it was empty. The last thing he needed now was to make small talk. No one was in there. He sat in a stall for several minutes waiting for the sweat to dry, and then splashed water on his face and washed his hands. He checked himself in the mirror. "You're a freak," he said.

It was raining when he exited the building, and he didn't have his umbrella with him. "It figures," he said out loud. He started jogging toward the car and then remembered that he had just gotten lucky. He could see himself now, sitting in the meeting with the other Medical Directors, reviewing Lisa Simmons policy templates and casting his vote to approve. Though he wasn't able to squash the panic attacks, he would have some control over what got approved in the committee meeting without Ron Shay getting in the way. Just as he got into the car, the rain stopped, and the sun peeked through the clouds. His thoughts turned to Nathalie. It was Thursday.

CHAPTER FIFTY-SIX

B EN SAT IN front of the monitors. He watched Lisa Simmons in her office, working intently behind her screen. Although he couldn't see her hands moving, her body language told him that she was typing. He could see her dog laying at her feet, and stared at the sleeping pet. He had never had a dog, but he liked the idea and could envision himself devoted to a loyal companion.

"Time to make shit happen," he said to the monitor. He opened his burner phone and sent a text to Lisa and Ken.

"92lbs."

Then he watched Lisa. Her phone sat on her desk, and she immediately picked it up and studied the message. She held the phone with two hands and starting texting quickly using her thumbs. He hoped the information would allow them to finish this job. It had only been a day, but he was more than ready to take his money and move on. He watched Lisa set the phone down for a few seconds, and then pick it up again and start texting. He knew that her husband was probably still home, though he hadn't seen him on camera. Ben just assumed that she had told him what was happening. It didn't matter. Lisa and Ken were cooperating.

CHAPTER FIFTY-SEVEN

"FINALLY." KEN READ the message on his phone. "41kg". No other information. But he didn't need anything more. She weighed enough to be considered in the adult range. However, children's bodies were not the same as adults, which is why the FDA didn't give broad approvals when there was no research to back it up. None of this was his concern, though. He only cared about bringing his mother home. He opened a text to Lisa, but before he could type his phone was ringing.

"Did you get a text?" Lisa asked.

"Yeah. 41 kilograms puts her in the adult range. I think the only way to do this is to remove the word adult from the policy and hope that your company approves it. I don't know what else to do. There is nothing I can do on my end. Weston already did the work. There's nothing here for me to change. What do you think?"

"I don't know," Lisa replied. "It's a crap shoot. I can send it through to the approval committee that meets tomorrow, but I have no control over whether they will approve it. If any of them know about this drug, they will pick up on the ambiguous language and kick it back. Even if they never heard of the drug they might notice the language. Then what?"

"I am not seeing any other options, short of finding where they are keeping my mother and rescuing her."

"We're working on that too. My husband is discretely trying to have your mom's cell phone traced. I don't know if it will come up with anything, but it's worth trying. I will let you know if I find out anything."

"Assuming your company gets the drug approved tomorrow, how long do you think it will be before they let her go? Won't you be able to tell who requests the drug?" Ken asked.

"If the drug gets approved tomorrow, the benefit will be published, then added to the medical pharmacy drug list. After that, it will be easy to find out who ordered the drug. I'm guessing that the person behind this doesn't care about being caught at that point. Once the kid starts the treatment and it's working, no one is going to stop giving it." It will just be a matter of time before the police put it all together."

"Okay, well let me know what happens, and if you hear anything else. I wish they would let us see her again."

"I know. I'm so sorry, Ken. I hope this is all over tomorrow morning. The meeting is at nine o'clock, and it should be quick. I will know pretty quickly if they approve it. Cross your fingers," Lisa replied, and then said goodbye.

The policy template was open on her screen, and in one motion she highlighted and deleted the word 'adult', and then saved the document in a PDF format. She reviewed the agenda for the meeting and attached each template that needed approval. There were only three drugs so the meeting should be quick.

Lisa sent the meeting invitation with the templates attached, barely holding her mouse steady.

"There goes my job," she said facing the TV.

* * *

Ken stood in the window gazing at the view of Boston in the distance. There was nothing more he could do. It was all in Lisa's hands or the hands of whoever was approving these things at Unified. He pulled his phone out of his lab coat pocket and started a text to his wife.

"I'm going to Florida. I want to be there in case anything happens." A minute later she texted back.

"OK, we should both go. I'll start checking flights."

Ken read her reply and then responded.

"No, you stay here. I don't want you caught in the middle of anything. If anyone ever asks any questions, I don't want your name to come up."

It took her a while to reply.

"Fine. I'll stay, but you have to promise to tell me everything that's happening."

"Promise. 143. I'm going home", he texted back. He knew their special 'I love you' number would make her smile, even though she'd have to take the T to get home.

Ken sent an email to his boss letting him know that he needed a couple of days off for a family emergency and then he left the Weston Pharmaceuticals' office.

The traffic was light at midday, and he made it home quickly. He unplugged the TVs in the living room and bedroom, and then packed a bag and walked to the T station. He hoped they assumed he was at work and wouldn't be watching him, but he didn't want them watching Laurie either. He knew he was taking a risk. As soon as he was on the train, he made his flight reservations. In six hours, he would be at his mother's house in Florida. He sent a text to Lisa.

"I'm flying down now. I will go to my mother's house." A moment later a text came back.

"Come to my house. Only one TV in the back office and you

can come in through the garage and stay with Dan. Hoping we hear soon about the cell phone."

Ken considered the idea. Maybe it would be better if they were together, and he liked the idea that Dan was a retired cop.

"OK. Text me your address."

As soon as he got to the airport, he changed his ticket to fly into Sarasota and forwarded the info to Lisa. He settled in at the gate, anxious, but relieved he wouldn't be alone in dealing with whatever was coming next.

He sent another text to Laurie. "TVs unplugged. They can't watch you."

She texted back, "143. Call me when you get there."

CHAPTER FIFTY-EIGHT

ARIUS RODE HIS bike quickly along the chain link fence and then stopped at the corner to push the walk button at the traffic lights. He looked both ways, and since all the traffic was inching slowly toward the parent pick up line, he decided not to wait for the light and instead wove his bike between the cars, across all four lanes until he reached the sidewalk on the opposite corner. He didn't have any lunch money that day, and since Hanna had stopped coming to school, he went most days without eating a full meal until he got home. He imagined her lying in a hospital bed, and his heart sank. He tried to think of himself laying in a hospital bed, with needles stuck in his arms and he pushed the thought out of his head.

His home room teacher passed out several notes from Hanna just before the end of the school day, and he hoped that whatever she had written included some positive news about returning to school before the end of the term, but he knew it was unlikely considering there was only a short time left.

He rode his bike into his dirt driveway, ditching it at the side of the house, and then made a fist and snapped his arm in. "Yes!" His mother's car was gone. He entered through his grandmother's door and yelled, "I'm home" and waited for a response. There was none. He went into the kitchen, didn't see

Wendy Weiss

anything cooking on the stove, and the sink was empty. He opened the refrigerator and found a tin-foil-covered dish with a yellow sticky note.

"Mac and cheese for my sweet boy."

Darius took the dish out of the refrigerator and pulled back the tin foil cover. He grabbed a large spoon and dug into the mix, shoveling it into his mouth so fast that food fell out of the corners. His eyes closed and he chewed, enjoying the delicious flavor. He considered continuing to eat the casserole cold, right from the dish, but then remembered how good it tasted hot, and grabbed a plate from the cupboard. He heaved four large spoonfuls onto the plate and set it into the microwave for two minutes. He knew it probably wouldn't be very hot, but two minutes was all that he was willing to wait.

He took the oven mitts from the hooks above the counter, set the plate on the table, and then opened his backpack and took out Hanna's note. He ate another spoonful of the macaroni and then set the spoon down. He used both hands to smooth out the folded paper, and then read it word for word.

Hanna was still sick, and she was still in the hospital. His eyes hung on her words, '. . . don't know if and when I will go home'. It sounded bad. He read the note two more times and then folded it up and put it in his pocket. He finished his meal, set the dish in the sink and then went to his bedroom, barricading the door with the bookcase. He took out the phone. It was now fully charged since he was able to connect it to an iPad charger at school without anyone noticing. He opened the book app and saw he only had two hours of Cujo left to go. He would finish the story and then send a text to Ken, the owner's son. He knew all along that he would do the right thing. In his own time.

CHAPTER FIFTY-NINE

T HE PLANE TOUCHED down at Sarasota-Bradenton International Airport at four o'clock Thursday afternoon. Ken could see that the sky was dark off to the east and a storm was about to settle in the area. He was glad to be back on the ground. Dan had sent him a text before he left Boston and was waiting for him outside. He disembarked and walked quickly to the exit. His eyes swung left and right, and then he heard a car horn, spotting the red Mustang that Dan had described in his text. Ken jogged to the car, jumping into the passenger seat and tossing his backpack behind him. Dan reached out and patted him on the shoulder.

"Hey, Ken. How was your flight?"

"It was fine. It went quick. Is anything new?"

"No, nothing new. I'm really sorry we have to meet like this, but we're going to find her. Lisa has everything all set with the meeting today. It's at nine. In the meantime, I'm waiting for a call from one of my buddies at the police station who is trying to trace your mom's phone. I'm hoping we'll get lucky."

"You didn't tell him why you wanted it traced did you?" Ken panicked.

"No, no . . . I didn't say a thing . . . just asked if he could do me a favor."

They rode a few miles in silence and then Dan's phone rang through his car radio. He pushed a button on the steering wheel.

"Hello?"

"Hey, Dan, it's Bob. I found the phone you asked me to trace."

Ken's eyes widened, and he motioned Dan with his hands to share the conversation.

"Really, that's great. So where is the phone?"

"I got an address in Fort Myers. I can text it to you if you want."

"Yeah, that'd be great. Thanks, Bob. I really appreciate you doing this for me."

"Sure, no problem. Tell Lisa I said hello."

"Will do." Dan pushed another button on the steering wheel and ended the call.

A moment later Dan's phone chimed with a text message, and he handed the phone to Ken.

"Do you recognize the address?" Dan asked him.

Ken studied the phone.

"No."

He set Dan's phone down on the console, opened his own phone pulling up Google Maps, and then he thumbed in the address.

"It's downtown Fort Myers . . . a couple of miles from my mother's house. Do you think she's there?" Ken asked hopefully.

"Wait, let me see if there's a street view."

He adjusted the map view and brought up the image of a duplex.

"It's a duplex. Looks like a dump."

"Okay. Let's go back to my house and do a little research and see who owns the house. I don't want us to jump to any conclusions yet."

Ken continued staring at the image on his phone and then

remembered he hadn't texted Laurie to let her know he'd arrived safely.

"I have to call my wife," he announced tapping Laurie's image on his phone.

*   *   *

It was just under forty-five minutes later when they reached Dan's driveway. The traffic was heavy in the Sarasota area, and on the way Dan explained the impact of 'snow birds' on the traffic patterns in the area. He laughed when he talked about it, telling him that no matter where he went, people were talking about the traffic, and then when all the northerners leave, the place is empty and everyone complains about the heat.

"It's a strange place to live."

"My mother says that sometimes too."

"Lisa tells me that you and your mom are close."

"Yeah, it was just us when I was growing up. I still can't believe that she moved down here." He shrugged.

"That must have been tough. Well, I'm from upstate New York. Mostly everyone in Florida is from somewhere else. Somewhere north. Guess people get sick of the cold and snow. I actually like the cold, but my wife hates it . . . so that's why we're here." Dan chuckled, but Ken could sense that he didn't think it was funny.

"We're gonna go through the garage and stay away from Lisa's office. We think that the assholes who are doing this are watching through the smart TV."

"Yeah, the same at my house. I unplugged them before I left so they couldn't spy on my wife."

Dan's eyebrows went up.

"That was a risky move, don't you think?"

"I don't think they are interested in what I was doing at home.

They knew where I worked. I got a couple of hang ups on my business line. I think they were checking to see if I was at work."

"You're probably right."

Dan and Lisa's house was a modern Florida style single level home. It was large, had a bright ceramic tile roof and lots of large windows. The entryway to the front of the house was an elaborate path of stone pavers, and a long hanging light fixture over the front door gave the home a grandiose effect. The garage had two standard stalls, and then one smaller one, which Ken guessed was either for a tiny car or perhaps a golf cart.

Ken followed Dan into the garage which led to the kitchen, where Missy greeted them with a wagging tail.

"Cute dog. What's her name?" Kenny asked.

"Missy. She's a good girl."

"Yes, she is!" Lisa whispered with a smile as she entered the kitchen. "Hi, Ken. So sorry that we have to meet under these circumstances." She hugged him close, holding him tightly.

"Thank you," he whispered back. "And thank you for fixing that template. I know you are putting your job at risk for mom."

"I'm not worried about it. We'll get your mother back and then straighten all of this out. I've worked for Unified for twenty years. They will understand. I'm sure the police will explain everything too."

She stepped forward opening her arms again sensing he needed another hug . . . and he did. Ken held on to her, eyes filling with tears as he pulled away.

"We have a room ready for you. Last door on the right. We're keeping our voices low and texting each other while we're in the house. We shouldn't take any chances."

"I agree. I'm going to go wash up and then, Dan, can we find out about that house in Fort Myers?"

"What house?" Lisa replied, trying not to raise her concerned voice.

"Bob traced Lindsey's cell phone. It's at a duplex house in Fort Myers, somewhere downtown. We have the address."

"You're not going there," she insisted.

"No, not yet. I'm going to do some research and see who owns the house."

"What do you mean, not yet?" she asked.

"Let's just see who owns the house, and then we'll figure out the next step. Go back to your office and work. I don't want them thinking that anything is going on."

Lisa walked down the hall and into her office, and Dan went into the den and waited for Ken. He opened a web browser and typed in the address from Bob's text message. Just as Ken described, it was a duplex-style single level home in a run-down neighborhood. The street view showed cars nearby up on blocks and the possibility of some nearby abandoned buildings. It was unlikely that the kidnappers would keep her phone, but Dan knew never to make assumptions when it came to criminals. They were all uniquely stupid, and nearly all made a critical mistakes in thinking they wouldn't get caught. It was always just a matter of time.

A few minutes later, Ken sat down in a chair next to Dan at the computer.

"Here's the house. It is a dump just like you said."

Dan opened another browser and Googled the Lee County Property records website, then worked his way through multiple menus before he was able to enter the address.

Mrs. Ronita Williams owned the property. It was, in fact, a duplex and after entering the 'A' and 'B' address, he could see that she owned both units. He highlighted her name with his cursor, right clicked 'copy' from the menu, and then opened a new browser and pasted in her name.

Mrs. Ronita Williams was a sixty-two-year-old woman. There was only one other name associated with hers at either address, Rhonda Williams. He copied her name, then opened another new browser and pasted it in. This time several links appeared, along with a mug shot.

"Geeze, do you think that woman has my mother?" Ken asked staring at the computer screen.

"I don't know. Looks like she has an arrest record for drugs and prostitution. Seems unlikely though that she would be involved in kidnapping for a pharmaceutical cause. People like her tend to stay in the drug world. I mean the illegal type of drugs."

"So what should we do?"

"I'm not sure. It's possible that someone at the house just found the phone somewhere. Maybe we should just call the phone and see what happens?" Dan said.

"Actually, I called and texted. Well before I knew she was kidnapped, but I think it was after it happened. It was late on Wednesday morning or early afternoon. I can check my outgoing calls and messages."

"Obviously, you got no response," Dan said watching Ken scroll through his phone log.

"It was late morning. She had texted me before six am."

"So early?" Dan asked.

"Yeah, she walks in the morning and sometimes she will send me a text."

"Do you know where she walks?"

"I think so. The last time Laurie and I visited she got us up early, and we walked with her. It was along some chain link fence. There were schools, I think."

"I see. I think it's likely that someone else picked up the phone."

"But we don't know for sure," Ken questioned.

"No, we don't. I'll see if I can have one of my cop buddies in Fort Myers do a drive by and see if anything looks out of place."

"Thanks." Ken patted Dan on the shoulder.

Dan spent a few minutes on the phone making calls and then reassured Ken that they would hear some news soon.

* * *

Lisa signed off her computer at five o'clock and joined Ken and Dan in the kitchen. They spoke quietly, assuming that whoever was watching might be able to hear their conversation. Lisa set her phone on the table and texted a message to Dan. He pulled his phone out and read, "Let's take Missy out and grab some dinner."

Dan showed Lisa's text to Ken, and he nodded his head in agreement.

Lisa grabbed Missy's leash from the counter and called her over. Her tail wagged in anticipation. They exited into the garage and settled into Dan's car.

"It's better if we stay out of the house," Dan said.

"I agree!"

"I could certainly eat," Ken admitted. "What do you do with Missy when you go out? You can't leave her in the car in this heat."

"Never. We always find dog-friendly places to eat."

"Really? The restaurants let you bring in your dog?"

"We mostly eat outside, cafe style and just tie Missy to one of our chairs."

Ken patted the dog on the seat next to him and thought about how he and Laurie would manage taking care of a dog with their full-time jobs. He knew it would be difficult.

He took his phone out and took a picture of the dog and texted it to Laurie, then added, "My dinner date." He stared at the phone waiting for her to reply, but then a text came in, from his mother's phone.

"On my God! Look!" Ken held up the phone to Lisa. The text read, "I found your mother's phone."

"I'm going to call her number." Ken was breathless in his excitement.

"No! Wait!" Dan instructed.

"Why? We should talk to this person and see who it is."

Dan swung the car into the restaurant parking lot and parked on the edge, away from the other patrons.

"Let me see."

Ken handed him the phone.

"I will call and put whoever this is on speaker," Dan said.

He tapped the 'Mom' icon on the phone.

"Hello, you have Lindsey Blake's phone?" Dan asked.

There was a moment of silence, but they could hear someone breathing on the other end.

"Yes, I have the phone."

Dan hit the mute button on Ken's phone.

"It sounds like a kid!" Dan said.

He un-muted the call.

"What's your name, son?" Dan asked.

"Darius Williams. I found the phone in the grass near my school."

"Okay, I see. I'd like to come and pick it up. Is that okay?"

"When?" the boy asked.

"Tonight, if possible. Where are you located?" Dan tested him.

"Near the Lee Middle School," he answered.

Dan hit the mute button again.

"This kid must live in the house we found on Google Maps."

He unmuted the phone again.

"Could we come tonight to pick it up? We're about two hours away, so that would be around eight o'clock."

Again, there was hesitation.

"You can't come to my house tonight. I will get in trouble

if you come here. I can give you the phone back tomorrow morning, near where I found it."

Dan's eyes shifted between Ken and Lisa.

"Okay, Darius. That sounds good. Can you text me a location and a time?" Dan asked.

"I have to be in school at nine o'clock, so it has to be just before then."

"That works perfectly for us. Just don't forget to text the location and we will see you in the morning. Thanks, young man, for doing the right thing. I'm sure your family will be very proud of you."

Darius didn't answer to his comment.

"Are you still there?"

"Yes. I will text the location. Bye."

"I can't believe this!" Ken exclaimed. "We're going to get her back! I just know it!"

Then he thought about the sight he had witnessed. His mother tied to a chair, a gag in her mouth and two black eyes. His ears were ringing and his vision blurred. Lisa turned to the back seat and noticed Ken's distress. She reached back holding out her hand to him.

"We're going to get her back tomorrow. You'll see."

CHAPTER SIXTY

ARIUS LAY IN bed and listened to the last wondrous moments of Cujo. He knew it was now time to contact the owner's son. Hanna would be proud of him, and his grandmother would be proud if she had known what he was about to do. He lifted his ankle and rested it on his other knee, and then holding the phone above him, earbuds still in place, he thumbed in the text to Ken. Then he waited. When the phone rang a moment later, he suddenly panicked, nearly flying off the bed. But he settled back down staring at Ken's face as it rang and then swiped to answer the call.

It was over in under a minute. The guy was grateful to him for wanting to return the phone, and said he would meet him in the morning at the fence. He laid back on the bed and once again tapped each of the apps. Then he remembered the fitness app and how it honed in on a location up the coast. He didn't mention it when Ken called, but he would say something in the morning. He tucked the phone under his pillow and then pulled his backpack onto the bed to start his homework. But he was startled again, standing up as he watched his brother pushing through the door, once again knocking over his bookcase.

"What the fuck, little bro? Why you keep blocking the door?" Darrin's face twisted in anger.

"Aww, man!" Darius stomped his foot. "Why do you keep knocking down my stuff?"

"Whatchu hiding in here anyway?"

"Nothing! I told you that the last time. I have nothing that you want."

"You lying to me, boy."

And with that Darrin started tossing his room. He kicked the books in every direction and opened all of his dresser drawers.

"Stop! Stop! You're wrecking my room!"

Darrin pushed him back on the bed and then straddled him, pinning his arms at his sides. He moved his face in close and Darius could smell old beer on his breath.

"Either tell me whatchu hiding or I'm going destroy this whole house."

Darius turned his face away.

"Nothing! I told you. Nothing!"

Darrin climbed off the bed leaving Darius lying flat and then with both hands pulled the edge of the blanket sending him flying to the floor at his feet.

"Ow! That hurt!" Darius rolled onto his side and rubbed his back.

"Get outta my room now!"

Darrin wound up and slapped him on the side of the head.

"Don't you order me. I'm the boss of you. Get it?"

Darius rubbed the side of his head and started to cry.

"You little cry baby," he teased as he tossed the pillows off Darius's bed.

"Well, well, what's this, little bro? I thought you wasn't hiding anything. When you get this fancy phone?" Darrin picked up the phone and examined it.

"Don't touch that. It's not mine! I have to return it in the morning!"

"This is one of them new iPhones. This is worth some serious money. Don't worry, little bro. I'll make sure you get your share."

"No, you can't take it. I have to return it in the morning," Darius insisted.

Darrin stuffed the phone in his pocket and then kicked a pile of books into the air.

"Clean up this mess before Ma sees it. Where's she at anyway? I got somethin' for her."

Darius didn't answer. His eyes were filled with tears, and he was fixed on his brother's pocket. He wanted to launch himself at him and somehow get the phone back, but he knew it was futile. He started to sob.

"Please gimme back the phone. I promised I'd give it back before school tomorrow. I have to give it back."

Darrin hesitated for a moment gawking at his brother sitting on the floor, and then he pushed his way out the door, pulling it shut behind him.

*   *   *

Darius pulled himself up from the floor and pulled a tissue from the box on his desk. He blew his nose and wiped the tears off his face. He had to find a way to get the phone back. He could hear Darrin in the kitchen and considered pleading with him one more time, but then decided he would probably end up getting hit again.

He cupped his hands, looking out his bedroom window and didn't see a car in the driveway. Darrin must have walked to the house. He decided he would wait, and then follow him. He stepped over the mess in his room and went through the back door of the house. The air was hot and sticky. It had rained earlier, which cooled the temperature a few degrees, but then it always went up again.

The lights from the house drew in the mosquitos and at this time of year they were particularly large. Darius had to keep slapping them away. Finally, his brother was on the move. He waited and watched until Darrin reached the end of the street and then took a right.

The streets were well lit, and getting caught would put him in danger, but he suspected that Darrin wasn't going far. He jogged along the side of the road and slowly approached the corner, crouching down and leaning forward just enough to see his brother's legs ahead in the distance. He held his position and waited. The mosquitos were making it difficult to be still, and he swatted and slapped them away. Darrin reached the end of the block and then crossed the street walking left. Darius knew he was heading for their mother's boyfriend's house. A known drug den.

He had no plan as to how he was going to get the phone away from his brother, but at least he had a location. As soon as his brother turned the next corner, he followed, crouching in the shadows. Finally, he got close enough to confirm his suspicions. It was his mother's boyfriend's house, and his mother's car was parked in the driveway.

Darius knew what was going on in the house, and fear crept up the back of his neck making the hairs stand to attention. He was just a kid and did not consider himself to be street smart, despite having been raised by a drug addict mother and her drug dealing boyfriends. He tried hard to insulate himself from that world by staying focused on school, being with Hanna and Gia, and staying on his grandmother's side of the house as much as possible.

As he got closer to the driveway, he could hear activity in the back yard. There was a bonfire, and he heard Lil Wayne rapping his profanities in the distance. He never understood how people could like those lyrics, describing girls using those gross words.

It made him embarrassed. It would never occur to him to think of girls' body parts in such a vulgar way.

As soon as Darrin entered the home, Darius again crouched low and sneaked up the driveway. He wanted to look in the front window and see where everyone was. He thought about just announcing himself and asking to speak to his mother, but he had never done anything like that before. Maybe he could make up a reason to talk to her, which would get him safely in the house. But then Darrin would know why he was there. He decided to wait and watch.

The front curtains blocked most of the view, but he was able to see through a sliver where the curtains met in the middle. The couch on the opposite wall was body to body, and body on top of body, with women sitting on men's laps. A chair nearby also had two people jammed into it. Another woman sat on the floor. He didn't see his mother or brother, but he did see her boyfriend with another woman sitting on his lap. Darius watched with disgust. Drug paraphernalia covered the various tables. He spotted smoking bongs, small glass pipes, ash trays and assorted lighters, spoons and small tin foiled wrappers. His skin crawled.

He skirted quietly around the side of the house still slapping at his exposed skin. He thought by now he must have been bitten at least a hundred times. The shrubs were thick, and he scraped his arms and legs as he sidestepped with his back against the house. When he reached the back corner, he bobbed his head quickly to peek. He saw his brother and his mother sitting in beach chairs in front of the fire. There were other people around the fire too, and the music was pumping loudly. He wondered how the neighbors tolerated the noise, but then figured in this neighborhood, they were all in on it. Now what? He stood there for a moment shoeing away the bugs, peeked again and then saw Darrin showing the phone to their mother. She took it from him and examined it, then handed it back. Darrin put the phone in his back pocket and walked into the house.

Darius turned and pinned his body against the house, then stood on his toes to peek in the side window. Darrin sat on an uncovered mattress and tied a tourniquet around his upper arm. Darius looked away, breathing hard, realizing he was about to witness his brother stick a needle in his arm. He peeked through the window again and held his eyes on the entire scene. It took less than a minute for Darrin to inject himself and then fall back on the bed. He appeared to be unconscious, but Darius wasn't sure. Do people that use drugs pass out after they inject, or do they lie there in some awakened state? He had no idea and never wanted to know. But if he was asleep, or whatever, it could be an opportunity to get the phone. He waited another minute and didn't see Darrin move. He decided to walk into the yard and talk to his mother. He would tell her that he was on his way home from a friend's house and saw her car and that he needed to use the bathroom. How could she say no?

He was sweating heavily, and the fear was making him nauseous. He hoped he wouldn't stutter and make her question him. More than likely she wouldn't even notice. He made his move.

"Hey, Ma," he called as he approached the blazing barrel.

"Darius! Whatchu doin here?"

"I was on my way home, and I had to use the bathroom. Is it okay if I go in?"

His mother studied his face and then started to laugh.

"Why didn't you go in the trees like all the other boys?"

"Ma, it's not like that." His voice got quiet, and his eyes met the ground.

"Yeah, go inside. Darrin is in there somewhere."

The door to the back of the house had a torn screen and bent frame. He thought about all the mosquitos that must be in there but then realized that the druggies probably didn't notice. He entered the house and turned right down the hall to the bedroom where Darrin was laid out on the bed. The door was cracked open, and he could see that his position had not changed. How would he get him to roll over without getting caught? He got down on his hands and knees and crawled into the room gently closing the door behind him, then on his belly, wiggled to the end of the bed. The floor was old wood that had a rotting smell, and he breathed through his mouth to avoid the stench. Darrin was lying flat, his butt was on the bed, but his legs hung all the way over, and his feet touched the floor. Maybe he could get underneath him and just slide the phone out. He crawled closer. He could taste the bile in his throat now, and his head pounded with the sound of his beating heart. His face was beginning to throb of from all of the growing mosquito bites.

He reached under his brother's sagging pants and could feel the phone in his pocket, the top wedged against the mattress. He would have to wiggle it up and sideways to get it out. He pulled his hand away, sank lower, and considered crawling completely under the bed. But he quickly dismissed the idea since he couldn't see how it would help him. He lifted himself again slightly, just high enough to see his brother's face, and he still appeared to be sleeping. For a second, Darius considered the possibility that he had overdosed and was dead. Though the thought was fleeting, he had no particular feelings if that was the outcome. He urged himself to continue.

He reached up again feeling the bottom edge of the phone in his brother's pocket and slowly started pushing it. Like coaxing out a splinter, he pushed the phone slowly until he was sure that it cleared his brother's pocket. Now all he had to do was get underneath his brother's back and grab it. Once again, he peeked at his brother's face and saw no movement. *This is it,* he thought, *all or nothing, or worse.* He pushed his hand into the mattress, hoping he could avoid contact with his brother's backside, and secured the edge of the phone between two fingers. It took a little wiggling, but he did it. He had the phone.

The adrenaline rush was both good and bad. He had the urge to pee his pants, but he grinned with pride and a sense of accomplishment.

He crawled back to the door and pulled it quietly shut behind him. He stuffed the phone down the front of his pants and walked straight out the front door. He didn't care to say anything to his mother in the backyard, and figured by now she'd forgotten that he'd even been there. He ran as fast as he could, all the way home.

CHAPTER SIXTY-ONE

THE DOCTOR DID not let Hanna go home on Thursday afternoon as Donna and Jason had hoped. By nine o'clock that night her kidney function was poor, and her liver was failing. Donna laid on the hospital bed next to her, spooning her and patting her head. Jason heard her whisper, "I love you so much, Hanna. I'm right here with you, baby."

He caught her eye for a second and could see her deep sadness. He sank into the small recliner, tired, wasted from the stress of the day and then the intensity of his time with Nathalie. He regretted not being at the hospital. What was he thinking? He wasn't thinking. He couldn't think. It was all too much. For an ugly moment, he thought about what he'd done, what he was doing, and if it would even matter. Maybe Hanna and Donna were right, and it would all be for nothing.

His shirt was sticking to his body, and he was aware of his heavy breathing. He was lifting again, separating from his body and looking down, watching the room, watching Donna with Hanna. The unbearable tightness in his chest was gone and relief washed over him. Why couldn't he be like this all the time? It was easy, natural. He drifted off to sleep.

* * *

Hanna was the only one still sleeping when the nurse flipped the light switch at seven am Friday morning. Donna was still in the hospital bed with Hanna, but sometime during the night she rolled onto her back, her hand resting on Hanna's hip. She was aware of Jason's presence but stayed silent.

The nurse was holding a tray full of tubes and supplies and stepped quietly to the bedside.

"Good morning. I need to draw some blood."

"She's sleeping so soundly. Do you need to disturb her?" Donna asked.

"I'm afraid so. I will try not to wake her," the nurse responded.

Hanna had an IV inserted in the right arm where the chemo was administered, so Donna pulled the covers back exposing her daughter's left arm. She glanced over as the nurse prepared the tender spot in the crook of her arm and cringed at the thought of the needle puncturing her daughter's tender skin. Hanna was poked so frequently that the bruises which ran the length of her inner arm never had a chance to heal. She didn't move when the nurse tied the rubber tourniquet on her upper arm and then inserted the needle filling two tubes.

Donna looked at Jason and watched him watching the nurse. Their eyes met for a second and then parted. There was nothing she wanted to say to him. Why wasn't he there last night until late? A few minutes later the Oncologist walked in.

"Can we step outside?" he asked them.

Donna rolled off the bed and followed Jason out into the hallway.

"I think it's time for you to prepare yourself. Hanna is not responding to any of the treatments and the cancer is shutting down her organs."

Donna started to cry as the Oncologist continued.

"We're going to keep her as comfortable as possible, but you need to prepare yourselves," he repeated.

Jason shook his head.

"You're giving up too easily!" he insisted.

"I've been in touch with the pharmaceutical company, and that new drug is going to be available for her," Jason blurted.

"I know how hard this must be," The Oncologist replied ignoring Jason's outburst of information.

"No, you don't! You'd don't know anything!"

The Oncologist turned to Donna.

"Mrs. Smith, stay with Hanna, and I promise we will keep her comfortable. She won't feel any pain."

Donna's eyes met Jason's with a fearful expression as if she heard the words, but they were too hard to understand. She reached out to Jason, grabbing his arm, and then her knees buckled, and she fell to the floor sobbing.

Jason went down on one knee and grabbed her with both hands and tried to pull her up but she couldn't move. He lowered himself fully onto the floor and put his arms around her.

"I can't do this. I can't do this," she cried.

The Oncologist stood over them, his own eyes glossing and said he would be back later in the day to check on Hanna.

"I can't live without her." Donna sobbed onto Jason's arm.

"You won't have to," he replied.

"I'm going to get her on that medication. I just need a few more hours. Come on. Get up and let's go back in the room. We'll wake her up and get her to eat some breakfast."

Jason pulled on his wife's arm and helped her to her feet. He kept his arm around her waist and escorted her into the room. They stood for a moment, eyes locked on their sleeping daughter.

"She's all I have in the world." Donna continued to cry.

"I know. I know. Me too. Let's wake her up."

They stood on separate sides of the bed, and Donna reached down and stroked her daughter's forehead. "Hanna . . . Hanna . . . time to wake up. It's breakfast time."

Just as she said the words, a hospital worker entered the room with a domed tray and set it down on the rolling cart at the end of the bed. Jason pulled the dome away.

"Look, honey, there's eggs and cereal," he coaxed.

Hanna's eyes remained still.

Jason moved in closer and spoke in her ear.

"Honey, time to wake up. You have to eat."

Hanna still didn't move. Donna's eyes filled with tears.

"Why isn't she waking up?"

Jason ignored the question and made a loose fist, then rubbed his knuckles over the middle of Hanna's chest. Still no movement. He pushed the call button tied to the bed.

"What's wrong? Why won't she wake up?" Donna's voice cracked with hysteria.

"They might have medicated her. Try to calm down. I'll find out what they gave her."

Donna stared at her daughter's motionless face, and then noted her chest was continuing to rise and fall. Jason turned and walked into the hallway and met the nurse as she approached Hanna's room.

"She's not waking up. What did you give her? I want to see her chart."

The nurse took a step back avoiding Jason's aggression.

"I need a minute to look. I just came on shift," she replied.

Jason followed her to the nurse's station and waited while she brought up Hanna's chart on the computer.

"She was given a very small dose of morphine during the night. The Oncologist ordered it."

Jason slammed his fist on the counter, and the nurse jumped.

"Mister Smith!" She stood facing him.

"I'm sorry. I didn't mean to scare you. I don't want her given any more morphine. Is that understood?"

"Yes, I'll make a note in her chart, and I'll send a note to the Oncologist."

"You do that," he demanded.

He went to Hanna's room and told Donna about the medication.

"I don't remember anyone coming in and giving her anything," she commented.

"Neither do I. We must have been asleep. She'll wake up on her own. It will just take a while for the medication to wear off. I'm going to run home and take a shower. Call me when she wakes up."

Donna nodded and laid back on the bed, pulling herself against Hanna's thin, sleeping form.

CHAPTER SIXTY-TWO

THEIR MEETING WAS set at eight-forty-five am, fifteen minutes before the school bell, but Dan suggested they leave a little early to account for traffic.

They ate a quiet breakfast with Lisa, sipping their coffee, and agreed that as soon as the meeting was over, Lisa would text them and let them know the outcome of the meeting. Assuming the medication was approved, Lisa would hold up a sign in front of the TV, and hopefully, they would let Lindsey go.

Dan stood up from the table grabbing Missy's leash and signaled Lisa to follow. Missy came running, wagging her tail.

The couple walked out to the street, letting Missy sniff the grass. He took her out earlier for a quick first-morning walk just before breakfast, so he didn't feel the need to escort her to every tree. Lisa put her arms around Dan's neck and hugged him close.

"Please be careful," she begged.

"Don't worry. We're just meeting a kid. He couldn't have been more than thirteen or fourteen. It sounded like his voice hadn't even fully changed yet. Once we get the phone, we'll come right back and see what we're going to do next. Just do what we agreed. Hold up the sign for at least ten minutes. Assuming they see it, we have to hope they will let her go."

Lisa was not convinced.

"But what if they don't?"

"We'll figure something out. I promise."

"I feel so bad for Ken. He could barely contain himself in the car last night. I know how close they are."

"I know, honey. We're going to get her back."

Dan looked down at Missy who had somehow wriggled herself between their legs.

"She's jealous," Lisa commented.

They both bent down to pat her, nearly bumping their heads together in the process.

A few minutes later they were on the way. Dan had returned Darius's text with the location, and let him know the make and model of the car. Ken ogled the leather interior and commented on how nice the ride was.

The car was new with black interior and red trims. Ken wiped his hand over the luxurious leather and listened to the purring engine.

"What kind of car do you drive?" Dan asked.

"Oh, we just have an old Toyota Camry. We recently bought a condo in the city, and it's expensive to park, so we probably won't replace it when it dies."

"You live right in Boston?"

"Yeah, well we lucked out on this condo and bought it just at the right time."

"Good for you. It must be hard for young people to get started after college. It sounds like you're doing well."

"We're trying," Ken said. "My mother was a big help teaching us about real estate. It was . . . is a hobby of hers." Ken caught himself.

"Lisa never mentioned that about her. I'm sure she'll be back into it in no time."

"I hope so," Ken replied wringing his hands.

Dan pulled the car off the exit about thirty minutes before their meeting time. There was no traffic on route seventy-five, and they sailed right through. The car's navigation system led them directly to Lee Middle School.

"Look." Ken pointed. "I see the fence."

Dan drove up slowly noting that the fence covered the length of the sidewalk on both sides of the block.

"This thing's gotta be at least a mile all the way round."

"I remember walking here before," Ken commented.

He circled the block twice and didn't see anyone waiting on a bicycle, but, then again, they were twenty minutes early.

"Do you know how to access your mom's gate?" Dan asked.

"Yes, I know the code. If you drive a little further, you'll see the gate."

Dan followed Ken's direction and then punched the numbers into the keypad beside the gated entrance. It took a few seconds for the gate to fully open, and they drove in.

"Take two lefts and then a quick right. It's the fourth house on the right," Ken directed.

Dan wove his way into the community and pulled the car into Lindsey's driveway, then checked his watch.

"We have ten minutes."

The men got out of the car and walked up to the front door. It was easy to see that the house was new and they heard construction noises nearby. A crane lifted and lowered roofing materials just one street away.

Ken punched the key code, a combination of their birthdays, into the lock and heard it click open. They entered the house and looked around. As expected, it was neat, clean and quiet. Ken stood for a moment at the sliding doors that overlooked the lanai and pool and imagined his mother on her favorite lounge chair. He put his hand on the door handle, pausing, and then turned to Dan.

"She loves this pool. She talks about how much she loves sitting outside and floating in the pool at night and on the weekends."

Dan held off the urge to comfort him and instead checked the time.

"We'd better go."

Ken nodded and followed him out of the house. He punched the key code in again and waited for the lock to engage and then got back into the car.

"You can go out the back entrance. It will bring us right across from the fence." Ken explained.

Dan followed his lead, and as described, the fence was right across the street from the back gate. They waited a few seconds for it to open, and then pulled off to the right. Cars were lined up along the fence near each adjacent entrance of the two school buildings. It appeared as if they had a rotation pattern for dropping off the kids. In the distance, coming from the far left, they could see a boy on a bicycle. Other children cluttered the sidewalk, but the boy made a wide arc, clearly on a mission.

"I wonder if that's him," Ken said.

They waited another minute, watching as the boy approached, and then he stopped near a tree that leaned over the fence.

"That's gotta be him." Dan's voice rose with excitement.

*   *   *

The two men got out of their car, waited for the traffic to pass, and then crossed the street, cautiously approaching the boy. He appeared to be just as young as Dan suspected. No older than twelve or thirteen. He was wearing navy blue Bermuda type shorts and a white polo shirt. He wondered if this was a school issued uniform.

"Hi there, are you Darius Williams?" Dan asked.

The boy nodded but didn't open his mouth.

Dan sensed his fear and kept his distance.

"My name is Dan, and this is Ken. The phone belongs to his mother. We really appreciate you finding it for us. Can you show us where you found it?"

Darius swung a leg off the bike and set it on the ground. He looked down in the grass and then up at the tree.

"It was right about here," he said.

"Do you remember what day and time you found it?"

"Yeah, it was Wednesday morning around nine o'clock. I was late for school, so I remember getting inside after the bell."

"Can I have the phone now?" Ken asked gently.

Darius reached into his pocket and handed him the phone with the earbuds wrapped around it.

"I charged it at school," he offered.

"Well, we appreciate that, Darius," Dan said smiling.

"Oh, also, if it helps, I looked at some of her apps, and she has one of those fitness trackers. I think it tells you where she is."

Ken sucked in a quick breath.

"I forgot about that! She has GPS on her fitness tracker. She must be wearing it!"

He pressed the home button on the phone.

"Are you looking for your mother?" Darius asked.

Ken didn't answer. His eyes remained focused on the phone, swiping through apps looking for the fitness tracker.

"Yeah, well she's been missing for a couple of days. Listen, Darius," Dan said reaching for his wallet, "here's some money for your trouble. You're obviously a good kid, and you did the right thing by calling Ken and letting him know that you had the phone."

He handed him a fifty-dollar bill.

Darius stared at the bill. "Thank you, sir." He smiled.

"Is there anything else you think we should know about?" Dan asked.

"Well, she has a lot of books on the phone, and I listened to Cujo. I'm sorry." Darius lowered his eyes.

Dan laughed. "It's okay. The important thing is that Ken has it back and now we can find his mom. I'm sure your mom is very proud of you."

Darius didn't answer, and Dan wondered if the boy was having a rough time.

"I have to go now. I have to be inside before the bell rings."

"Sure. You go ahead and have a good day at school."

Darius got back on his bike and followed the sidewalk along the fence to the entrance. As soon as he was out of sight, Dan turned his attention back to Ken.

"Did you find what the kid was talking about?"

"Yeah, I think so. Look."

Ken handed him the phone and pointed to the flashing icon. "Can you tell where this is?" he asked Dan.

"It looks like it might be near Long Boat or Casey Key." Dan raised his eyebrows.

"What does that mean?"

"Casey Key is an expensive area, lots of estates. Wealthy people come to vacation, though it's not as crowded in the summer. It's practically the end of the snow bird season so many of them should be gone already. Let's head back in that direction and see where this leads us."

They waited for traffic to pass and then jogged across the street to the Mustang. It was only nine o'clock, but the temperature was up near ninety.

"I don't know how you can stand this heat," Ken remarked.

"Air conditioning." Dan pushed the AC up to high.

"It's nine. I wonder what's happening in that meeting."

"We'll know in a few minutes," Dan replied. He pulled his phone from his pocket and set it on the console.

CHAPTER SIXTY-THREE

I T WAS HARD to tell if it was morning with the windows sealed so tightly, but Lindsey's inner clock was urging her awake. She pulled her wrist up and checked her fitness tracker. The battery was getting low, but it read nine o'clock. It's Friday, and I'm still here, still alive, and I'm going to get out of here today one way or another. She sat on the edge of the bed and glanced up at the camera. It was instinctive now. She raised her middle finger and mouthed the words, "Fuck you."

She had been in the same clothes for two days, and her skin crawled, but at least her hair felt better after her hand soap shampoo job in the bathroom sink. She reached into her left pocket and reassuringly patted the screwdriver.

She walked to the door, opened it, listened, and then poked her head quickly into the hallway. The fat one was sitting in front of the computer. She heard him belch, then belch again. She took a second look and spotted the beer cans. *Disgusting pig*, she thought, scrunching up her face. She took two quiet steps across the hall into the bathroom and closed the door behind her. The toilet seat was up, and she groaned. "Disgusting!" she yelled.

No footsteps could be heard in the hallway. She pulled a sheet of toilet paper off the roll and used it as a barrier to lower the seat. Her face twisted with disgust. She finished her business, taking extra time to wash her hands, and then went into the living room.

The fat one didn't notice her, but she could see past him. Two naked women undulated on the computer screen, and he let out an "Oh yeah!" as they tongued each other's mouths. Lindsey moved toward the kitchen hoping he wouldn't notice her, hoping she would find coffee, but he heard her light steps.

"Princeth bitch is awake," he lisped.

She wanted to say 'fuck you' again, but she was afraid of him. He could easily overpower her, hurt her, or even kill her. She resisted and pretended to ignore him, and took another step toward the kitchen. She adjusted her left pocket, jamming the contents behind her hip.

"It's my buddie's turn to get the coffee, so princeth bitch will have to wait until he gets back."

He was still gawking at the pornographic images.

She wanted to cry, mostly from fear in knowing she was alone with him, but she quickly calmed herself and went back to the bedroom. She listened for a moment and didn't hear any footsteps in the hall, and then climbed on the bed, rolling onto her left side, her body blocking the camera's view. She slid the screwdriver from her pocket and then tried to jam the edge under the plywood. It was futile. She slid the tool back into her pocket and lay on her back closing her eyes. Hopefully, the black guy would be back soon with the coffee. As bad as he was, the fat guy was even worse. Her skin crawled, and she hugged herself, rubbing her arms. The fat guy might be drunk, and he was watching porn, this could easily escalate. She turned onto her right side and watched the door. Then she heard his footsteps in the hall.

Please, please be going to the bathroom or the other bedroom. She watched the door knob turn, and she jolted upright.

"Leave me alone!" Lindsey yelled.

He stepped into the room.

"My buddy's been delayed. Sounds like a long line at the McDonald's, so it's your lucky day."

His tone was raunchy, and he was practically drooling. She knew what he had in mind, and her fight or flight instincts were in turmoil.

He took a step closer to the edge of the bed.

Lindsey backed up, bringing her knees up, her feet up in a position where she could kick him if she had to. He took another step closer. His eyes were fixed on her, crazed, and he grinned exposing his fleshy upper gum.

"There's no point in fighting this, princeth bitch. You gonna get what you gonna get."

She was backed up against the covered window. Her eyes moved left and right, searching for an escape route, but the fear and adrenaline were fogging her brain.

"If your friend comes back and you've hurt me he's not going to give you your money," she tried reasoning.

"I ain't worried about that. I'll just tell him that you got feisty and I had to put you down. He'll believe me cuz he seen you all crazy like that."

His knees were touching the edge of the bed now, and his hands hung less than a foot from her ankles.

"You been well taken care of here, bitch. Drinking coffee and eating our food, but you ain't given nothing back. It's time for princeth bitch to pay her to keep."

His words slurred together and Lindsey was sure he was drunk, which made him even more dangerous. She pulled herself back, pulling her knees in even tighter and felt the screwdriver jab her left thigh. Her hand went to her pocket, and she turned her fist and gripped it like a weapon. Cliff lunged forward and grabbed her right ankle. She pulled back and kicked with her left, punching her foot at him, but he caught it midair.

"Here I come, bitch, and you gonna love it."

He leaned into the bed, hunched over her and released her ankle, grabbing at the front of her sweat pants.

"Go ahead, bitch, fight all you want cuz I'm comin.'"

She got her left foot under his face and kicked up, landing a blow on his chin. He was unfazed by the impact. He had both of her legs now and yanked her toward him, pulling her flat. She screamed as loudly as she could, but then his left hand came up and slapped her hard across the face. The room went dim, and a cracking sound rang in her ears as if the sound of the slap was vibrating.

He placed his right knee on the bed, and she could smell his sweaty funk and rotten beer breath. His hand pressed her lips hard over her teeth, and the pressure caused a painful fissure. *Now!* She forced into her mind, and then all in one motion she pulled her fist out of her pocket and rammed the screwdriver as hard as she could into the right side of his neck.

He backed off and released her, his face converting into a twisted question. He swayed as he got both feet back on the floor. She watched in horror, the screwdriver protruding from his neck at a near perfect ninety-degree angle. Blood was oozing from around the plugged hole. Her hands went up to her face and lips in horror.

He reached up with his right hand, then cocked his wrist awkwardly as he gripped the handle and yanked it out. The blood squirted clear across the room in a rhythmic pattern. He instinctively tried to cover the gaping hole in his neck, but it was too late. His artery was severed, and his own act of removing it had finished him. He dropped to his knees, his eyes rolled back in his head, and he went face first to the floor, landing in his own pool of blood.

Lindsey could hear herself screaming but she couldn't stop. Her throat hurt, but she screamed until there was no sound left. Her eyes clenched shut, and she pulled her knees in, huddling herself deep on the bed. She breathed fast through her mouth, then slowed herself down as reality set in. She had to get out.

*   *   *

Her hands were shaking so hard that she had difficulty steadying herself enough to shimmy off the far end of the bed, away from the dead man whose blood still ran across the floor. There was barely a way around it. She got one foot on the floor and then stretched to step around the puddle, then hopped through the door way into the hall. The urgency to pee clouded her thinking. She ran into the bathroom and closed the door, her sweatpants already down around her knees before she reached the toilet. Relief. She checked her hands and didn't see any blood. No time to waste. "Keys! Oh my God." She realized the only way out was through the front door. She looked into the room at his body and retched. Her brain made the stomach connection faster than she could control it. It was just spittle. She had no food in her. She took a deep breath and then took a large step in the same pattern that she took before. The blood was everywhere, having left his body with such force that it made a bizarre pattern on the wall and bedding.

On the end of the bed again, balancing on her knees, she wanted to reach over him and dig in his pockets, but he was too far away. She laid on her belly and inched toward the edge of the bed, keeping clear of the blood splatter on the blanket. First, she patted his pockets, and then reluctantly reached inside and pulled them out. Empty! *What if they are in his back pocket?* Lindsey considered how she could get to his back pocket and then decided that it wasn't happening. He must weigh at least three hundred pounds! She stuffed her hand as far as it would reach on the side of him closest to her and felt nothing. He was wearing basketball type shorts. Did they even have a back pocket? She wriggled herself back onto the bed and rolled back upright. *Calm down and think! The screwdriver!* It was lying next to him in the puddle of blood. "Oh my God!"

She sat on her knees on the bed, thinking. The black guy would be back soon. She could hide behind the front door and when he opened it she would duck past him and try to make a run for it. But she wanted the screwdriver. She climbed off the end of the bed and flipped up the blanket covering the blood splatter. Then she stepped on the bed and walked to the opposite end. She dropped to her knees and reached for it. Her fingers caught the blade end, and she held it up, away from her body. She saw the blood on her finger tips.

"I got it, you motherfucker!" She was up on her feet again and jumped off the other end of the bed and made the same long steps out of the room, then back to the bathroom.

She turned on the water and dropped the screwdriver in the sink, then washed her hands, and peed again. She watched the blood run off the tool and down the drain and leaned over the sink thinking she might wretch again. *Concentrate!* She ran to the front door and stood in the corner, making herself as flat as she could. A car door slammed. Her heart was exploding through her chest as she tried to push herself flatter and deeper against the wall. The keys turned the lock, and then the door opened.

"Coffee's here!" He came through the door holding the coffee tray in one hand while he finished keying the lock. The food bag hung from his teeth.

Lindsey ducked under his arm, turned sideways through the narrow opening, and ran. She ran as fast as her shaking legs could carry her. Past the car and down the dirt road. She looked back only once, seeing him run after her, but then, he was gone.

Did he go back inside? She kept running for what seemed like a mile until she saw the gas station with the little store and knew she was going to be okay.

* * *

The gas station was further than she thought. Everything that appeared just ahead on a Floridian road was further than she thought. There was no contour to the roads, and the landscape blended. She had slowed to a jog and then a shuffle. Her split lips swelled bigger and stung with each step, and her breathing couldn't keep up with the movement of her pounding chest. She looked back, again and again, to see if anyone was following, but no one was there.

Finally, she reached the lot and stood for a minute. The word 'hyperventilation' flashed through her mind, but there was no bag to breathe into. She rested her hands on her knees and stared at a spot on the ground. Finally, she was able to catch her breath enough to look around. No one was pumping gas, and there were no cars parked in front of the building. Was it closed? On a Friday morning? It didn't seem possible. The tiny hairs on her arms and neck stood up. All she needed was a place to make one phone call. She squinted off into the distance and could see the main road up ahead, but her legs were heavy, and her mouth was parched. Up ahead probably meant at least another mile, so she shrugged off the bad feeling and entered the small store.

The air conditioning hit her like a barrel of cold water pouring down over her head. She stood in the doorway for a moment, under the blower and let the refreshing air coat her sweat-soaked body. The small store appeared empty, but there had to be someone here. No one would leave the front door unlocked like that. She spotted the raised check-out counter and approached. Maybe there was a camera or mirror, and someone would come. No one did. She walked to the back of the store and waited in front of the stockroom door. "Hello?" she yelled. No answer. Then she raised her fist to knock.

"Can I help you, ma'am." A quiet voice came from behind her, and she span around.

"Oh, thank God."

The woman was large and possibly in her mid-thirties, but it was hard to tell because the side of her face was black and blue. She immediately thought that this woman had been abused, and her expression changed to concern, but then she remembered her own plight. She had been hit in the face twice, after being kidnapped and now she had two black eyes of her own.

"Yes, please. I need to use a phone. I need to call the police." Her voice was desperate and pleading.

The woman gawked at her, unsure of how to respond. Lindsey repeated herself.

"I need a phone. Do you have a phone I can use?"

The woman shook her head no, and her eyes stared at the floor. Lindsey couldn't figure out which one of them was more damaged, herself or this beaten down store-keeper. She put her hands on her hips, breathing hard, and inspected the store.

"Do you sell any burner phones?"

The large woman opened her mouth to speak, but then her face changed to fear. She was staring past Lindsey, her eyes opened wide and her mouth was frozen as if she tried to speak but was forced to stop.

Lindsey spun around to see what or who she was afraid of, and then she froze too. A very tall bald man with a full beard stood in the doorway, blocking the exit. He wore a stained sleeveless undershirt and old, dusty looking jeans held up by a skull and crossbones belt buckle. He was holding a shotgun, the shortened kind, like Lindsey had seen in the movies. The gun hung in his right hand, aimed at the floor.

"Who's your new friend?" the man asked sarcastically.

"She ain't no one. She just walked in, looking for a phone."

The man studied her for a moment.

"That's quite a shiner you got there. How'd that happen?"

Lindsey's hand gripped the screwdriver in her pocket.

"I was kidnapped. I got away."

The man laughed loudly, and Lindsey could sense the woman next to her flinch.

"You was kidnapped? You expect me to believe that?"

Lindsey shook her head.

"Yes. I've been held for two days."

"So where are these kidnappers that messed up that pretty face of yours? Cindy, ain't her face pretty? She's prettier than you!"

Cindy continued to cower, nodding her head in agreement.

"Down the road a way. I ran here. Please, if I could just use your phone."

She tried not to sound vulnerable, but she couldn't hold back the desperation in her tone.

"Who you gonna call? The po-lice?"

Lindsey hesitated. If she said yes, then he might object, and who knew what this man was capable of? If she said no, then he probably wouldn't believe her.

"I want to call my son and let him know I'm alright. Please, Sir . . ."

He cut her off and glared at the other woman.

"You hear that, Cindy. You hear how she called me sir? That's how a woman's supposed to talk to her man."

Cindy's head moved toward her shoulder, and she was trying to make her large form smaller in his intimidating presence.

"Look, I don't want to cause any trouble. I just want to go home to my son. Please, sir, if I could just make a call and then I'll be on my way."

"What do you think, Cindy? Should I let this nice lady who

called me sir use the phone?" His voice got louder with each word.

Cindy shook her head yes and then no. It was evident to Lindsey that Cindy did not know the right answer and wasn't taking any chances.

"I'll just leave you both alone. I'm sure I can find another store nearby. I am sorry that I bothered you," Lindsey said.

She made a move toward the front door, but the man blocked her path.

"There ain't no other stores nearby. And now that you're here, you're gonna stay here and show my Cindy how a woman is supposed to treat her man. But first you both gonna do some woman's work. Cindy keeps this place like a shit hole, and the customers don't wanna come in here. The two of you gonna do some cleanin'. Cindy nodded her head in agreement and then went behind the front counter. She returned quickly with some Windex and some rags, then urged Lindsey with her eyes to follow. Lindsey was ready to burst into tears. The screwdriver in her pocket no longer gave her any power or comfort, and she didn't see any way that she was getting around this shotgun-wielding, angry wife beater.

She followed Cindy to the back of the store, and two women started wiping down the dusty shelving. The man settled in behind the counter to watch. Lindsey didn't see the gun but she assumed it was within his reach.

The shelves were clean after forty-five minutes of dusting and scrubbing, and by then Lindsey was hunched forward, with her thighs squeezed together, positioning herself anyway possible to avoid her peeing in her pants.

"Is there a bathroom I can use? I really have to go."

"Sure. Cindy, take our new friend to the bathroom and make it quick."

Lindsey followed Cindy to the back of the store and through

the stockroom door. When the door closed behind them, Lindsey turned to her.

"Is there a back door? I need to get out of here."

"Yeah, there's a door, but he's got the key," Cindy said pointing to the stockroom door.

"Fuck! Where's the toilet?"

Cindy pointed to the bathroom door, and Lindsey went in and relieved herself quickly.

"There must be some way out of here. Is there a phone back here somewhere?"

Cindy thought for a minute and then pointed to a small table in the corner, wedged between the wall and a mattress that lay on the floor.

"Sometimes he keeps a phone in the drawer."

Lindsey bolted across the room nearly knocking over a stack of boxes and pulled the drawer open. It was empty.

"We better get back, or he'll come after us."

Lindsey reluctantly followed her back into the store.

CHAPTER SIXTY-FOUR

J ASON ENTERED THE small conference room at two minutes before nine o'clock. An oval shaped table filled the center of the room, and six high-back, thickly cushioned chairs were neatly spaced around the perimeter. He had already received two texts from Donna letting him know that Hanna had still not awoke, and that the blood test results weren't in. He sent her a text back telling her he'd be there within the hour. Two of his colleagues entered the room, and they shook hands. Jason explained that Ron Shay, who was covering for another Medical Director, wasn't coming, but there was enough of them to approve the new medications.

A moment later the last two participants entered the room, and they all took a seat at the table. Jason reached for the bat-shaped conference phone in the center and dialed into the conference line. After a series of beeps, Lisa's voice greeted them.

"Hi, everyone, I'll take a quick attendance and then please refer the documents in your meeting invitation. Lisa collected everyone's name and then started the meeting.

"We have three new drugs today. Let's start with Cineth," Lisa suggested.

"I'll give everyone a couple of minutes to read the policy."

Jason felt his phone vibrating in his pocket but ignored it. *Just a few more minutes,* he thought. He had the Oncologists contact information as the number one position in his favorite's list, and he focused on tapping his finger on his name and sharing the good news. Hanna could have the medication. A tap on his shoulder snapped him back into the room

"Hey, I felt bad letting you cover. I can do this . . . you get to the hospital and be with your girl." Ron Shay whispered in his ear.

Jason cocked his head sideways to see Ron's face. He stared at him, shocked, in disbelief. The rubber band around his chest tightened to the point of breaking him in two, and the blood rushed in his head, pounding in his ears. His phone continued to vibrate in his pocket, and he reached in pushing the power button to silence it.

Ron moved to the other side of the table and opened his laptop, and then looked at Jason.

"Go. I've got this." Ron broke his gaze and spotted the bat phone.

"Hi, Lisa, it's Ron Shay."

"Hi, Dr. Shay, glad to have you with us. We're reviewing Cineth first."

"Oh good. I'm familiar with that one."

Ron began reading but then stopped, flexing his neck and then caught Jason's eye. His brow cinched in a question. Jason squinted back at him, willing him to stay quiet, but he didn't.

"Lisa, I think there's been a mistake. I did the research on this drug, and I don't think this is written correctly."

Jason tried to open his mouth to speak, but no words came out. He attempted to suck in air and take a breath, but his chest wouldn't move. The room grew dim around him. His phone vibrated again, and this time he took it out of his pocket and read the message.

"Come now. She's dying."

Jason read the words again and then stood up and walked out the door, leaving his laptop open on the table.

CHAPTER SIXTY-FIVE

A T TWENTY MINUTES past nine, Dan's phone rang through his car speakers. He pushed the answer button on the steering wheel.

"So, what happened?" Dan asked.

"Nothing happened! It was the craziest thing! We were just getting started and then Dr. Shay showed up. He said that he knew about Cineth and he could see a mistake in the template. Then it was quiet for a second, and then I heard the door close. I'm not sure who left.

"So it wasn't approved?"

"No! We just moved on to the next two drugs. What about Lindsey? What do we do now?"

"Did you hold up a note in front of the TV?" Ken asked.

"No! I didn't want to tell them that it wasn't approved, so I did nothing!" Lisa sounded out of breath like she had run a marathon.

"Okay, well sit tight. We might have some information. We got the cell phone back from the kid, and there's a fitness app that's flashing at a location on Casey Key."

"Casey Key? Do you think that's her?

"I could be. We're heading that way now."

"Is Ken alright?" Lisa asked not realizing that she was on speaker phone.

"I'm fine. Just want to get there already," Ken replied.

"I'm going to do a drive by and see what we can find out. You just do business as usual, and I'll call you as soon as I can. Love you."

"Love you too."

Dan ended the call and viewed the navigation system.

"We should be there before ten thirty. I'm driving as fast as I can. I don't want to get pulled over."

"It's okay; I know you're doing the best that you can."

Ken checked out Dan's car and saw he had a duffel bag in the back seat. He hadn't noticed that the night before when they went out for dinner.

"What's in the bag," Ken asked.

"I brought some extra equipment just in case. Go ahead and take a look."

Ken reached back and pulled the heavy bag into his lap.

"Geeze feels like lead in here."

He unzipped the bag and examined the contents.

"Wow, you come prepared. Is this a baton? I've never seen one of these batons up close. It's shorter than I thought it would be."

"Yeah, well you never know when you're gonna need it to bring someone down, and the baton is pretty effective. There is mace and pepper spray in there too."

Ken pulled out a set of handcuffs and fully extended them.

"I didn't realize how heavy they are."

Dan smiled. "Like I said. You never know when you're gonna need them."

Ken put the items back in the bag and lifted it over the seat into the back.

"Another hour and we'll be there," Dan said.

* * *

The north bound traffic was light, and Dan drove like a pro, carefully avoiding marked police cars and even unmarked cars that he intuitively knew were looking for speeders.

"Do you still see the GPS marker on the map?" Dan asked.

"Yeah, but it looks like it might have moved a little. I'm not sure."

He used the edge of his thumb and index finger to try and enlarge the screen and zoom in.

"I think this is it," Dan said.

They pulled the car forward into the gas station and parked on the street edge of the lot. Dan put his hand on Ken's arm.

"I want you to wait here. Let me check it out first, just in case."

Ken hesitated and then nodded his head in agreement.

"Keep your cell phone out. I'll text you if she's in there."

Dan got out of the car and walked in the front door of the small store.

"Sorry, man, we're closed," the man behind the counter said.

Dan studied him and could immediately sense that something was off. He took a step closer.

"I just wanted a bottle of cold water. Do you mind?"

"Yeah, I mind. Like I said, we're closed."

Dan stepped back and turned looking down the row of shelves, and then spotted the two women in the back. The shelves were high, but he was certain that one of them was Lindsey. He turned back to the man behind the counter just as he was pulling up the shot gun. He pointed the barrel at Dan's face.

"I changed my mind. We're open now. Girls, get up here. We have a customer."

Lindsey moved first, urging Cindy to stay behind her. The

two women walked slowly to the front of the store, Cindy's hand was on Lindsey's shoulder, and then Dan and Lindsey's eyes met. Like telepathy, they knew not to let on that they knew each other.

"The man wants a bottle of water. Cindy, get him one. Then he's gonna leave here and never come back."

Cindy pulled away from Lindsey and grabbed a bottle of water off a nearby shelf. She handed it to Dan.

"There's your water, mister. Best be on your way, and if you think you gonna call the cops, then these girls here are gonna get it. You understand?"

The man now had the gun aimed at the two frightened women.

Dan put his left hand on the door, but instead of pushing it forward he reached his right hand behind his waist and pulled out his Beretta hand gun, aiming it at the man. There was a loud click as Dan released the safety.

"Let these women go now!" Dan demanded.

The man was caught off guard and moved the shot gun away from Dan and aimed it at Lindsey.

"I wouldn't try anything with that toy you holding, else this bitch gets a big giant hole in her head."

Lindsey couldn't hold back any longer.

"Dan . . . run!"

The man flew a look between the two of them and then stepped out behind the counter holding his aim on Lindsey.

"Let's go. Move."

He waved them toward the back of the store while Dan kept his aim steady at the man's chest. The four of them side stepped down an aisle of canned goods until they reached the end.

"I don't see how this is going to end well," Dan said. "Just let the women go, and we'll forget this ever happened."

The man ignored him and moved the two women into the back corner of the store. Dan followed and positioned himself in the aisle with his back facing the store front.

*   *   *

Ken sat in the passenger seat of Dan's car waiting for his text. Nearly ten minutes had passed and nothing. No text. No call. Dan was still inside. His anxiety grew, thinking about all he and his mother had been through together. All that she had done for him to ensure his success. He got out of the car and pulled the seat forward, reaching in for the duffel bag. He unzipped it and gazed over the contents, shifting them around in the bag. He pulled out the baton, but he worried it wasn't enough. *Was there a gun in here somewhere?* Then he spotted Dan's baseball bat and softball glove on the floor. He pulled out the bat, closed the car door and crossed the parking lot to the store. *Why hadn't Dan come out?* Goose pimples ran up his arms, and he shivered. Something was wrong. The lower part of the door was wood, and old weathered glass covered the door from the waist up. He put the bat between his knees and held his hands around his eyes.

"Oh shit!" He could see four people toward the back of the store, and one of them, a tall man with a beard, was holding a shot gun. He could see the top of Dan's head, but from where they stood it didn't appear that the gun was aimed at him.

"Oh, shit!" He turned away from the door thinking and said, "Shit," again. Then he dropped to his knees, holding the bat under his arm. He pried the door open from the bottom and slithered snake-like along the floor. Relief washed over him when he didn't hear any bells or noise makers on the inside of the door. He crept on all fours down the outside aisle of the store, balancing the bat so it didn't crash to the floor. He could hear Dan trying to talk the man into putting down his gun. When he reached the end of the aisle he peeked quickly and saw his mother.

He mouthed the word 'shit' again and stayed where he was to listen and think. He poked his head forward again, and this time he was sure that Dan had seen him. He backed up again and waited a moment. Dan continued trying convincing the man to back down.

Ken crept forward on knees and elbows into the back aisle. Adrenaline filled his body, and the rush pushed him forward. His mother was just a few feet away now, but her eyes stayed focused on the man holding the shotgun aimed at her head. Ken's fear quickly turned to rage. He crept the last few feet until he was just behind the man, then tucked his toes under, raised himself up, and lifted the bat. He slammed it down as hard as he could on the tall man's bald head.

The sound was a sickening combination of a smack and a crunch, but the man didn't drop the gun or move. Ken wasn't sure what to do so he swung again and struck him a second time. Blood burst out in all directions, and the man's eyes bulged from his face. He dropped the gun and his knees folded, causing him to fall forward. The two women jumped back, and the other woman screamed, "You killed him! You killed my husband!"

"Mom!"

Ken's eyes met Lindsey's, and he dropped the bat. The sound of the heavy wood hitting the floor startled them still for a moment, but then she rushed into his arms. Tears streamed down their faces, and they held each other tight. Dan put his gun in the back of his pants and then moved in putting his arms around both of them.

CHAPTER SIXTY-SIX

J ASON STOOD AT the hospital entrance having no idea of how he got there. He had no recollection of getting into the car, turning on the engine, or navigating the roads to the hospital parking lot. He was out of his body like he was watching himself in a movie. He watched himself walk to the elevator and push a button. Was he dreaming? He touched the elevator wall, but his fingers didn't register any sensation. There was no movement. The doors opened, and he turned left, but who or what was moving his body? He didn't know. He entered the room, which appeared dim. Several nurses surrounded the bed. Words came out of his mouth but they came from far away, and he could hear what he said.

Their heads turned simultaneously, looking at him with sympathetic faces, and they took a step back, allowing him to see his wife sobbing on the bed holding Hanna in her arms.

"I'm so sorry, sir. She passed a few minutes ago."

He heard the woman's voice but couldn't distinguish who said the words. After that, there was nothing.

CHAPTER SIXTY-SEVEN

SEVERAL SHERIFF'S CARS, an ambulance, and a county coroner vehicle filled the small parking lot at the convenience store. One of the officers rolled out yellow police tape from the gas pumps to the sides of building forming a large triangle.

Lindsey sat on the gurney in the open ambulance while Ken and Dan remained in the store, describing the events to the officers. She hoped they wouldn't keep them too long. She wanted to wrap herself around her son again, memorize his face and thank him for saving her. The uninjured half of her face smiled.

Cindy sat in the back of a police car still sobbing. The car's windows were up, and Lindsey could only see her anguish-filled expression. Lindsey felt sorry for her. Nothing that happened was her fault, and she hoped that someday she would understand that her husband would have likely killed her at some point.

Finally, she saw Dan and Ken exit the store, and behind them, a gurney with the battered man connected to an IV. Lindsey was shocked that he was still alive. She turned her head away not wanting to retain the image. Ken climbed into the ambulance and sat beside her.

"Are you okay? Does anything hurt? Did they hurt you?"

He rolled his eyes at his own stupid question. Obviously, they had hurt her. She had black eyes and a hand print on the side of her face that was rapidly turning black. She was a mess.

"I'm going to be fine." She smiled and wrapped her arm around his back putting her head on his shoulder.

"You saved us you know. Do you realize that? You saved all of us." Tears were flowing again.

"I'm just so glad you are okay." He squeezed her.

"The police want to talk to you about where you were held and what happened there."

Lindsey let out a big sob.

"Honey, I killed a man." she blurted. "He attacked me, and I had no choice!"

Ken pushed back from her, shock rising in him.

"Mom, oh my God. Mom, we have to tell the police now!"

She grabbed his arm pulling him back down onto the gurney next to her.

"Just give me another minute. I want to be with you and pull myself together before I talk to them. Just one more minute."

He settled his arm around her again and squeezed her close.

Ken spotted one of the officers heading their way.

"Mom . . . he's coming over now. You have to tell him what happened."

The officer approached and asked her if she wanted to go to the hospital and get checked out. Lindsey declined.

"It looks worse than it is. I'll be fine."

"My mother was kidnapped on Wednesday morning from near her house in Fort Myers. She was held in a house not far from here. One of the guys is dead."

The cop stepped back surprised, taking in the information and then speaking into the microphone attached to his uniform.

"We've got another body nearby. Ma'am, can you tell us the address?"

"No, there was two of them, and one went out this morning and left me alone with the fat guy, and he attacked me. I got away and ran. I think I can show you where the house is."

The cop spoke into his mic again.

"Victim thinks she can show us the house. I'll take her in my car."

"Wait here," he instructed, and he walked to where another cop was still interviewing Dan. He said a few words and then the three of them came back to the ambulance.

"My partner and I will take you in our car. You can come along too, sir, if you'd like," he said to Ken.

"I'll follow behind," said Dan.

Lindsey and Ken followed the two cops to their police cruiser and climbed in the back. A thick shield cut the space between the front and back seat. Lindsey held Ken's hand.

"Go down this road . . . it's not far!" she shouted, not knowing if the shield blocked sound. "I think I ran for about fifteen minutes."

The cop drove slowly until Lindsey directed him to make a right turn down a narrow dirt road.

"I think it's down there . . . at the end."

She was right. Seeing it from the outside gave her a whole new perspective of the horror she had survived, and she started to cry again. Ken put his arm around her.

"Mom, it's okay," he said holding back his tears. He laughed a bit and said, "You always make me cry when you cry."

The steel door to the cottage was open, and it was clear that the black guy had taken off.

"Stay in the car," the cop instructed, and the two men exited the vehicle and drew their weapons. They watched as the cops went into the house, one at a time, covering each other's movements. About five minutes later, they returned with their weapons holstered and stood by the car. Lindsey could see one of them talking into his mic, and then they got back in the car.

"We're going to have to bring you down to the station and take your statement. I'm sorry, Ma'am. I know you've been through a lot."

Ken squeezed her hand again.

"Will you tell our friend behind us that we are going to the station and we'll see him later?" Ken asked.

"Sure." The cop went to Dan's car and spoke to him through the window. A moment later Ken received a text from Dan telling him to come back to his house when they were done.

*   *   *

It took more than four hours for Lindsey to describe in detail, over and over, every moment of her two-day captivity at the Casey Key cottage. She was able to give a clear description of the exotic looking black man, and mention that just before she escaped, he had been at McDonald's. The Sheriff expressed confidence that they would see his image on any local CCTV and be able to track his location.

Lindsey was exhausted. By the end of the fourth hour, she had trouble keeping her eyes open, and her face had continued to swell. The throbbing made it difficult to hold her head up.

"I think my mother has reached her limit. If you need any more information can you just call her? I'd like to take her home."

The Sheriff nodded in agreement.

"Ma'am, please don't make any plans to leave the state, just in case we need you here."

Lindsey's heart skipped.

"Am I under suspicion for anything? Do I need a lawyer?"

"No, ma'am. It's just routine. Nothing to worry about."

Ken held on to Lindsey helping her stand, and then he remembered that they didn't have a car.

"We don't have a car. Can someone give us a ride to Sarasota?"

"Let me see what I can do."

The Sheriff made a phone call, and then instructed them to wait in the front of the building. An unmarked car pulled up and waved them in. Ken gave the address, and Lindsey closed her eyes, leaning on Ken's shoulder.

"Are you sure you don't want to go to the hospital?"

"No, nothing's broken. It will all get better on its own."

Ken patted her hair. He hadn't realized exactly how tough his mother was and his face expressed a prideful grin.

* * *

Lisa and Dan were waiting in the driveway when their car approached. Ken could see Missy wagging her tail and running back and forth with excitement.

"Mom, we're here." Ken patted her lightly on the shoulder.

Lindsey tried to smile, seeing Lisa through the window but her face hurt, and she held back.

Dan opened the door helping her out, and he and Lisa wrapped their arms around her. She started to cry, but that fell back to a whimper. The throbbing in her face had worsened.

"Oh my God, Lindsey." Lisa squeezed her.

"She didn't want to go to the hospital," Ken replied.

They escorted her into the house and went into the kitchen. Lisa pulled a cold compress from the freezer and handed it to her.

"Put this on your face. You're so swollen! Did this just happen?"

Ken sensed she was having trouble answering; her words were jumbled.

"She was attacked this morning by one of the guys who kidnapped her."

He held off on telling the rest of the story, not wanting his mother to hear the words again after her lengthy interrogation.

"I'm so sorry this happened to you. Tell me what I can do."

"I just need a shower and some clothes."

"Of course. Come with me."

Lindsey followed her down the hall and into her bedroom. They hugged tight, and Lisa started to cry causing Lindsey to whimper again. Lisa released her and apologized.

"I'm sorry. I can't imagine how much that hurts. I'll try not to cry again." She smiled and then pulled some clothes from her drawer and led her to the bathroom.

"There's plenty of towels in there. Let me know if you need anything. I'll be right in the kitchen."

Lindsey took her time in the shower, and when she finally emerged and entered the kitchen, Lisa, Dan, and Ken were digging into a freshly delivered pizza.

"Do you think you can eat something, Mom?" Ken asked.

"I don't know, but it smells good."

She took a few bites and then started to whimper again. Ken reached for her hand.

"Mom, it's okay . . . you're safe now. It's over."

"I want to go home."

"Dan, would you drive us home?"

"Absolutely. Just let me grab the keys."

Lisa cleared the table and walked them to the door.

"Please text me later and let me know you're okay."

Lindsey nodded and reached down to pat Missy's head. She looked back at Lisa and tried to smile.

CHAPTER SIXTY-EIGHT

ONNA LAID IN the hospital bed, holding Hanna's body in her arms. She had been sobbing so hard she had trouble seeing who had entered the room, but she sensed Jason's presence. She wiped her eyes and tried to focus.

"Mr. Smith?"

The nurse who had just delivered the news of Hanna's passing was becoming concerned. Jason's body was still, and his face was expressionless. She had worked long enough on the pediatric oncology floor to know when a parent was in distress. She approached him.

"Mr. Smith?" This time she touched his arm, but he remained still and unresponsive. The nurse moved toward the bed.

"Mrs. Smith, your husband might be in shock. I'm going to call for help."

Donna's brain couldn't register what was happening. All she knew was that her daughter was gone and nothing else made sense. What kind of help could she call for?

One of the nurses standing by the bed sat down and put her hand on Donna's arm.

"I'll stay with you, and you can stay with Hanna as long as you need to." Donna thanked her and put her face back on the pillow next to her daughter's head. She was quieter now and wanted to clear the fog from her brain. She needed to figure out what to do next. It had all happened so suddenly. Why, she kept asking herself? Why did this happen? She was up yesterday morning, writing letters to her friends, and then today she was gone. Just like that. The thoughts and questions brought back the sobs, and she felt the nurse stroke her arm again.

Suddenly there was a commotion in the room, and Donna lifted her head. A woman in a white coat that she assumed was a doctor was in front of Jason.

"Mr. Smith?" Her voice was loud.

She turned to the nurse standing next to her and told her to bring a gurney and one of the male aides.

"What's wrong with him?" Donna skipped a syllable, sobbing through the question.

"I'm so sorry for your terrible loss, Mrs. Smith, but it looks like your husband is in shock. He's probably going to need some medication to help him come out of it."

Donna set her head back down without commenting. She didn't care about Jason. The only thing she cared about was her last moments with her daughter.

*　*　*

It took two male aides to lift Jason's rigid body onto the gurney. The men lifted the side rails in unison and wheeled him out of Hanna's room, followed by a nurse in blue scrubs. They paused in the hallway as the psychiatric attending physician approached. She lifted each of his eyelids, flashing a penlight at his pupils, and then called him by his name again. "Mr. Smith!" Her voice carried.

"Give him two milligrams of Lorazepam and if you don't see any change in the next two hours, give him two more. I'll be up tonight to check on him."

The nurse nodded her head and led as the two aides pushed the gurney into the elevator.

"His thirteen-year-old daughter just died," the nurse explained to the aides.

"Wow, that's tough. No wonder the guy is in shock," an aide answered.

The elevator stopped, and the nurse punched a four-digit code on a keypad to open the doors to the psychiatric floor. Jason remained mannequin-still, his eyes blinking at long intervals.

They wheeled him into a stark white room, and the aides secured his wrists and ankles with Velcro cuffs while the nurse supervised.

"Make sure they are not on too tightly. He's not a prisoner," she added.

"I'm all set now. You guys can go."

She nurse reached into her pocket and pulled out a syringe and an ampoule of medication. She shook the tiny bottle, popped the plastic top off, and then pulled the needle cap off with her teeth, spitting it into the waste basket next to the bed. She inserted the needle into the rubber stopper and pulled back the plunger until all of the liquid was collected, then pulled an alcohol square from her pocket.

"Here you go, Mr. Smith."

She inched up the sleeve of his polo shirt with her pinky finger, rubbed the square on his exposed skin, and then injected the liquid into his deltoid muscle. She waited a few minutes to check for a reaction. There was none, so she left the room.

An hour later the nurse returned and found that Jason was still not responding. She pulled a notepad out of her scrub pocket and noted the time, then left the room again. She returned an hour later and then administered a second dose. At the fourth hour, she paged the attending physician.

"He's had four milligrams and still isn't responding."

"Start him on IV Diazepam and keep me informed."

The nurse followed the order and worked quickly gathering the intravenous supplies and medication. Another four hours passed and Jason was still not responding.

"No change yet," she reported.

"Let's do a Head CT and see if it shows anything. I'm off at midnight, but I'll leave a note for the next attending. Where's the wife? I should go talk to her."

"I'm not sure. Their daughter passed away earlier today."

"Was she oncology?"

"Yes, AML. She was only thirteen."

"That's sad, the doctor added.

"I know."

The attending sat at the nurse's station and searched for Hanna's chart. She located Donna's phone number and dialed.

"Mrs. Smith?"

"Yes," Donna answered in a quiet voice.

"This is Doctor Clarke. I am very, very sorry for your loss today."

"Thank you."

"I wanted to let you know that your husband has been admitted to the psychiatric unit and we are giving him medication to help get him moving again. He hasn't responded yet, but we're running some tests and watching him closely."

Donna hesitated, and the doctor could hear her breathing.

"Mrs. Smith?"

"Yes, I heard you." And then the line was disconnected.

CHAPTER SIXTY-NINE

LINDSEY SLEPT FOR nearly sixteen hours, though it wasn't a deep sleep. She woke up several times, scared, sweating and shaking, repeating the last two day's events in her mind. It was noon on Saturday before she finally emerged from her bedroom. Ken sat on the living room sofa playing a video game on his computer and glanced up when he heard her bedroom door open.

"Finally! I was getting worried. Woah, your face is really swollen."

It was hard for Lindsey to talk. Her right eye was swollen shut and her inflamed cheek distorted her mouth.

"It doesn't hurt any worse today, but I need some ice . . . and some coffee."

"The coffee is still hot. I'll get you a cup, and an ice pack."

She sat on the sofa and picked up his laptop, watching the fast-moving images on the screen.

"What game is this?"

"League of Legends. Why?"

Lindsey started to cry.

"Mom, what's wrong?" He grabbed the ice pack and carefully carried the coffee cup to the sofa.

"The guy . . . the black guy . . . he played a game with you."

"What?"

"He could see your computer, and he knew your screen name or whatever. You and he were playing a game together!"

Ken put his arm around her.

"Try not to cry. It's gonna make it hurt more." He held the ice pack up to her face and handed her the coffee cup.

"I remember playing with a guy a couple of times. I kinda had the feeling that he was looking for me, but I didn't think too much about it. The game moves so fast. Wow." Ken was shaking his head. "I'm changing all of my passwords. Can I do anything for you? Do you want anything?"

"No, honey. I'll be okay. I'm hoping the police call with some news. Just knowing that guy is still out there . . ."

As if she willed it to happen, her cell phone rang.

"I got it." Ken jumped up. "I think it's the police."

He swiped to answer and then put the call on speaker.

"Ms. Blake? It's Deputy Rodriguez from the Hillsboro County Sheriff's office.

"This is Lindsey, and my son Ken is here also. You are on speaker."

"I'm calling to let you know that we picked up Ben Griffin. We believe he is the other man who held you at the cottage."

Lindsey grabbed Ken's arm.

"Oh my God. How? Where?"

Based on your description we were able to get a match from the CCTV at the McDonald's. From there we tracked him to a cruise ship in Tampa that had just left port. We sent the Coast Guard out, and they picked him up. We have him now in the county jail. He's already talked and told us that a man named Jason Smith had hired him to kidnap you. Do you know him?"

He spoke in a matter of fact way with little inflection in his tone.

Lindsey launched herself off the couch and stared down at the phone.

"Yes! I know Dr. Jason Smith. He's a medical director at Unified where I work. Oh my God! Why did he do this to me?"

"Ma'am, we don't have too many details yet. We do know that his daughter died yesterday and Doctor Smith has been admitted to the hospital. We're not sure why yet, but we have a Lee County detective down there looking into it. We'll let you know as soon as we have some more information."

Ken thanked the Deputy and ended the call.

"Mom, why would this guy want to kidnap you?"

"I have no idea! I hardly know him! I need to call Lisa."

Ken searched the contact list on his mother's phone and tapped on Lisa's name.

"Lindsey?"

"It's Ken. Mom's right here. She just got up, but the deputy from the county sheriff's office called and told us that they caught the other guy. He also told us that Doctor Jason Smith hired him to do it."

"Oh my God! Jason? Lindsey . . . are you okay?"

"I don't know what to think. The deputy said his daughter died yesterday, and now he's in the hospital, but they don't know what's wrong with him."

"The drug, Cineth, it must have been for his daughter. He had you kidnapped to force us to approve the drug for his daughter. This is so crazy. I never even knew that he had a daughter!"

"Me either," Lindsey said. "I'll call you later. It's hard for me to talk."

Lindsey laid down on the couch and put the ice pack on her face.

"I need some time to soak this all in. I can't believe this happened."

"It's okay, Mom. I'm going to stay down here for a while, and Laurie is flying down tomorrow. We can both work remotely for the week, or as long as you need us to. We don't want you to be alone until you're ready, and you know you can always come back to Boston and stay with us if you want."

Lindsey nodded in agreement, then closed her eyes and dozed off.

Ken picked up his laptop, looked at the game on his screen and then shut it down. *Maybe it's time to take a break*, he thought.

CHAPTER SEVENTY

INDSEY'S FACE WAS almost healed after two weeks, leaving her with just a small yellow area along the side of her cheek. The pain was gone, and she felt confident that there wouldn't be any physical scars. The shock of her ordeal had faded to some intermittent post-traumatic stress, which made her teary, but she was ready to get back to work, back to a somewhat normal routine. The distraction of work was what she needed.

Ken and Laurie had returned to Boston the day before, but the tearful goodbye was still stinging. She loved having them stay with her, and now the quiet left her with a pit in her stomach and no appetite. But she forced herself to eat and knew her strength was returning.

She sat behind her computer and stared at her dark screen. She wasn't sure why her hands were shaking, and her heart was beating so fast. She felt insecure as if Unified would think she was damaged and she would lose the job she loved. They had no reason to terminate her employment. *It wasn't my fault!* But fear slowed and scrambled her typing and it took several tries before she successfully logged in. She let out a sigh of relief and opened her chat communicator. Lisa was already online. She typed, "Good morning!"

Her phone rang immediately.

"Welcome back! I'm so glad you logged on. The team has really, really, really missed you. How are you feeling?"

"I feel much better. Most of the bruises are gone, and the kids left yesterday, so it feels like the right time to come back to work."

"Well, I'm happy you're here."

"Has there been any talk about Dr. Smith?"

"Not much. We heard about his daughter, and we know that he was admitted to the psychiatric unit but no one's talking about his condition. No one knows anything about his wife either. I guess he was friendly with Ron Shay. I did hear that the police interviewed him, but it's all hush hush."

"Yeah, well, I guess the important thing is that they caught the other guy and it's all over . . . well mostly. I'm still getting calls with questions about what happened with the fat guy, and Ken is still getting calls with questions about what happened at the convenience store. But it will all die down eventually.

It's strange how everything can be fine one minute, and the next minute everything blows up. I'm in the trunk of a car, and people are dying." She held back the urge to cry and took a deep breath.

"Lisa, I wanted to thank you and Dan for everything you did for me. You were both so brave. I am so sorry that you had to be involved." She sniffled back tears.

"You have nothing to be sorry for. We love you, and we'd do anything for you. Missy too." Her laugh broke the tension.

"Let's plan a work day together this week at our usual place. I'll bring the grapes," Lisa offered.

"Sounds like a plan."

CHAPTER SEVENTY-ONE

ANNA'S MEMORIAL SERVICE was held three weeks after her passing at a beach side event hall just before sunset. The rain had already moved through, temporarily dropping the steamy temperature, and the sky had a beautiful pink and orange hue. Large crowds gathered inside and outside of the building, some laughing, some crying, but mostly just being in the moment to remember the beautiful and generous person that Hanna was.

Donna had Hanna's body cremated two weeks earlier and held a private ceremony that included just the immediate family at the Smith's home. Donna was glad that she had the two weeks to prepare herself for the event. She had a bit more energy, and in a way, looked forward to being around people who knew and loved her daughter.

Within two days after Hanna's death, her phone blew up with calls from reporters. Media trucks parked outside her door despite the gates that were supposed to provide safety and privacy to her neighborhood. She did her best to ignore them, but it wasn't easy. She had to leave her house to make Hanna's final arrangements and each time they swarmed her like angry hornets. She had nothing to say because she knew nothing except that her daughter was gone. They eventually lost interest, and she was glad not to be bothered at Hanna's memorial event.

Donna was overwhelmed by the sheer number of people paying their respects. The evening passed quickly with many hugs, condolences, and offers of support. She thanked Hanna's teachers and school administrators and all her classmates and their families that were in attendance. It was hard and emotional but she powered through it, 'like a champ' her father said hugging her close.

Her parents had flown in from California and had stayed with her since the day after Hanna died. She was glad for their company. They made her feel safe and grounded despite her deep sorrow.

Her father dealt with the reporters and the police that were constantly ringing the doorbell. And her mother slept in the bed with her, comforting her, crying with her, and assuring her that in time, she would come to terms with Hanna's death and learn how to move on with her life. Donna gradually believed that she would, in time.

As the memorial gathering ended, the three of them waved off the stragglers and drove in silence back to Donna's house. Her body felt heavy, and her feet dragged. She slowly climbed the stairs and went straight to bed.

The next morning Donna lay in bed, taking her time, thinking about all that had happened. She started to get emotional, imagining that Hanna was sleeping in her bed just down the hall, but pulled herself back to reality and swallowed back her tears. She rolled onto her right side and considered the empty half bed that she once shared with Jason, and remembered the metal box in the drawer. It was time to finally open it to see what secrets she might find.

She threw back the covers and walked around to the right side of the bed and opened the drawer, pulling out the box. It was locked, but might not be too difficult to pry open. She dug through the drawer and found a large pair of nail clippers.

She unfolded the thin blade and wedged it near the lock, then wiggled it back and forth until she heard the lock release. Inside the box were several envelopes from medical practices, and all dated within the last year. She opened the first one and read.

"Dear Dr. Smith,

Thank you for your interest in joining our practice. However we have located a candidate that better meets our requirements. Best of luck in your search."

The woman who signed the letter identified herself as the "Practice Manager."

Donna examined the second envelope, and then opened it, reading a similar rejection. She didn't know he was applying for jobs, but then she really didn't know her husband at all. She was married to a stranger, a mentally unstable man, who was an incompetent physician and resorted to criminal acts in Hanna's name.

She laid back on the bed and wondered if she could forgive herself for being so stupid. How could she not have known? She never got the opportunity to search his laptop and cell phone. The police searched their home, taking nearly everything out of his office. No one was able to confirm that he was having an affair.

On the day before Hanna's final arrangements were made, Donna went to the hospital and met with the social worker assigned to Jason's case. She signed paperwork making herself his legal guardian, which made her responsible for his care but also gave her access to all of his bank accounts. She printed all of the statements and quickly picked up on the weekly hundred dollar checks. The online check image revealed Nathalie Serbo's name. At first, she thought that this must be the woman he was seeing, but then she googled her and discovered she was a massage therapist. It occurred to her that Jason was receiving more than just a massage, but a few days later Nathalie called to offer her condolences and explained that Jason was a client, and that she had offered many times to assist her and Hanna with stress management. Donna believed her.

She decided to let it all go. It wasn't a hard decision. It was time to think about herself, and how she would deal with her grief.

She showered and dressed and went down to the kitchen, where her father sat already on his second cup of coffee.

"Good morning, sunshine. Did you get enough sleep?"

She leaned over and kissed her father's cheek.

"Yes, I slept. I feel okay this morning."

Donna poured herself some coffee and sat across from her father.

She could sense he wanted to say something and, holding her steaming cup, she faced him head on.

"What? I can't tell you to want to say something, so just say it."

"Honey, I'm just curious about Jason. You haven't said a word about your plans and I want to help you. That's all."

Donna shrugged and got up from the table.

"I need some cream," she announced.

"Honey, let's just talk about it."

"What do you want me to say, Daddy?"

"What is the hospital telling you?"

Her face dropped as she considered the question and then decided to answer.

"He is still catatonic. He's made no progress. They've tried shocking him . . ."

Her father cut her off mid-sentence.

"Shocking him? Like what you see in the movies?" His voice escalated.

"Yes! He's had several shock treatments, and he still doesn't respond. They think he had a full psychotic break and there's no telling if he'll ever recover."

"Oh, my!" He set his coffee down and leaned back in his chair.

"I think we should get you a lawyer . . . get you out of this mess."

"I thought about that but I can't right now. I can only deal with one thing at a time."

"Okay, you're right. But when you're ready, that's what we should do."

Donna finished her coffee and went out onto the lanai. She sat with her feet dangling in the pool and thought about Jason as she watched the ripples move across the water. Maybe being catatonic wasn't such a bad thing. He wouldn't have to deal with the grief, and they certainly couldn't throw him in jail, not that he didn't deserve it.

She noticed her thoughts about Jason were calmer, and her body was more relaxed. Her father was right. She would call a lawyer. The sliding door opened behind her, bringing her back into the moment.

"Honey, there's a young man at the door that wants to talk to you. He said his name is Darius."

Donna got up and dried her feet and went into the house.

"Darius! I'm so happy that you came by." Donna opened her arms to hug him.

"Hi, Mrs. Smith."

"I have some things for you. Come in and sit down. This is my father."

Darius reached out, shook his hand, and greeted him respectfully calling him 'Sir'.

Donna returned a moment later with a tote bag.

Her voice started to crack.

"Honey, Hanna wanted you to have these, and I hope you will accept them and use them. She talked about you all the time and thought of you as her best friend." She handed him the bag. His eyes welled up with tears, and he hugged the bag to his chest, then looked inside at the iPad and cell phone, and then back to Donna.

"Please, honey, just enjoy them. Don't worry about the cell phone bill. It's all taken care of."

"Thank you very much." His voiced cracked holding back a sob.

"I also heard about what a hero you were in returning that woman's cell phone. Did you know that your actions helped to find her?"

"I found the phone two days before I gave it back. Hanna and I wrote letters about it, and she wanted me to return it even though I thought about keeping it," he confessed.

"I know, honey. She told me. But she also told me that you knew all along that you were going to return it, so you really are a hero. You saved a woman's life, and you should always be proud of yourself. Come here; let me hug you."

Donna wrapped her arms around Darius and held him tight. Tears ran down her cheeks, and she felt his body sob against hers.

"You will always be welcome in my home, Darius. I want you to know that I will be here for you if you ever need anything . . . and I mean anything. Carry Hanna's memory with you wherever you go in life. She loved you, Darius, and that means I love you." She pulled back and admired his face, then kissed his forehead. Come, let's make some breakfast.

<<<>>>

92
105

230

Laura/Laurie

231

259

Sympathetic to characters
page turner
suspensful
engaging